Limb of the Judas Tree

Aux Arcs Novels

Best wishes & Happy Reading

Bob

6/24/03

Eldon

Limb of the Judas Tree

A novel of mystery
and suspense in
old Linn Creek

ROBERT DEAN ANDERSON

Robert Dean Anderson

Published by:

Aux-Arcs Novels
26183 Indian Creek Lane
Barnett, MO 65011
E-Mail: bdanders@socket.net

First Edition 2002
Copyright © 2002 by Robert Dean Anderson
ISBN: 0-9720680-7-4 $25.95
LCN: 2002091775

Cover Design by Beth Mix

Set in Palatino

Printed in the United States of America by
Central Plains Book Manufacturing
Winfield, KS

For Carol, of course

Introduction

The Osage River flows out of the eastern prairie land of Kansas into western Missouri where it is joined by several large rivers and many small tributaries to form a major watershed for the central and western part of the state. The Osage was a major navigable stream in the eighteen and early nineteen hundreds and had a growing stream of riverboat traffic from the Missouri River to trading posts and dram shops that sprang up along the river. In the 1830's and 1840's a settlement began where the Osage and Niangua Rivers and Linn Creek meet in a wide bend of the Osage. This settlement came to be called Linn Creek—named after the creek which in turn was named after the linn or basswood trees that grew plentifully along its banks. The town became a major port on the Osage and grew as trading by river traffic expanded.

Because of the terrain—steep hills and deep valleys—sudden storms common in the spring and late fall, often resulted in flash flooding. The town grew more or less accustomed to the frequent floods—sometimes as frequently as three out of every five years saw the dusty streets of the town running brown with belt-high floodwaters—but much talk circulated about means to control the sudden gushing of the high waters. Early on, part of the town relocated several hundred yards away from the Osage alongside Linn Creek to distance the main businesses and residences from the flooding where the three bodies of water came together.

Being the trade center for the area and the central location for budding tourism to the springs and attractions of a stone, castle-like building in an area known by its Indian name, Ha Ha Tonka, led to relative prosperity for the town.

The earliest mention of the possibility of damming the waters of the Osage and its tributaries in this region surfaced in 1911. The idea was scoffed at by the residents of the area, but electricity was much in demand across the country and success with the building of dams elsewhere to provide a free energy source to drive electrical generators gave speculators incentive to begin serious planning for such a project.

The residents of Linn Creek—the largest town in the path of flood waters that would be produced by such a dam—went through many emotional roller coasters of the on again-off again project. Talk and promises flowed and receded for the next eighteen years until—in 1929—the Osage Project reached a crossroad. It would proceed or it would die. Many people in the area were supportive of the dam, given the promise of high prices for their land and employment opportunities in a region where thin soils and rocky, forrested land offered little else. Others talked disparagingly of losing all contact with their roots and those of their ancestors. Most of the residents of Linn Creek had been born there and so had their parents and their parents' parents. The thought of never being able to go home again was devastating.

As you read *Limb of the Judas Tree*, written of the time and of the people of Linn Creek, though fictional, you will experience the same swing felt by the residents between the anguish over the imminent death of their town and the jubilation over problems that threatened to curtail the dam.

Several people ended up in prison for their manipulations and criminal activities in trying to launch the dam project. This was the last effort by a private enterprise to construct a major electrical-producing dam on a navigable stream in the United States. All such subsequent projects have been engineered and financed by the government.

The story herein about a fictional sheriff, his wife and her former lover was based on historical fact from another region in the state. Nevertheless, though based on actual events—the names, characters, places and incidents are either the product of the author's imagination or are used fictitiously, and any resemblance to actual persons living or dead, or to business establishments, events or locales is entirely coincidental.

I thank the people and the organization of the Camden County Museum for material that was used as guidance and inspiration for the ideas in this book. If this book similarly inspires the reader to know more about the history of old Linn Creek, I urge you to visit the Camden County Museum in Linn Creek, Missouri.

PART ONE
THE ARREST

The year 1929 brought on a stock market crash at a place called Wall Street in New York City; a tragedy barely noticed in my hometown of Linn Creek, Missouri, engaged as we were with our own string of calamitous events. I guess you could say the trouble commenced when Shorty Mickleson got himself killed about the same time talk heated up about building a dam on the wild Osage River. A dam that would create the largest lake ever built in the whole country. Some in Camden County were exhuberant over the possibilities, but that enthusiasm did not extend to the people in Linn Creek. Such a dam would put our town under thirty feet of water.

The dam builders faulted our ancestors for choosing a location where the wandering Niangua and mercurial Linn Creek met the Osage, forever tying the fate of our town to the whims of running waters. Lord knows we endured enough floods to put us on a level with Noah, but we loved our town, its beauty and its people. Were we supposed to sacrifice all that just so folks in St. Louis and Kansas City could have more light bulbs?

Another change that happened recently was that women here had finally begun to vote. Not that I had any notion of disagreement with that, it just changed what happened in ways no one could have anticipated. When the women of Camden County got organized and voted as a group they elected every female on the ballot.

A chapter in the Klan had been organized several years before, but 1929 was the year they came to play a role that was to be as devastating as the dam threatened to be. I never could figure why we needed a Klan—less than a dozen colored lived in the whole county—but the fashion was to have one so we did.

And, of course, we had prohibition. Illegal whiskey prices were up 500 percent, inspiring the stills in our county to step up production by the same amount. Whiskey running became more profitable than distilling the stuff, but at a considerable risk. You could have asked Shorty Mickelson about that, but as I mentioned, Shorty wasn't with us anymore. He was the first bootlegger shot in our county.

I was a deputy sheriff pulling the graveyard shift at the sheriff's office inside the jail house the night Shorty died when a boy, Sam Studdard's youngest, came rapping on the door at 2:48 a.m. by the Gregory family watch. I opened the door, looked around and said, "Where is everybody?" because all I saw outside was one swaybacked mule. And the boy, of course

Now the Studdards didn't own a motor car, nor even a buggy as far as I knew. Didn't own, in fact, much of anything except a reputation for sloth and drunkenness. And well earned at that. But none of that was the boy's fault. At least not yet. As thin as a blade of grass, he had big frog eyes that looked as if you could rake them off with a stick. His home-sewed chambray shirt and Osh-Kosh-B-Gosh overalls had been passed down for the last time and wouldn't go through another round of Studdards if they happened into the world.

He acted possessed or something, he was that excited. He babbled on and on about the thunderous racket they'd heard.

"Tat-tat-tat," he said, imitating the sound with his tongue. I thought the boy was caught up in a stutter he couldn't escape from, but he wasn't. Turned out he was trying to sound like a Thompson sub-machine gun.

His breathing was so heavy by then that when he took in one large gulp of air I thought his skinny body might lift right off the floor. He ceased talking for a moment to let his breath catch up so I just stood watching him twitch. I couldn't do a thing until he told me what was wrong in a way I could understand. When he continued he said they had waited as long as they could and when they went outside to investigate they saw the motor car with the engine still running and more than twenty holes from the front end of the car to the back. Or so he claimed. Then—and his bulging eyes got saucer sized and started to blink rapid fire—they saw the man inside. And the blood.

And the boy ran right out of the jail house and threw up on the ground.

Now that last act was pretty convincing, though I kept in mind the Studdards were powerful liars and that none of them, as far as I knew, could count past ten. But his story sounded serious enough for me to wake the sheriff.

Ora Mitchell's a damn good sheriff if I do say so. Of course, he is married to my sister Addie, but I would think the same even if he wasn't. From the time I pinned on the badge, no one thought I could do the job. I was young and lean and all I had to recommend me were a few months studying the law in Springfield. Some said that was a detriment to being a good deputy.

The thing that pleased me, and probably the reason all the kidding I got about me being hired by my brother-in-law never got to me, was that Ora believed in me. He really did. And so I believed in me, too. I was never going to let him down.

Ora was a hard featured man with a drooping mustache who could flat scare the hell out of most people just by looking at them. I stood over six feet and he was nearly a head taller than me. Already he was a legend. Down at the Dutchman's Barber Shop and in Potter's Garage probably not a day passed that one of his feats of strength or courage wasn't retold. As with most legends, a lot of the stories had been unduly magnified. Nevertheless, he was the biggest man I would ever know and I wasn't just speaking about his size.

15

LIMB OF THE JUDAS TREE

Ora had absolutely no tendency toward excitement and when he asked the Studdard boy flat out, "Are you lying, boy?" the dead calm of Ora's face, instead of scaring the boy, seemed to settle him down some.

"No sir, Sheriff," he said. He told the tale again, the same way he told it to me. That made me wonder if he really was a Studdard. I couldn't recall his given name and I wasn't sure just when I had seen him in the company of other Studdards, but family features were as easy to read in his face as rabbit tracks in fresh snow.

We sped out past the schoolhouse on Bagnell road as fast as Ora's Chevrolet sedan would go, taking the boy and Doc Hardesty with us. The ride was a daring one in the dark, dodging possums, raccoons and occasional deer as well as rocks big enough to tear up the motor car. A lot of talk had been going around the courthouse about paving the road with concrete and building a bridge over the Osage at Bagnell so that people could make the drive from Springfield to the Capitol in Jefferson City in any kind of weather. I suppose that plan would happen some day, but I wasn't holding my breath.

Some holes were so deep that if you let a wheel fall into one of them, you had a busted axle on your hands, or at the very least a blown-out tire. But Ora had strong hands and the Chevrolet had exceptionally bright headlights, so he guided us safely and in pretty good time to the spot where the boy said the shooting had happened. Our headlights caught the car still sitting in the middle of the road. It had been a shiny new, gray 1929 Buick, but, boy, not any more.

The Buick was pockmarked all over on one side with so many bullet holes I figured they had to have been made by an automatic weapon. Or an army. Plus two tires were blown out and the windows shattered. And, just like the boy had said, the bootlegger Shorty Mickelson lay dying on the front seat. When I got around to looking where the back seat had once been, I counted nineteen stacked five gallon lard cans. I suppose when Shorty had started the trip they'd been full of whiskey, but now they were full of holes. Unless a person had no nose at all, guessing wasn't necessary about what had been in the cans.

Doc Hardesty couldn't do a thing for Shorty who died a couple of minutes later. Doc said it was a plumb damn miracle Shorty lived as long as he had since any one of the six bullets in him would have been fatal.

Doc held a medical flask under one of the leaking cans and caught it full of whiskey. Figuring to collect his fee, I guess.

Come daybreak, after Lonnie Harper towed the car into Linn Creek and parked it by Volly Newell's Shell Oil station, people flocked to see it and run their hands over the bullet holes and stare at the seat all stained up permanently with Shorty's blood. Ora said string some wire around the Buick and Lonnie did, but one guy no fence was going to keep away was Yawley Earnhardt. See, Yawley owned the Buick *and* the whiskey. Shorty now, had only been hired and Yawley was too busy a man to pay attention to things he didn't own.

Some families—the Hatches, the St. Clouds, the Norfleets and the Cargroves to name a few—came to Linn Creek with money, but most of the town's ancestors, my own included, came with nothing and looking for a way to make a living. The majority of them found they could do it hacking railroad ties. They cut down large groves thick with oak, hickory and sassafras and hewed the ties out of them for ten cents apiece. The Earnhardts had been the contractors, the middle men, buying the ties for a dime and selling them for thirty cents at the railhead in Bagnell. You didn't have to be an airplane scientist to see where that would be a lot more profitable—not to mention easier on the back—than tie hacking. But the whole family had been prone to unfortunate accidents leaving Yawley the only Earnhardt left in town. Except for his tantalizing daughter Estelle.

Yawley shoved people out of his way until he got to the wire

17

around the Buick. He was big enough to do that. I don't just mean in size, though he was almost Ora's weight with a lot of it fat, showing how he liked to eat and drink and how he hired out too much of his heavy work.

He got his finger pointing at the car and his face right up in Ora's and he said, "Ora, I paid three thousand dollars to get that car fixed up the way I wanted and I had three hundred dollars in good charcoal filtered mash whiskey in the back seat. Something's got to be done, Ora. Man can't squeeze out an honest living in this county anymore."

"Running whiskey's a dangerous occupation," Ora said, towering over Yawley by a good four inches. You couldn't help but compare Ora's tanned, leather-like face next to Yawley's pink cheeks. Ora sliced a chaw off his plug before offering it to Yawley who just stared at it.

"That whiskey was medicinal, Ora. Make sure you put that down in your report. I was sending it up to St. Louis to some doctors. How many men you reckon it took to shoot that many holes in my car?"

"One could have done it," I said. I held out my hand with a half dozen .45 caliber spent cartridges in it that I had picked up off the road where we'd found Yawley's Buick. Yawley stared at the brass shell casings. "Probably a Thompson sub-machine gun," I explained, hoping to make an impression on him because of his daughter Estelle.

He ignored me and looked at Ora. "Who you think done such a terrible thing?"

"Musta been some fellow who knew you, Yawley. One of your enemies I reckon."

Yawley said, "Well, that don't narrow it down much." He got back into Ora's face. "I heard Champ Gowan was paroled last week. Wouldn't surprise me none it turned out to be him."

"Could be," Ora said, stroking his mustache. "I got a notice from the parole board he'd been paroled with a Buster Workman

18

from up around Audrain County and a fellow named Wilbur Crowder from Kansas City. Wilbur, they said, was a machine gunner for the mobs up there."

"Well, hell, there you are," Yawley said. "What more proof do you need?"

"Champ has seven days to report in to me as his parole officer," Ora said. "We'll see what he has to say when he does."

"Maybe the Klan ought to just take care of him," Yawley said. "Save the county a whole lot of bother and money trying him."

"Justice don't wear a bed sheet and hide under a hood in my county, Yawley. Not as long as I'm sheriff."

"Damn shame," Yawley said. "The Klan gets things done."

Before the tie inspectors for the contractors started using a branding hammer to mark the ties they bought, they used paint to mark them on each end. For those disinclined to cut their own ties, chopping off the paint marks and reselling the ties back to the same contractor was an easy feat. The first person caught doing that was a Gowan. He was hanged from a cottonwood tree by an irate lynch mob. Now that was harsh punishment, but it sure cut down on tie thieving for awhile. The branding hammers practically did away with it. Since that hanging, every time something was stolen or broken into in Linn Creek, a Gowan was blamed. Probably with justification. Champ was the youngest of the Gowan clan and had been sent to the state prison at Jefferson City three years ago for stealing Yawley Earnhardt's brand new Packard motor car.

I lived at Minton's Boarding House, sharing a room with my

best friends Lonnie Harper and Volly Newell. Lonnie would remind you of a rail fence he was that thin. There was nothing that wasn't humorous to him. For recreation Lonnie crawled around inside dark, damp caves and collected snakes that he kept in cages in back of Volly's station. Volly on the other hand was shorter and wider and as serious as daybreak.

The evening after the shooting the conversation at Rose Minton's supper table was all about Shorty and speculation about Champ Gowan. I usually took my meals at the jail house because they were free—cutting down on my monthly bill at Minton's—but I enjoyed supper at the boarding house on occasion just to catch up on the gossip and the news from the rest of the world.

The dining room at Minton's was bigger than a lot of houses in town. Rose Minton was known to set as many as 28 people at her table at one time. The table was what people called a harvest table. Extra leaves were stored underneath. To add them to the length you turned a crank and one end of the table extended until the last leaf was in place. Rose said she thought the table would be good for her business because she could make it shorter during the week and longer on weekends when tourists flocked in to visit the millionaire's castle at Ha Ha Tonka, a few miles away, along with the springs and caves surrounding it. But Rose was too good a cook and the news spread. She hardly ever set a table for less than twenty people.

The wallpaper in the room had a pattern of big red roses that I always found myself admiring as I listened to the talk around the table. The curtains were a cheerful red with a layer of lace over them. A big gas chandelier that had been converted to electric after Yawley Earnhardt got a power plant up and running, hung over the massive table.

Sympathy was expressed for Shorty Mickelson's family. Uncle Billy Jack Cummins—uncle to nobody as far as I knew—who had rode the tie rafts down the Osage with Granddad Gregory, recounted the history of the Mickelson family, where they came from, when they came and which ones married into which families. Everyone listened respectfully because Uncle Billy Jack was regarded as the historian of the county. There wasn't anyone in town he didn't know and there wasn't anything any of us did that he didn't know about. I guess Uncle Billy Jack had been around when the first shovel of dirt was turned in Camden County.

Lonnie Harper said, "I hear it was Champ Gowan who filled old Shorty and Yawley's new Buick automobile full of holes."

I was sitting between Oma Thornbush, a full blood Osage if there was such a thing, and Jane McGann. Oma was a distant cousin of Ora's and had taken in washing and ironing before she became too frail. Jane was an elegant lady of eighty who dressed every day as if she was calling on the Queen of England. On the street she always wore wide brimmed straw hats in the summer and every man she came to tipped his hat to her without even thinking about it.

I could feel everyone's eyes on me and I can't say I didn't take a small amount of pleasure in the attention I was getting. I was the only person at the table who actually saw Shorty die. Doc Hardesty stayed at Minton's too, but on this night he had remained in his room, probably sipping on Yawley's free charcoal filtered mash whiskey.

I was always practicing my speech making and facing the public, hoping to get my struggling law practice going. I had a chance now to do some practicing and talk about something exciting. After all, when you're twenty-four and you haven't had much happen to you, something like a bootlegger getting shot is a major event.

"We haven't proved anything," I said. "That is, no one has except Yawley who has tried and convicted Champ in his own mind. I think Gideon Norfleet would like to have at least one piece of evidence before he took Champ to court."

Uncle Billy Jack said, "If something was stolen or somebody

21

killed, it was more than likely a Gowan who did it. I watched every one of those boys grow up and get sent off to jail. Their daddy, too, but I hear he escaped from prison and never heard from again. Never came back here, anyway, to help raise that family."

"People can change, Uncle Billy Jack," Jane McGann said. "You can't convict somebody in court on account of what their daddy did."

"That's the way they pick race horses," Uncle Billy Jack said.

"You people down here having a whiskey war?" one of the drummers across the table asked.

Rose had three drummers from St. Louis and one from St. Joseph staying for the night. Our town had a hotel, but Rose's place was the favorite for the drummers who had a regular beat in town. They kept us informed on what was going on in the world and Rose fed them the best food they could get on the road.

Volly Newell said, "It wasn't a war until Shorty got killed last night. The Monger brothers over in Miller County have been trying to horn in on Yawley's suppliers here in Camden County. They were probably behind it. Maybe hired Champ. He and Yawley never got along."

"You don't have Prohibition here in the hills?" the Stetson hat drummer from St. Joseph wanted to know.

"That's what made the prices go up," I said. "The market is gone for railroad ties and mining is too expensive and risky. So whiskey distilling helps people make a living. Places they call speakeasies in St. Louis and East St. Louis pay a dollar a gallon for any kind of whiskey and a dollar fifty for really good mash whiskey aged in a barrel."

"When you get the dam put in, the free electricity will draw factories and all kinds of businesses here," another drummer said.

"They lie like a dog under a shade tree," Lonnie said. "They're backing off on the promise of free electricity. Now all they're promising is jobs for a couple of years."

22

Uncle Billy Jack banged the table with his fork and snorted through his nose. "There is not going to be a dam on the Osage," he said. "I don't know why people think it can be done. Might as well try and dam up the ocean. People here would never stand for it anyway."

"What if the other counties want to do it?" the drummer asked.

"Let 'em try," Uncle Billy Jack spat out. His face had taken on a hard set. He always got that way when talk started about a dam. Once he'd been so upset at two drummers telling how deep the dammed-up water would be on Main Street in Linn Creek that he had gotten up from the table before dessert was served.

"It's a corporation," the drummer went on. "They're selling stock in it. Thousands of people are buying shares. I bought some myself."

Uncle Billy Jack's eyes narrowed to slits as he looked at the drummer. "Why would you want to do a thing like that?"

"Why? Why to make money, of course. After the dam is finished and the turbines start running, they'll be selling electricity all over the country. You want to make money these days, invest in electricity or motor cars."

"What will you do with all the money you make?" Uncle Billy Jack wanted to know.

"Buy a bigger house. A nicer car. One of those big LaSalles or Packards."

"Can you buy a town full of friends? Can you buy the respect of your fellow man?"

The drummer was getting set to answer, unable to detect the obvious extent of Uncle Billy Jack's disgust with him, but Uncle Billy Jack's dessert was saved when the telephone jangled on the wall, ringing out two longs and a short.

"Oh, that's me," Rose said, and got up from her end of the table where she always sat and ate with her guests. She talked on the telephone for awhile, then hung the receiver back on its hook and returned to the table.

"Joel Dean," she said, looking at me. "That was Ora at the sheriff's office. You better get over there. Someone took a shot at Yawley's other whiskey runner."

Lud Harris said he had been hauling a load of medicinal whiskey to St. Louis for Yawley Earnhardt when he heard a bunch of people shooting at him, all at the same time.

Or it could have been one person with a Thompson automatic submachine gun.

"It's getting too dangerous, Ora," Lud said. "I got six kids to feed, but I can't do it if I'm dead."

While Ora was asking if Lud had gotten a look at who did the shooting, Lud just sat hunched over in the chair, turning his hat brim around and around in his hands and nodding his head at Ora with each word. Then he said without hesitation it had been Champ Gowan and the two who'd gotten out of jail with him.

"How'd you know about them?" Ora asked.

Lud looked up, straightened his shoulders some and said Yawley had warned him to be on the lookout for them. Ora let that go by without saying anything.

Lud sneaked in a drink of whiskey and that calmed him some. When Ora got back to asking him about the two men with Champ, Lud first said they were big, then changed his mind and said they were short and skinny, then ended up saying he really hadn't gotten a good look at them because he'd been busy watching Champ and that Thompson submachine gun.

Ora said, "How do you know it was a Thompson submachine gun?"

24

LIMB OF THE JUDAS TREE

Lud said he'd read about it at the Dutchman's Barber Shop in the *Police Gazette* and that all the really bad gunners were using them nowadays.

Minutes after Lud left the office Yawley was there, puffing like he'd run all the way from his big house way up on the hill.

"Ora, you can't sit around here waiting for Champ to report in. I'll be out of drivers by then. You've got to go out and bring him in before he kills somebody else."

"If you wasn't to run any more whiskey, Yawley, I doubt anybody else would get killed," Ora told him.

"What the hell you saying?" Yawley demanded. "You saying I got to quit making a living?"

"I'm saying it ain't the sheriff's job to protect illegal whiskey running in Camden County," Ora said.

Yawley came right up into his face. "By God, Ora. By God, you know what you're asking?"

"I ain't asking, Yawley."

Things got a little tense right there. Yawley's face turned a few different colors and he cocked a finger, ready to shake it in Ora's face, changed his mind and let it drop.

"I'll go busted, Ora," he said, close to pleading. "I got a contract with these doctors and . . ."

"You'd have to have a prescription to make it legal," Ora said.

"You know I ain't got that, Ora." Yawley looked hurt. He turned his eyes down to the floor and collapsed into a chair. "Damn sure I'll lose the hardware and feed stores. The furniture business and the grocery store'll probably be gone too. Might even lose the flour mill. You know what happens to a town they come in and tear the mill down? You got no idea how much money I got borrowed to buy them two Buicks. And I got two thousand gallons of good whiskey all over the county promised to me. Ora, you'd be taking bread out of little children's mouths were you to shut down the whiskey running in Camden County."

25

"That's what I'm doing Yawley. It's shut down from now on."

Yawley shot to his feet shedding his act of humility.

"You can't do this, Ora. You try shutting down this whole county and you'll be drummed out of office so fast. . ."

"Take more'n that cowardly bunch you call the Klan."

Yawley kept clenching and unclenching his fist, then he pounded it into his other hand. Ora just stood watching him, no more concern showing on his face than if Yawley had been whipping up a cake. I knew Yawley wasn't going to hit Ora. I'd never seen or heard of anybody in Camden County dumb enough to do that.

Yawley's eyes went wild, racing all around the room as if he was looking for help. Then he remembered the finger he'd been cocking before and this time he shook it at Ora.

"I'll get you for this, Ora. This county can't afford you for sheriff no more."

He stomped from the office, banging the door on his way.

Ora didn't appear particularly annoyed by the incident.

"Going to have a new job for you tomorrow night, Joel Dean," he said. "You'll have to stake out the Bagnell road and watch for whiskey runners and hijackers."

I remembered the tat-tat-tat sound the Studdard boy had made.

"What'll I do if I find any?"

Ora said, "Same as you'd do to any lawbreaker. Arrest them or shoot their ass off."

"How many bootleggers you figure there are in the county? Present company excluded," Noah Lamb asked at the breakfast table next morning. Noah had a few years on Ora and had been his deputy since Ora was sworn in.

The prisoners at the table chuckled amongst themselves and glanced over at Gideon Norfleet, Camden County's prosecuting attorney, who was a visitor at the jail house for breakfast.

Gideon, looking tall and dignified next to the prisoners, sawed away at his ham, then worked it over in his jaws. "You ain't including me in that assessment are you, Noah?

"Talk down at Toby's pool room is that you might be one of Yawley's silent partners," Noah said.

"That's scurrilous talk, Noah," Gideon said, his eyes leveled at Noah who was stuffing biscuits and jelly into his mouth, leaving a little of the jelly on his fluffy white mustache.

"Notice I didn't say it was the truth," Noah said. "What I said was that was the talk. Thought you'd want to know so's you could protect yourself. Or whatever needs to be done."

"Rumors like that could damage a man's reputation. I'd be honor bound to take some sort of action against a man if he was to accuse me of something like that."

Gideon, who hoped to be a judge one day, looked as serious and sober as one. He was a thin man with thin features and a fine head of hair. My guess was that Gideon had been born looking stern. The prisoners all had a smile on their faces as their eyes shot back and forth between Gideon and Noah like people watching a Sunday afternoon tennis match in Springfield.

"Oh, I'm not so sure it would hurt a man," Noah said, piling some fresh peach jam on another biscuit. "We had a preacher once in Neosho that stayed a bachelor till he was nearly as old as I am. He was an ugly cuss. Then the story got started around that he'd tried to accost one of the widder women in the rectory. You know, after that the rest of the widders in that church just wouldn't leave the poor man alone."

The prisoners chuckled and guffawed as Gideon glanced sharply at them, one by one. He was responsible for them being there, see, and he wanted to make sure they didn't forget it.

We had a unique situation here in the Camden County jail house. The cells were all upstairs and the sheriff's office occupied one room downstairs with a large kitchen and Addie and Ora's living quarters in the rest of it. Addie ran the kitchen with the help of Birdie, the colored maid. The county paid Addie and Ora for each meal served to the prisoners. The prisoners sat on one side of the table and the deputies and any visitors on the other side. Ora sat at one end and Addie at the other. The prisoners had to clean up and shave or they couldn't show up at the table. And if they didn't show proper respect for Addie or any other lady who might be present, or if they used coarse or vulgar language, they would be taken back to their cell without a meal.

"Ora," Gideon switched his attention away from the prisoners. "Yawley complains to me that you aim to stop the whiskey running in Camden County."

"He's right about that," Ora said. "You might have to call on Joel Dean to help you out if I have to arrest every whiskey runner in the county."

Ora was referring to the fact that Gideon was sort of my mentor and had helped me in getting admitted to the bar a few months back.

"How many more men you going to deputize?" Gideon asked.

"I got enough," Ora said.

Gideon looked at me and Noah. "Two? You think that's enough? And Doyle? Where *is* Doyle?"

He was talking about Doyle Savoy, the other deputy. If I could choose one person in Linn Creek I'd most enjoy being like, it was Doyle Savoy. I mean, I admired Ora and Gideon, but I could tell you, Doyle had a whole lot more fun out of life. And I said that without even knowing what all it was he did for fun.

I answered for Ora. "Doyle's got two days off. Says he's going to St. Louis and raise hell."

"Well, he's good at that," Gideon said. He pushed his plate

28

away and rose from his chair. "Good breakfast, Addie."

She looked at his plate and said, "You don't eat much, Gideon. I may start worrying about you."

"Stomach's been acting up lately," Gideon said from the door which I unlocked to let him through. As he turned he nearly collided with Doyle.

"Thought you were in St. Louis," Gideon said, looking at Doyle's suit coat over his denim pants and plaid shirt.

"On my way," Doyle said, motioning with the guitar case he carried. "Just dropped by to get Birdie to fix me some dinner to eat on the way."

"Gonna make some music in St. Louie, Doyle?" one of the prisoners asked.

"That I am. More ways than one."

"Stay out of trouble," Ora said.

"Don't worry, Cap'n, I do my hell raising across the river in East St Louis. That way it's out-of-state charges if any are brought."

In a biting voice Addie said, "Fix your own dinner. Birdie's busy."

It puzzled me why Addie had never seemed to like Doyle. They had a running quarrel that never boiled over, just sort of simmered on the back burner. Part of it, I'm sure, was Doyle being a foreigner. I mean, not only was his daddy not born in Camden County, Doyle wasn't even born here. And that's something you can't ever live down and your children can't either.

Doyle worked his way around the table in that slow, easy manner of his, eyes kind of twinkling out from under the short, two-inch cattleman's brim on his hat. The room was big, maybe thirty feet square with support posts on each side of the table and the kitchen area at the other end where a big oil stove stood, a double sink, and enormous food safe and a cooler against the wall. Doyle set the guitar case down next to the chopping block and searched the cooler until he found a ring of baloney and a wheel of cheese. He pulled a drawer open, searching through the knives until he pulled it out too far and the drawer and all the utensils in it went clattering to the floor.

Heads turned to look at Doyle who wore a sheepish grin.

"Oops," he said.

Addie walked slowly over to the mess on the floor and began picking it up along with Doyle. The prisoners and Noah were naming all the moonshiners in the county and Ora was listening and correcting them where necessary.

Addie laid the baloney ring on the chopping block and started cutting slices with a long, black handled butcher knife. Doyle's left hand came into contact with Addie's hip, then slid all the way around the curve to show it hadn't been accidental. Addie jabbed the knife into the chopping block just before Doyle jerked his other hand away.

"Mind if I get some more coffee, Sheriff?" one of the prisoners asked.

Ora looked at me. "Joel Dean, pour us some more coffee you don't mind."

From across the table I saw Doyle say something to Addie and smile. I went directly to the stove and the coffee pot trying not to look at them. I couldn't help hearing Addie say, "Forget it, Doyle. Addie Mitchell with a fire inside is something you don't want to see."

Addie and Champ Gowan had been gone three days when Pa had a stroke. When we got the card from Addie saying they were going to be married, Ma telephoned the hotel in Joplin where the

30

two were staying and asked Addie to come home, Pa was dying.

"Doan mare Gown," Pa said to her when she got back. His slurred speech and the waving of his gimpy arm brought on a lot of sympathy from all of us.

"We're in love, Pa," Addie had said, tears already starting to run down her cheeks.

"Gowns no dand goo," he said, then he started crying too. The first time I'd ever seen that.

"I lub oo," he continued and they hugged and Addie said, "But, Pa, what if someone had told you not to marry Ma? You mean you wouldn't have?"

He hadn't an answer for that, just sat and bawled like a baby.

Finally, after a week of that, Addie agreed to wait until Pa recovered and they could talk about it. The hospital bills came in and lots of others Ma couldn't pay because Pa hadn't been able to work in the lead mine for some time. I was a skinny kid then, about like the Studdard boy, and I wasn't much help. Ma cleaned houses for the banker and for Sid Hatch, the former governor who lived in our town. It wasn't enough. So Addie went to work at the jail for Ora while keeping Champ at a distance in deference to Pa's feelings about the Gowans. Pa died on a bleak February day, a lightning storm hit the house in March and a few weeks later a windstorm took part of the roof away. It broke Ma and before the year was out she was gone too. But not before Addie made one last attempt to save the house and the family. She married Ora.

I lived a few months with Addie and Ora and I would say at that time they were in love and doing what I thought married couples did, trying to have a baby every night. Ora had his mind set on having a son, but I guess things didn't go right. I spent several years in Springfield living with Ma's sister and her husband who was a clerk in a law office. I got a job helping out there, got interested in the law and ended up taking some courses at Drury College. I came back to Linn Creek for a visit, saw how Estelle Earnhardt had filled out and asked Ora about a job.

Things seemed to be different between Addie and Ora from what they had been before I left.

Addie was a right pretty woman, though I couldn't call her beautiful. She was too tall and skinny for that. Her face had the Gregory shallow cheeks, all sunk back into her head with cheek bones sharp and prominent, and the eyes so big they nearly had to bend around to the sides to get them into such a narrow face. If I was to say she *wasn't* pretty it would mean I wasn't much to look at either since we favored each other a good deal.

All that ran through my mind because I had to have something to think about while driving Ora's Chevrolet up the schoolhouse road to the top of Rifle Ridge. I stopped at a pullout to let the Chevrolet cool down and then, coming around one of the switch backs, I met a motor car coming downhill so I had to back all the way back to the pullout because the road was too narrow for us to pass.

I stopped at the top of the ridge and watched the sun set over some of God's proudest work. I'd never been able to put it into words just why I didn't think more of Springfield, but the view from the top of that hill said it for me. Springfield was too flat. Flat land was like a plain woman; nothing to get excited about.

Looking down on Linn Creek and the 800 or so people scattered around the town, I realized that fellow that set up the dram shop eighty years ago picked the prettiest spot in the Ozarks for his business—and for a town—but not the most sensible one. The creek that the town took its name from emptied into the Osage right where town began and the scenic splendor of the Niangua River was only a hundred yards upstream. Summer visitors to our town were captivated by the view that surrounded us. Photographers were in awe of what they could capture on their film. But none of them knew that three out of every five years our little town was covered with water from the three streams.

The thought of plain women brought Estelle Earnhardt into mind because she was anything but plain. We had started seeing

32

each other on a semi regular basis. A few weeks later I began the night shift. I was hoping for understanding from Estelle, but I was still trying to decide what she'd said when I told her I wouldn't be by each night.

"I suppose I'll get by," she had said and sighed dramatically. She put a cigarette into one of those long holders, lit it up and started puffing and blowing smoke into the air right away without inhaling. Then she waved the holder in elaborate motions, drawing pictures in the air with the smoking end and said, "Maybe I'll get spiflicated every night."

She was Yawley's only child so she was acting no different from what you would expect of a rich man's daughter who had been indulged her whole life. Spoiled or not, I was always thinking about her. About the little rosebud mouth and the button nose and the pencil line eyebrows over eyes that were dreamy and sleepy. Boy, her beauty just kept me awake at nights.

I'd picked a perfect spot to watch the road. And a perfect night to do it. Hard white light still ran along the horizon on the west behind the line of trees on the bluffs across the rivers. Behind, to the east, stars began to pop out to define the sky. Nights have a special beauty all their own, but I was thinking Shorty Mickelson might have had the same thoughts.

I saw a set of lights winding through the draw at the foot of the ridge, then weaving in and out of the oak and hickory on their way to the top. I stepped out and put up my hand like you're supposed to do and the motor car stopped. It was Ernest Raines who made the best whiskey in the county according to just about everyone.

Ernest smiled out the window in the center of the beam from my handheld battery lantern. He had a lean, chiseled jaw and a thin nose that he twitched ever now and then.

"What's the problem, Joel Dean? Bridge out over the Glaize?"

"I got orders to stop the whiskey from leaving the county, Ernest," I said.

He blinked his eyes rapidly, a habit he has, and leaned out of his early model Ford.

"What the hell for?"

"It's against the law, Ernest, to be selling whiskey."

"That's a federal law, Joel Dean. It ain't got nothing to do with us down here."

"Well, I'm afraid it has, Ernest. If you're hauling whiskey, I'll have to ask you to turn around and take it back home."

"How you know if I've got whiskey? You going to search my car?"

"No, I'm not, Ernest. If you tell me you're not hauling whiskey you can go on."

Ernest took his hat off and slapped it against the door of his Ford.

"Hell's fire, Joel Dean. Of course I got whiskey in here. Why in tarnation would I be driving on this road at night?"

"Then I'm going to have to ask you to turn around and take it back home with you, Ernest. Those are my orders."

Ernest pulled his hat down on his head and leaned way out so he'd be closer to my face.

"What am I supposed to do with it, sell to Yawley Earnhardt or the Monger brothers for thirty cents on the dollar? Sheriff tell you that?"

"Yawley ain't buying and the Mongers ain't coming over here in Camden County for whiskey no more," I said. "Somebody shot and killed one of Yawley's drivers and fired some shots at another one. Ora don't aim to be put in the position of providing protection for an operation that's illegal to begin with."

"Who was it got shot?"

"Shorty Mickelson."

"I'll be damned."

Ernest got out of his car and paced back and forth, taking his hat off and putting it on, blinking his eyes and spitting on the ground. He stopped in front of me.

34

"I see Ora's side of it, all right," he said. "Now, I hope he can see mine. Look out yonder and tell me what you see."

Dark mostly was all I could see. I could just barely make out the crests of the hills.

"Trees," I said. "Hills. That's all."

"And that's all there'll ever be," Ernest said. "You ain't never going to see wheat fields a waving, nor skyscrapers, nor boats dragging in nets full of tuna. You tell me how the hell we're supposed to make a living out here."

"Cutting cordwood," I said. "Tie hacking. Barrel staves. Raising hogs. Milking cows. Digging in the lead and iron mines. Raising strawberries is big now. That and feeding chickens."

"Tried 'em all," Ernest said. "Like to starved. I got seven young uns to feed. Making whiskey is the only way I can do it. I'll go back home tonight, but I'll be back tomorrow night and ever night after that. You tell Ora I'll keep turning around when I'm ordered to until the kids are out of food. Then, by God, you tell him I'm going through to Jeff City and for him not to try and stop me."

Ernest got back in his Ford, turned it around and I watched his taillight all the way back down the hill into the draw below. He had succeeded in making me feel bad about what I was doing.

I spent about an hour after Ernest left with no company except the tree bugs chirping and the sound of the bullfrogs croaking deep in the draw below. A time for thinking, but I had exhausted my list of pleasant things to think about. I started to wondering if Champ Gowan had really killed Shorty Mickelson and I decided he didn't. Why would he do that, I asked myself. I remembered Champ as having this grin on his face that always covered up the orneriness everybody knew was there. In school, I couldn't even remember him being in a fight with anyone.

The lights and sounds of one of those long haul trucks echoed through the draw, then crawled slowly up the side of the hill, back and forth on the switch backs. Some trucker must be mighty late because they usually don't drive this part of the road after night. Too dangerous with a heavy load. I let him get to the top before I stopped him. He was stopping anyway to let his radiator cool.

The driver seemed as glad to see me, as I was him. He said his name was Buck Newland and he was hauling a load of furniture squares for some furniture factory in Mexico, Missouri. He'd made an unscheduled stop in Linn Creek and acted rather proud about it.

"You from Linn Creek I 'spect you know why I stopped," he said with a wink of his eye. "Little old gal name of Nita something or other. . ."

"German," I said.

"How's that?"

"Her name is Nita German."

"Don't know her last name. Know everything else about her, you know what I mean. I see you know her, too." He laughed with a kind of "Hah, hah, hah," sound with his tongue hanging out.

"I'm acquainted with her," I said.

"Bet you are, young buck like you."

He brought out a vacuum insulated bottle full of coffee he had and offered to share it with me. Since I was hoping to hear more detail about his visit with Nita, I accepted. Instead he started talking about trucking and I was glad when his engine cooled enough for him to go on.

I swatted bugs and mosquitos for about an hour or maybe two before another set of lights spoiled all that darkness stretched out below me. These lights were coming fast and I mean dangerously fast. They came flickering through the trees coming up the hill so fast my throat tightened up. It had to be some kind of powerful motor car that could pull the hill with the speed it was showing.

If I was running whiskey with the fear of being stopped, that's just the way I would drive.

I had to stop that car. I mean, what else was I there for? That's what I did, that was my job. Stick my neck out and let somebody try and chop it off.

I drove Ora's Chevrolet into the roadway and pointed the headlights straight at the oncoming car. It was the only way I knew to stop it the speed it was coming.

The Thompson submachine gun sprang to mind, all right, but I had to stand in the headlights just the same.

I stopped worrying when I made out the little yellow roadster with the black fenders.

"Hello Estelle," I said after she skidded to a stop.

"Well, well. Joel Dean. Fancy meeting you here," she said and her laughter rang in the night and rolled across the hills, tinkling like the notes of a music box.

When I got closer I could tell she'd been drinking.

"You were driving pretty fast, Estelle. This is a dangerous road."

"Oh, poo. You're not going to scold me, are you?"

Her dainty face was shaped like commas curling in from each side of her head and ending under cheek bones that framed a perfect nose and held two gray, pouty eyes aloft. The chin was pointed and delicate and her mouth shaped like a small, red, red heart. Each time I looked at her I was struck momentarily speechless by her beauty.

"Just hate to see something happen to you," I said, helping her out of the car. "Hate to see that pretty face of yours end up in a wreck."

"You do say the keenest things, Joel Dean. You really think I'm pretty?"

"Just about the prettiest I've ever seen."

"The bee's knees?"

"How's that?"

"The bee's knees," she repeated. "You think I'm the bee's knees?"

"Yeah, sure I do," I said without having the slightest idea what it meant.

"Say it then."

"Say what?"

"Say you think I'm the bee's knee's. The berries. The cat's meow. A darb. Say it, Joel Dean. Say all those things to me."

"You've been drinking," I said instead.

"Oh, Joel Dean. I had hopes for you," she said. She twirled an exquisite looking purse with long strings around her fingers. She walked back toward her bright colored little roadster.

"Please move out of my way. I'm going to Jefferson City. Maybe I can find one person who appreciates me."

"I don't think that's a real good idea, Estelle."

"Joel Dean!" She stomped her foot in the dust.

"How about staying here and keeping me company."

"Why? You lonesome?"

"Sure."

"What would we do out here in the dark all by ourselves where no one can see us or ever know what we did here?'

"Talk," I said.

"Talk?" her laughter tinkled in the night. "About what?"

"About a picnic tomorrow when I'm off duty."

"A picnic? You mean with those dreadful ants and those smelly cow things around?"

"Well, I thought we could go down on the Niangua. It's awful pretty down there and. . ."

"Drag me in my satin slippers through the dirt and brush, is that it? In my new short dress I just bought in St. Louis. You want me to go tearing through thorns and thistles, ripping it from me,

38

leaving me naked down on the Niangua?"

Her idea was beginning to sound a whole lot better than the one I had.

"Joel Dean, answer my question. What would you do to me in that condition?"

"What if you don't like my answer?"

"I know what you'd do to Nita German in that condition. Of course, you'd have to pay her five dollars. Isn't that what she charges now? Have you ever given Nita German five dollars, Joel Dean?"

"Estelle, I. . ."

"Do you want to kiss me?"

"Right now? I'm on duty. . ."

"You don't really."

She started back to her roadster, but I caught her hand and whirled her to me. She flew into my arms and her hands came right up to clasp tightly around my neck. The little rosebud mouth was all over mine, hot and fiery. Her perfume filled my breath while my knees got rubbery and the skin started burning on my face.

My arms slipped around her waist and I pulled her soft little body to me. She was eager, holding me even tighter around the neck. Then she broke free and stepped back.

She was breathing fast, as was I, and her eyes glowed in the moonlight.

"What now, Joel Dean?" she whispered in a husky voice. "What now?"

Well did she think I was going to say it? Before I could though, or even think of how to put it, she was pulling the all white linen dress over her head. Underneath she wore nothing. I was struck dumbfounded. I had a glimpse of the Garden of Eden, but before I even had time to admire her nakedness, she grabbed my hand and pulled me to Ora's sedan, opening the back door. She slid across the seat and all I could see of her was a silly little cloche hat over the full head of curls and the pencil lines over eyes no longer dreamy.

"Get your clothes off, ninny," she whispered to me, and without really thinking about what I was doing, without building up to it the way I would have preferred, I did as she said. I crouched and slipped through the door of Ora's Chevrolet. My hand closed on a smooth, warm thigh.

The top of the hill lit up like daytime and a klaxon sound shook my nerves until my head started to vibrate and my heart tried to work its way out of my chest.

The lights swerved around Ora's Chevrolet with the sound of rocks sliding under tires and I came out of the back seat with nothing on, groping on the ground for my pistol. The gray 1929 Buick was even with us and I looked through the window at the laughing face of the driver. Doyle Savoy.

"Give it hell, Joel Dean," he shouted. Then the laugh died away and the Buick and its lights faded out of sight on the way to St. Louis.

You know, an experience like that I didn't even want to think about. I don't remember exactly how we got our clothes on, but I can remember I hadnt done anything I'd set out to do. As I watched the lights of Estelle's little yellow and black Jordan Playboy roadster growing smaller, I had a sickening feeling in the bottom of my stomach. I'd let Ora down.

I saw no need to stay where I was any longer. The fox had fled the chicken coop. On the way back to Linn Creek I tried every way I knew to sort it all out in my mind. Trying to get myself off the hook. Why was Doyle, a deputy sheriff like myself, driving a whiskey run for Yawley Earnhardt? The thought occurred to me that Estelle might have intentionally occupied me so that her daddy's whiskey could get through the roadblock, but I didn't want to believe that.

The obvious thing I had to do, it seemed, was to go in to see Ora, tell him what happened, then turn my badge in. I didn't want to do that, I liked what I was doing. I liked working for Ora. I liked the respect I'd been getting. So, there I was with an important decision to make—a serious decision—and all I could focus my mind on all the way back into town were those rosebud lips turned up on the end of a soft, warm body. And the feel of a smooth, naked thigh.

I opened the door to the office quietly, not sure but what Ora might be the one keeping watch tonight, but it was Noah. Noah was short and stout as a good mule, and had the best head of white hair in town according to the Dutchman at the barber shop. Noah's wife had died along with their firstborn son during his birth. I guess Noah just never gave them up as he didn't marry again. He was curled up on the cot in the corner, a loud snort coming out of him every now and then. I started to close the door when I noticed an envelope lying on the floor where I suppose it had been slipped under the door. On the outside of the envelope was the word SHERIFF.

I wasn't sure whether to open it or not, but on the chance it might be urgent, I lifted the flap and pulled out the note. The fragrance that hit me was one I'd smelled before. It was the same heady smell I noticed every time I met Nita German on the street.

The note was printed and unsigned. It said simply that if the sheriff wanted Champ Gowan he could find him in the abandoned barn on the old German place. Nita was turning in the man the whole town said she was in love with.

Once again I unlocked the door going from the office to the kitchen, a door that was always locked, even during meals. I turned on the electric light over the large eating table and walked to the door going into Addie and Ora's bedroom. When I pushed the button on the wall, I could hear the buzzer through the door.

I poured myself a cup of the coffee Addie always kept on the stove, sat down at the table and was halfway through the coffee when Ora came out of the bedroom hitching up his suspenders.

I handed him the note without a word. After he'd decided what to do about it, when he was a little more awake, I'd have to tell him about Doyle. And about Estelle.

"Where'd you get it?" he asked.

"Somebody slipped it under the door."

Ora held the note to his nose, but he didn't say anything.

"What time is it?" he asked.

"One thirty."

"They ought to be sleeping real nice about right now," Ora said. "Be a good time to take 'em."

Now that's what I thought he would want to do. That's why I'd woke him. And why I had that nervous twinge inside me. But to tell the truth, I was anxious for it.

"Could be a trap," I said. "She's pretty thick with Champ."

"I'm taking that into consideration," he said. "Go get Noah and take a couple of shotguns and a 30-30 in case one of 'em runs. I got a couple of dry cell lights in the cabinet. Put everything in the car and wait for me."

I was glad for the action and decided Doyle and Estelle could wait until we came back. If we came back. I got nearly to the door.

"Joel Dean, go over to the boarding house and see if Doyle maybe never left for St. Louis. We could use him."

And so, I had to tell him.

"Ora, I saw Doyle at the top of Rifle Ridge. He was going toward Jefferson City in Yawley's other gray Buick."

Ora gave me a quick look, his eyes squinted to a thin line the way they did when something didn't set right with him.

"Why didn't you stop him?"

And so, I had to tell him all of it.

"I stopped Estelle Earnhardt in that little yellow and black roadster of hers. I was sort of engaged with her, you might say. Doing what I had no business doing while I was supposed to be on duty."

Without thinking anymore about it, I reached to my shirtfront and unpinned my badge. I held it out to him, trying my damnedest to keep my hand steady.

"So, Yawley's using his daughter and my deputy to get around us," Ora said, squinting even more.

"I've thought about it Ora. About how it happened," I said, still holding the badge out to him. "And in all fairness to her, I don't think Estelle knew she was a part of it. She'd been drinking, is all. Her being there when Doyle came by was just a coincidence."

"Her being with you, him driving by. Count that as a double coincidence." He looked at the badge in my hand. "If you're ever going to be fit to wear that thing, you got to remember: one coincidence is unlikely, two is on purpose."

It was real quiet inside the Chevrolet on the way to the old German farm. For once, Noah didn't have any jokes to tell nor any funny stories he'd made up. Ora drove while I held the two shotguns and the rifle between my legs pointed straight up.

The Germans had gone broke. When the house burned, though it wasn't much, it was the end for them. They'd abandoned the place about the time my pa had died. Nita, sixteen at the time, already had wild ways. I remember the older boys laughing and snickering whenever she passed by.

Nita and Addie had been enemies. They even had a fist fight

43

on the school grounds. It was not your typical girl type name calling, hair pulling fight. That one was between two girls who knew how to slug it out like the boys. Addie suffered a bloody nose, but she had won. I never paid much attention at the time, but the other kids said it had been over the rights to Champ Gowan.

But the end of the line could have arrived for Champ. If he was involved in Shorty's killing it meant his crimes just kept getting bigger and bigger. I wondered how Addie would feel about it.

Ora killed the headlights a quarter mile before we came to the old barn standing in weeds nearly up to the roof. The Chevrolet coasted as close as Ora dared, not wanting the sound of the engine to wake Champ.

"Remember," Ora said quietly before we got out of the car. "That Thompson ain't very accurate and it has a tendency to climb and shoot high. So try and stay low if they start shooting."

We each took a battery light and Ora and I had the shotguns. Though the night was cool, I could feel the sweat between my hand and the smooth, walnut stock. And a trickle down my backbone.

Noah stayed just outside the big center doorway where both doors hanging from a strap hinge looked ready to fall off. I worked my way as quietly as I could through the weeds around to the back of the barn, cussing to myself the cockleburs and the tangle of smart weeds. By the time I got there my eyes were getting accustomed to the dark. Through the length of the barn I saw Ora starting inside. I sucked in a long, deep breath, clenched the shotgun tighter and went through the doorway.

Ora went down one side of the barn, I took the other. He stopped suddenly and made a circling motion with his arm. I went across to where he stood, pointing into a stall where three figures the size of men lay on a pile of hay. I looked at Ora and he nodded his head.

We both turned on our dry cell lights and the three men came scrambling up out of the hay.

"Easy," Ora said. "This is Sheriff Mitchell and I got three guns on you boys. Don't do anything foolish and things'll be all right."

I recognized Champ Gowan. Slab-sided face, almost as thin as my own, long dark hair that fell in strands across dark eyes with long lashes and bushy brows. Thin nose and jutting chin used up the rest of his face. With both hands he combed his hair through his fingers into a center part, and I could see that prison life hadn't destroyed any of his handsomeness.

Of the other two, one was big with some fat on him, bushy hair and the start of a beard, sort of rusty in color. His eyes were small and lost in his fleshy face. The other one was short with wild looking eyes and nervous, twitchy fingers that kept clenching and unclenching.

"What's this about, Ora?" Champ asked. "We just got out of stir. We ain't had time to do nothing."

"Yawley thinks you been picking on him again," Ora said.

"Hell," Champ said with a grin starting to form on his thin lips. "If Yawley's missing a car again, it sure wasn't me this time."

"He's missing more'n that," Ora said. "He's missing Shorty Mickelson. Got himself killed running whiskey for Yawley."

Champ gave it some thought.

"You giving Yawley protection nowadays, Ora?"

"Killing's agin the law, Champ. Even bootleggers."

"And you think we did it?"

"Thought we'd talk some, down at my office," Ora said. "You had to come in to see me on parole anyway. I'll give you a ride into town."

"Damn decent of you, Ora," Champ said. "You start your days a little early for me, though."

"You'll get used to it," Ora said. He looked around the stall with his light while I kept mine trained on the three. Not spotting anything, Ora said, "Let's put the cuffs on them, Joel Dean. Then you can look through the hay for the Thompson."

The big one spoke for the first time. "Just what is it you're lookin for?"

"I thought you might have one of them Thompson submachine guns layin around," Ora said. "Like the one killed Shorty."

The little guy let out kind of a snort for a laugh. "You think I had a Thompson you birds woulda got within a hundred yards of this place?"

While I was putting the cuffs on Champ, he looked me over.

"Joel Dean Gregory, ain't you?" He didn't wait for me to answer. "How's Addie doing?"

"Sound asleep last I seen her," I said.

"Addie still cooking that good food in the jail house, Ora?" Champ asked.

Ora said, "She is."

Champ shook his head in disapproval. "Good looking woman like that, Sheriff, ought to be sitting down to eat in one of those fancy restaurants in St. Louis or Sedalia instead of cooking for a bunch of criminals like us."

"I'll tell her you admire how she looks," Ora said. "Maybe she'll fix you something extra special on the day of the hangin."

The day was still an infant when Ora stopped the Chevrolet under the redbud tree between the jail and the courthouse. I got out and opened the back door to motion Champ, big Buster Workman and little wild-eyed Wilbur Crowder out of the car.

Through the pass high in the valley to the east of us, I could see the sky turning a lighter shade of gray with a glow line along the horizon behind the fringe of trees. Down Main Street that ran in front of the courthouse and jail, a dewy mist rose over the Osage River, and way out in midstream I could make out the Rasher brothers being swallowed up in it along with their ferry.

Champ stretched as best he could with the handcuffs on and looked up at the redbud which some professor from Springfield had once called the largest he'd ever seen of that species.

"Judas tree," Champ said. "Big enough to hang a man from. Fits me, I guess. Seems like I hang myself everything I do."

While the others dismounted from the Chevrolet, Champ's eyes swept the length of Main Street, the sixteen buildings in a row, then across the street where a grove of linn trees, oak and hickory bordered Linn Creek. His eyes came back to rest on the vapors rising and evaporating in the August morning heat over the Osage.

"A pretty spot," he remarked to no one in particular. "Damn shame they had to ruin it by building a jail house here."

Wilbur looked around, a sneer on his face. "What's the name of this dump?"

"Wilbur," Champ said, "talk like that will get you hanged in this town faster than shootin a bootlegger."

"I didn't shoot no bootlegger," Wilbur said.

I motioned them inside the building where I helped Noah search them and lock them away in a cell upstairs.

I offered to stay in the office until breakfast, more than an hour away. Noah thanked me as he left. I should have been tired as I'd had no sleep at all, but I wasn't. I had too many things to think about. Estelle. Doyle. Ora. And about me.

I was getting comfortable in Ora's oak swivel chair when I heard the lock turning on the door coming from the kitchen. I looked up expecting Ora, but it was Addie bringing in two cups of coffee.

"You're up early," I said. "Not time to start breakfast yet, is it?"

"You think I could sleep while you and Ora and Noah was out

47

huntin people wanted for murder."

"You knew it was Champ?"

She sipped at the coffee, then smiled at me. "Good old Champ Gowan. Something bad happen? Go hunt up Champ Gowan."

"You think he's innocent?"

"Champ ain't the kind anybody'd call innocent."

"Just wondered how you felt about him now."

Another sip. Another smile.

"Champ Gowan. He was a long time ago. A long, long time."

"Well, they were asleep. Didn't give us any trouble. No need to worry about us."

"Well, it sure didn't bother Ora's sleep any. He's back in bed snoring."

I wasn't going to say anything to that. Husband and wife talk, well that was something I didn't want to get in the middle of.

She stared out the window where the mist had been reduced to thin, wispy curls hanging in the rays of the lemon yellow sun. Her voice now barely a whisper.

"I remember once, not long after we were married, Ora floating down the Osage where a crazy man killed his wife and threatened his kids. Ora had to shoot that man in order to save the kids, then he rode horseback all the way home, getting here just before sunrise. I was waiting up for him, so nervous I couldn't even hold a glass of water in my hand."

She took a drink from the cup and when she lowered it, I noticed ripples on the surface of the coffee.

"We stayed up that morning for hours, just talking. When we finally went to bed. . ." She paused, smiling to herself at the memory, "It was almost another hour before we got any sleep."

She smiled some more, still staring out the window. I shifted around in the chair, leaning closer to her cup and I smelled the whiskey in it. That surprised me because I realized then how little I really did know about my sister. We were raised in a house

48

where whiskey drinking was looked on with no amount of tolerance. I had tried it several times in Springfield, just to be part of the crowd, but the early years had left too strong an impression on me for it to be any source of enjoyment.

"That was some night," she continued, speaking louder now. "At least I got rid of my tensions."

She continued to stare out the window in front, looking off down the row of tin roofed store buildings setting on rock foundations as clay colored as the dust that powdered up from the street in a slight morning breeze.

"But that was a long time ago, too. A lot of water has flowed under this old bridge. A lot of mornings I sat and waited for them to bring him in full of bullet holes layin on a slab."

With her back to me, still looking out the window, she said, "I can smell the heat already this morning."

She turned around, facing me. "Smell it out there? Layin in the grass just waiting for us to come outside so it can spring up off the ground and suffocate us."

"Never looked at the heat quite like it was a panther or something," I said.

"August," she said in disgust. She dropped into a chair beside the desk, looking me straight in the eye. "I seen thirty of them, now, Little Brother. All of them the same. All of them hot. All of them dreary. All the wrong things happenin."

She got up and walked over to unlock the door into the kitchen.

"I got married in August," she said, a hand on the door. Then she closed it gently and the lock clicked into place.

Addie wasn't in the kitchen when I brought the prisoners

49

down for breakfast. Something was burning on the stove and Birdie was talking to herself. Not a good time for me to ask her anything.

Champ had cleaned up like he was headed for a ball instead of a jail cell. The gray suit pants with the chalk stripe he wore didn't look slept-in and his shirt still bore the marks of a hot iron here and there. It was downright remarkable how neatly Champ could keep himself, even in jail.

He looked around the kitchen at intervals as if he was looking for someone.

Wilbur was looking around, too. He took in the two other doors leading out of the big kitchen and just about everything he could lay his eyes on. Filing it all away, probably, along with all the other stuff that had gotten him into trouble. He got around to looking the length of the table at Ora who was paying no attention to anything except the mound of scrambled eggs and bacon Birdie had piled on his plate.

"Don't make no sense, men eatin and not workin," Birdie mumbled as she brought the coffee over to the table. Champ looked across the table and smiled.

"Birdie, you don't look a day older'n you did the last time I was in here."

"I's old, all right," Birdie said. "Workin way I do, co'se I get old. Jis cause I's colored no sign I don't get old."

"Thad Turpin told me once you was a right smart lookin' gal when you was young," Champ said. He stuck his cup across the table so Birdie could pour.

She snorted. "Thad Turpin, lot he know. Wadn't good fo nothin. Nevah put in a honest day's work. Always tootin on that ol horn o his. Think he's a music man. Ain't seen no music man was good fo nothin."

"Just the same," Champ said, "I'll bet you were some fancy lady. . ."

"Ain't nevah been no *fancy* lady." Birdie's voice rose and she

50

pointed her finger across the table at Champ. "Don't call Birdie no fancy lady. Cause I ain't nevah been that kind. Now you talkin fancy ladies, you talkin bout Nita German. . ."

Too late Birdie realized who she was speaking to. She retreated to the stove with her coffee pot leaving Champ holding an empty cup over the table. He withdrew it slowly and set it down.

"Nita's fancy all right," he said, more or less to himself. He buttered a biscuit and spread some jam on top. "Nita's only problem is she's got an awful big mouth."

Ora ran his hands over the mane of his black walking mare, then climbed into the saddle. Without a word he set off down Main Street. Ora liked to ride when he had some thinking to do.

Addie's mare was smaller than Ora's, and not as smooth in the front-legs-walking, back-legs-trotting gait. I had to nudge her a little to catch up.

Ora's eyes shot back and forth, scanning the street, searching the storefronts for something different, something changed since last night.

Postmaster Bill Schuyler stopped in his tracks, holding the flag he was about to fasten to the pole. He stared at the man who'd captured Champ Gowan and a machine gunner from Kansas City as if it wasn't the thousandth time he'd seen him riding down the street.

"Jesus," I could almost hear him saying to himself and to everyone who came into the post office that day. "A machine gunner from Kansas City. Imagine that."

LIMB OF THE JUDAS TREE

Lonnie Harper was standing in front of Volly's Shell Station, a snake writhing in each hand, while Volly filled the tank of a Model T Ford belonging to a farmer north of town. The three of them waved a hand as we rode by.

"Get a horse," Lonnie yelled out, trying to make a joke. "Cheat old Volly out of gas money."

We had an audience that morning. Shopkeepers came to the doorway, stepped into the street, lifted a hand, nodded a head.

Our sheriff, by God. He's something now, ain't he?

We rode to the river's edge just as the Rasher brothers were bringing their ferry ashore, Jack pulling in the rope and Mutt dropping the ramp down to rest on the hardened, clay pier. We rode onto the ferry and stayed in the saddle as the trip across would be short with the river so low in August. Both brothers always wore short billed military type caps they had brought back with them from France in the Big War. Mutt made a note in a dog-eared spiral wound notebook to bill the county for our crossing. Jack, the talkative one, asked Ora about capturing Champ Gowan and the other two ex-convicts. Ora told it with few words, leaving it to Jack to color it up some in the retelling.

We rode off the ferry onto a dusty road that connected with the state road that went to Gravois Mills and Versailles. Motor cars mostly used the toll bridge that crossed the Osage downstream, but horses and pedestrian traffic stuck with the ferry at a nickel a crossing. Ora rode off the road, following a game path to the top of a slight hill, then dipping back to the main road. Ora never spoke—as was his custom on these rides—nor did I. By the time we got back to the ferry crossing, the horses were lathered and I could feel a sweaty dampness on my shirt. Addie had been right about the heat. It sprung right up and grabbed you.

We had to wait for the ferry. We dismounted and loosened the girths for the horses' comfort. Across the river, high on the bluff where the Niangua and the Osage came together was a rock promontory everybody called Lover's Leap. An old Indian legend about Lover's Leap had fair Indian maiden Winona leaping to her death rather than be betrothed to Okema, chief of the Osage. Okema then had plunged after her, locked in mortal combat with Winona's real love, Minetus. On top of the bluff overlooking Lover's Leap was the picnic spot I hoped to take Estelle to.

My mind was so engaged with thoughts of Estelle I failed to see the motor car approaching until it stopped suddenly at the river's edge. The cloud of dust following the car settled slowly, coating our horses and our clothes with a fine, clay colored powder.

The driver left the motor running. I saw why. Nita German stepped out on the passenger side and the vehicle backed up, turned around and sped away. I recognized the driver as a shopkeeper from Gravois Mills.

Nita wanted us to think she was embarrassed, but I couldn't see that she was. She pushed at her hair with one hand and fussed with a belt on her white dress with red flowers of some kind running in rows around it. Her face was too made up, her lips too big and too bright red, her eyes outlined with black on the eyebrows and under the lashes. But it was difficult to take your eyes off of her. I suppose the quality of her attraction was due to every man looking upon her as a conquest for certain. I was no exception.

"Certainly is hot for so early in the morning," she said. She dabbed at her face with a delicate looking lace handkerchief.

I agreed that it was. Ora said nothing.

"I haven't seen you around much, Joel Dean, since you came back from. . .wherever it was. Springfield? Where you been keeping yourself?"

She wore that big, friendly business smile of hers. Every conversation was made personal, which was her way.

"Working I guess, Nita," I said. "I was pretty busy with Hobarts making tie rafts, but that didn't last long. Clerked at the

53

courthouse some."

"Oh, I know all that. I mean I haven't seen you sporting any of the young ladies around."

"Well," I said, stalling a bit, then shrugging. "Maybe they just don't cotton to me."

"Oh, I know better than that. Tall, good looking man like you. You put me in mind of your daddy. He was always such a handsome man. And a real gentleman, too."

She stole a sideways glance at Ora who was watching the Rasher brothers bringing the ferry back across the river.

"I'll bet young ladies in the county come knocking your door down."

I laughed along with her. She dabbed at her face some more, then dropped down to dab at her throat and let her hand trail downward into the sharp V of her dress between her breasts. Naturally my eyes followed.

"Come to think of it, Joel Dean, I saw you with some young lady in Ora's car two, three nights ago. I couldn't recognize her from where I was standing. It was too dark."

I didn't have to tell her, in spite of her prying, but I had no reason not to. A man likely wouldn't have asked, but a woman, well, they had to have something or someone to talk about. Some do anyway.

"I believe you must mean, Estelle Earnhardt," I said.

Immediately her eyes turned cool and her hand dropped away from her front.

"My, she certainly does get around now, doesn't she?"

She turned away to watch the ferry come ashore.

I was holding Ora's black mare Katrina and she didn't like the commotion the Rashers were making as they tied up. I turned the horse away, then led her along with Addie's mare, Sunray, back up the road twenty feet or so to calm her down. When I walked back to the ferry with the horses, Nita was talking to Ora.

Jack Rasher helped me board the horses and as we shoved off

from shore, he began telling me about the channel cat he'd caught the evening before in one of the old pools along the river that had been made for holding ties. I wasn't trying to pry, but I half listened to Jack and half listened to Nita talking to Ora.

". . .used some stink bait that Old Man Hadley made up for me. . ." Jack was saying.

". . .miss seeing you, talking with you, Ora. How long's it been now. . ." Nita said, her voice low, barely carrying.

". . .thought the danged bamboo pole was going to pop right in two. . ."

". . .anytime you want, for coffee, anything, you know. I always could talk to you, Ora. . ."

". . .my old handscales are rusty, but they read seven pounds. Now did you ever. . ."

". . .more'n fifty, Nita." Ora was talking now. "Some say I can't keep up with my thirty-year-old wife. . ."

". . .as big as that one you caught that time, Joel Dean. Joel Dean, you listening to me, boy?"

". . .don't know Ora Mitchell when they say that," Nita snapped. "Not like I do."

She was lying perfectly flat on the lounge that sat on the wrap-around porch of the Earnhardt's impressive home. The sun bounced golden rays through an elm close by, lighting her face then shading it as the wind-blown leaves dipped and dodged in the breeze. She made no movement, even from her breathing. An electric fan buzzed at her feet and the hem of her white dress rustled in its draft.

"Hello Estelle," I said.

Only silence. The cigarette holder hung limply from her fingers, the unlit cigarette overbalancing to the point of nearly dropping from her hand.

"I wondered about the picnic," I said. Why was I so nervous? "You never said."

"Do my breasts show through the dress?" she asked.

I hadn't even been looking at her breasts. Why did she ask? She wasn't even watching me.

"No."

"Good."

She sprang up from the lounge as if motivated by some urgent need.

"Now do they?" she asked, standing as straight as a soldier in front of me.

I was embarrassed of a sudden and I could feel the color rushing to my face. I looked. Nowhere in sight was any sign of her breasts under the sailer-like middie blouse.

"No," I told her again.

"See," she said, and grabbed the bottom of the blouse and pulled it up under her chin. She had a tight band tied around her chest just above silky underpants that were scandalously short. Her breasts were smashed completely flat and the two nipples were only small bumps under the sash.

"What do you think of it?" she asked, not identifying the 'it.'

"Uh. . ." I stuttered. "Think of what?"

"The dress, you ninny." She let it fall back into place. "It's the latest. they had a picture of one in *Colliers*. Perfectly flat. That's the way it's supposed to look. And I got a little sailor hat to go with it."

She picked up a white hat from the lounge and held it for me to see. It was a sailor's hat, all right. One blue star in front.

I could not hold back a smile.

"A lot you know," she snapped, turning away in a huff.

56

"I don't like it," I said. "I mean, I like the way *you* look, but. . .but, well, anybody could be underneath there looking like that. Even I could look straight up and down that way."

"I don't like people making fun of my new things," she said. She took up her reclining position on the lounge once again.

"I'm sorry, Estelle. I'll work on it and I'll probably get to liking it before long. Especially with you in it."

"Humph," she said without moving.

"I just don't understand why, all of a sudden, girls want to look like boys. Like they didn't have any shape to them at all."

She turned her head to stare at me.

"Would you like to be a girl, Joel Dean?"

It was the first time I'd ever considered it.

"No," I confessed after a very short study of the question.

She was back to staring at the ceiling of the porch again.

"You can walk down the street smoking a cigarette if you want. . ."

"Don't smoke," I interrupted.

"And take a drink of whiskey anytime you want. . ."

"Don't drink whiskey."

"And take your shirt off in public. . ."

"I'd feel funny."

"And take a pee out in the alley, standing up, holding it in your hand." She sat up, swinging around to let her legs dangle off the edge of the lounge. Her voice was sharp and demanding. "You do pee, don't you."

"What's that got to do with anything?" I asked.

"I'm tired of being a nice little girl."

I had nothing to say to that.

"You want to make love to me?" she asked. "You want to be the first one, Joel Dean?"

I wanted to answer that as soon as I caught my breath.

But I didn't get to. Footsteps pounded on the porch behind me. I froze, waiting, then felt a hand clasp my shoulder and I

LIMB OF THE JUDAS TREE

jumped.

"Joel Dean," Yawley said. "How've you been, boy?"

"Fine." What else could I say. Had he heard?

"I see you and Stell are getting along good, here," he said with a laugh, squeezing my shoulder. "She's going away to college, but of course she's told you that. Stephens College up in Columbia. Gonna make a lady out of her."

Yawley laughed at that as if he had doubts it could be done.

"Say, Joel Dean, I been looking for you to come by one of the Klan meetings. We need young fellows like you. Somebody's got to keep things going after us old guys wear out. Gonna be somebody in this county, then you gotta be one of us."

"I'm not much of a joiner," I said.

"Heard Ora's got you on the night watch for whiskey runners. You're going to freeze your tail end off on that ridge in a month or so. Early fall and cold weather coming on. What you're going to need is some long handled underwear."

Yawley stuck a bill in my shirt pocket. I could feel the crinkle of it. Before I could say or do anything, he was walking away.

"Don't forget about the Klan, now. We'll be looking for you."

I didn't like what was happening. I didn't like it at all. First there was last night with Estelle and Doyle, now this. Angry, I pulled the bill out of my pocket and looked at it. Fifty dollars. Half a month's pay.

I whirled on Estelle, looking for someone to spill my anger on. She was gone. I put the fifty dollar bill in her little sailor hat lying on the lounge. The one she'd bought to go with the shirt that made her look like a boy.

"Figuring to break into the whiskey business were you,Champ?" Ora was asking.

Champ sucked on a matchstick. "I'd be drinking myself out of business, Ora."

"Where abouts did y'all have your personal stuff stashed away?"

"All I got is what I got on me," Champ said. "I even threw the suit coat and tie away that the state gave me. I'm traveling light."

"Except for them two," Ora nodded towards the cell area where I'd left Buster Workman and Wilbur Crowder.

"They'll get tired of the hills," Champ said. "Nobody with any sense stays around here, do they? This ain't exactly a tourist stop."

"Don't mean for it to be," Ora said. "Still, it draws some we'd as soon not have."

"You asking me to move on, Ora?"

"Maybe you ought to stick around till things are settled about Shorty."

"Here? In jail?"

"I hate to see you sleeping in some barn, Champ."

Champ spent about a minute looking square into Ora's eyes, neither one blinking.

"You got the wrong man, Ora."

"We'll see what Noah finds when he gets back from searching the barn," Ora said. He took out his watch, looked at it, then put it away. "More'n an hour yet till we eat. You want a cup of coffee?"

Champ took the match out of his mouth, looked at it and threw it in a trash can by Ora's desk.

"I'd like that, Ora," he said. "Heavy on the cream and sugar."

I unlocked the door into the kitchen, went through and locked it back. Addie was helping Birdie with the meal. I stacked up three cups of hot coffee, added the cream and sugar in one for Champ, and let myself back into the office.

I'd just set the cups down when I heard Noah drive up and park the Chevrolet under the redbud tree. We each had a sip from our cups before the door opened and Noah came in carrying a gun that looked like a rifle only it had a large cylindrical chamber under the barrel and a pistol type grip under the stock. Half of a leather sling hung down from the barrel. A Thompson submachine gun.

Ora said, "Where'd you find that, Noah?"

"On the joists over top of where them boys was sleeping last night," Noah said, looking at Champ. "You fellows are lucky it didn't fall down on you in your sleep. Coulda got hurt."

Little Wilbur Crowder's squinchy eyes fastened on the three doors leading out of the kitchen again—just as they had at breakfast— while Ora was giving thanks. Addie glanced up from her plate at Champ and he was looking at her. Their eyes held until we mumbled Amen.

As we passed the food around, Wilbur still hadn't gotten over the unusual situation confronting him. He just couldn't take his eyes off the doors.

"In case Noah didn't explain it to you," Ora said to Wilbur, "all the doors are locked. And the only way to get out without being let out is to take the key off me after I'm dead."

Wilbur swallowed hard, his eyes darting back and forth between Ora and Champ. Champ looked at Wilbur, and if I read his meaning right he was saying go ahead if you think you can. But you can't.

"How you been, Addie?" Champ asked, looking into her eyes again.

"Doing fine, Champ. Staying out of trouble."

He smiled. "More'n I can say."

A moment later he said, "Still cooking a mighty fine meal, Addie. Wouldn't mind jail so much if they'd let you cook for me."

"County pays a dollar a day for feeding you," Addie said. "Stay as long as you like."

The lock clicked on the door from the office and Doyle came through wearing the same jeans and plaid shirt he'd had on the day he drove Yawley's car to St. Louis. He took a place at the table without a word. Those around him passed the bowls of food to him.

Ora always ate faster than a starved dog after a hunt. He was usually through with his dessert before most of the others were through the main meal. When he shoved his dessert dish away from him and drew his coffee cup closer, everyone put on a spurt at eating to hurry and finish.

Doyle was cleaning up his plate with the crust of his light bread when he looked over at Champ.

"You must be Champ Gowan."

"Must be," Champ agreed.

Doyle pulled the peach cobbler over and helped himself.

"Spent some prison time on the farm, I hear," he said to Champ.

"Didn't much care for it," Champ said, grinning. "Never wanted to be a farmer."

"I spent a couple of years at the Wall myself," Doyle said, and Champ did a double take, looking at him with mild surprise.

"Do tell," Champ said.

"That's right. But I was pardoned. That's how come I can wear a badge."

Champ said, "Good for you."

"Good for Doyle. Good for the governor," Addie said. I waited for the rest of it, knowing what was coming. "Seems ever time the governor needs a little spending money, somebody gets a pardon."

Doyle smiled at Addie. "Addie sees to it I don't forget I was inside."

"What were you in for?" Wilbur asked.

Doyle turned his attention to the little man, looking him over thoroughly before turning his eyes back to Champ.

"I killed a man," Doyle said.

Champ pushed his slicked out cobbler dish away from him and stuck a matchstick in his mouth. When he looked back at Doyle his eyes were smiling along with his mouth.

"Had it coming probably," he said.

Doyle scooped the last bite of cobbler out of his bowl and Birdie reached over his shoulder and whisked it away before he could entertain any thoughts about seconds.

"He was a bootlegger like Shorty Mickelson," Doyle said.

"You wouldn't happen to have shot Shorty, too, would you?" Champ asked, still grinning.

"No such luck for you," Doyle said. "Word is, around town, that crime's been solved."

"Sounds like you might have been framed, too. Like I was," Champ said. The grin was gone now and his face took on a serious look.

"I shot him all right. Thirty-eight caliber. Twice in the heart. The jury said it was manslaughter, but the governor decided it was justifiable."

"How did that happen?" Wilbur asked.

Again Doyle turned his attention to the little man, then back to Champ before answering.

62

"Caught him in my bedroom."

"Sounds like manslaughter to me," Champ said. "I had some experience in law. Did some graduate work while I was up in Jeff on the farm."

"Well, see, common law says you can kill a man if you catch him in your bedroom."

"What about after he's left your bedroom?" Champ had his grin working again.

"That's a gray area," Doyle said. "Ask Joel Dean. He's a lawyer."

Champ looked at me, his eyebrows raised a bit. "You don't say."

"Tried three cases," I said. "Two for chicken thievery—lost those two— and one for breach of promise. Settled out of court. Doyle's right about the gray area and common law. Or unwritten law, as some call it. Two different juries could see the same case two different ways if common law is involved."

Wilbur said, "You mean you could kill a man and get off by saying he was tampering with your woman?"

Champ took the matchstick out of his mouth and pointed it at Doyle. "You just heard the man. He *did* it."

"Well, then," Wilbur said, "why don't we say this Shorty guy was tampering with one of our women."

Champ turned on Wilbur with a real stern look. "We didn't kill Shorty."

"I know that and you know that," Wilbur said. "But they don't act like they do."

Addie said, "Doyle, you told that story plenty of times, but you never said what happened to your wife."

"I left her," Doyle said. "She went back to work. North of the tracks in Sedalia where the lights all turn red at night."

He drained his cup and set it down. He looked at Addie who was watching him intently.

Doyle finished his story. "Back where I found her."

Ora put Doyle on suspension, though he agreed that Doyle might not have known about the roadblock—Doyle smiled over at me—but he said Doyle shouldn't have been engaged anyway in an activity that was illegal.

Doyle shrugged it off and produced a flask, offering Ora and me a drink.

That night I was on the roadblock again and turned back Lud Harris who was willing to try Yawley's run again, now that he thought Shorty's killers were safely in jail.

I stopped Eddie Simmons, who, according to Main Street blabber was selling to the Monger brothers, Artis and Griff, over in Miller County. Some said Eddie distilled a low grade of lamp oil he sold for whiskey, but it was better than the rest of the Monger brothers' stock. I didn't know anything about that. The Monger's grade of whiskey, I figured, was the same as the rest of their reputation, which was something they couldn't take to the bank. But I guess they didn't need to. It was said they ran double what Yawley did, but Yawley had a higher grade of clientele with a more refined taste. And he got twice as much per gallon as the Mongers did, if the hangers-on in the barber shop knew anything about it.

I'd gone to grade school with Eddie, had a fight with him and whipped him if I remembered right. Anyway, he didn't give me any back talk when I explained why he couldn't go through. Just said Artis was going to be mad as hell and would probably tell Ora about it. I said Artis was going to have to stand in line.

I turned away Ernest Raines again. I did have one small sip

with Ernest, he was feeling so down.

The trucker who had hauled furniture squares to Mexico came through going south for another load. He asked if I knew whether Nita was home for the evening. I didn't.

I came dragging in the next morning just as everyone else was getting up from the breakfast table. Birdie said I looked so tired, kissed me on top of the head and gave me an extra big plate of bacon and eggs. While I was finishing it off, I heard Yawley's voice through the door. It wasn't hard to guess what it was about. I heard Yawley mention my name so I guess he'd found the fifty dollar bill by now in Estelle's silly little hat.

I thought about going to see Estelle, but my butt was dragging through my tracks. I wanted to hear about her plans to go away to college. I was hoping it was only wishful thinking on Yawley's part and that she would be here all winter.

And I kind of wanted to continue the conversation with her about being first.

Roommates Lonnie and Volly were working during the day and I had our room all to myself. I checked that Lonnie hadn't left any of his snakes in the room, then I slept like a coon in a hollow tree.

That afternoon, sitting in front of Volly's Shell Station, across from the courthouse, I saw Ora go into the side door to Judge Cargrove's office. The judge was over the other two county judges and the three of them made all the decisions for the county, except for the ones Ora made as sheriff and Gideon made as prosecutor. I'd worked for several months in Judge Cargrove's office doing clerical work and got along famously with him. I think that was why he didn't give Ora any trouble when I was made deputy.

But it was no secret Yawley and the judge were as thick as Sears and Roebuck. Pretty soon it was Yawley going into the judge's office so he was going to be in on whatever it was the judge wanted to talk with Ora about. I didn't know if it was true about Gideon and the judge being in on Yawley's whiskey running—I was a whole lot more skeptical about Gideon being a partner than I was the judge. Ora sure got called on the carpet pretty fast.

But, see, Judge Cargrove really couldn't do anything about Ora's decision to stop the whiskey trade. Ora was elected by the people, same as the judge, so they were the ones he answered to.

Another reason could be that somehow Doyle was tied in with the judge and Yawley. It was the judge who pushed Doyle off on Ora, shortly after I was hired. So, maybe it was tit for tat. Me for Doyle. But Doyle was a good deputy and I would welcome him at my back in any kind of trouble.

It could be the judge and Yawley didn't like Doyle being on suspension.

I lost interest in the affair when Estelle pulled her little roadster into Volly's for a fill up.

"Where you headed, Estelle?" I asked. I walked over to pump some gasoline into the upper chamber of the pump while Volly finished up with a Ford coupe from Lebanon.

"St. Louis. The Famous Barr has some new styles fresh from Paris. I expect I'll buy everything that fits me."

"Big dance tomorrow night at the picnic grounds across the creek. Hope you'll be back for it. Some kind of dancing contest. Want to be my partner?"

"Daddy's mad at you," she said.

"I don't expect Yawley'll be going to the dance."

"Well," she said coyly, drawing it out. "Depends on whether a certain person makes fun of my new dress."

"I expect that a certain person is going to tell you the truth," I said. "And without even seeing the dress yet, I know you're going to look stunning."

"In that case. . ." She left it hanging.

Volly said, "Joel Dean, you going to pump the lady's gas or are you going to stand around looking like a sick puppy?"

I was starting to snooze under my hat brim, rocking back and forth in one of Volly's rocking chairs when I heard the slam of a door at the courthouse. I looked up to see Ora on his way back to his office in the jail house with Yawley right on his heels, yapping like a rat terrier.

"I'll see justice done in this county, Ora," Yawley said, his voice carrying from one end of Main Street to the other. "One way or the other, by God, I'll see justice."

Ora walked under the redbud tree and to the front door of the jail house. Unlocking it, he turned to look at Yawley who was coming in a trot behind. Yawley pulled up short of the door.

"You won't always be sheriff of Camden County, Ora," he said.

"As long as I am, I'm all the justice you're going to see," Ora said, and shut the door in Yawley's face.

It was a good year for the locusts. Their noise was a piercing din on top of Rifle Ridge in the dark. Off in the deepest part of the hardwood trees I heard an owl hoot, then another. The whippoorwills added their mournful call to the sounds of the night. I leaned against Ora's Chevrolet, catching every sound, listening for trouble. But not much trouble comes to man in the hills.

No black bears had been spotted in these parts for thirty years. One woman called the sheriff's office a few months back and swore a black bear was in her back yard. When I told her no one had shot a black bear in Camden County for thirty years, her reply was, "Well, that ought to have give them plenty of time to multiply."

Ernest didn't show up at my roadblock, which was cause to wonder. One could follow the back roads, cross the Glaize at a dry ford, and make his way to Jefferson City if he was willing to risk a broken axle, blown out tire or smashed radiator. I didn't think Ernest would run the risk nor would Yawley put his new $3000 Buick on those roads.

Or you could take the long road across the toll bridge or the ferry—neither of which was open for business at night—to Gravois Mills. Or you could go south to Lebanon, then over to Rolla where the School of Mines was, and on to St. Louis that way. But the road to Lebanon was being worked on during the summer and to risk it at night was maybe worse than being shot at.

No, if you wanted to make a run to St. Louis with a load of whiskey, you'd best do it at night over the Bagnell road. And that's why I was where I was.

I got to hoping someone in a bright yellow roadster with black fenders would come by. Which started me to thinking about Estelle.

I admitted her mysterious and unpredictable ways attracted me. But I did wish she had been more open with me. I still wondered about the other night; the coincidence with Doyle. And why hadn't she told me about going off to college? I had been looking forward to the winter, to snuggling up to the fireplace, sliding down the hill on a toboggan for two, ice skating on a

68

frozen Linn Creek—and if it was really a cold winter, a community skate on the Osage with lanterns sitting all over the ice, hot chocolate around the roaring brush fires on the bank, cuddling up in the dark with a blanket and a pair of heart shaped red lips.

My mother had taught me that thinking about something by yourself could lead to brooding. I was beginning to brood about the whole thing with Estelle when I saw a string of lights from about ten motor cars coming down the hill toward the Glaize bridge from Miller County. I watched them wind their way up the ridge toward me, heading, it appeared, for Linn Creek.

I counted the cars as they went by, filled with tight-faced men who barely looked my way, uninterested in my position on the hill. My curiosity was peaking and I began to worry about what might be going on. I looked toward Linn Creek, but saw no light in the sky. It couldn't be they were going to a fire. A straggler came along after the others, about a half mile behind. It was a Model T Ford that wasn't running quite right. I stepped out in front of the car.

"Where you headed?" I asked the driver, then, getting a good look at him, recognized Artis Monger. He had a jaw as firm as iron covered with black stubble that looked like each whisker had been driven in with a hammer.

He spit out the window in my direction. "Linn Creek," he said, getting a good look at my uniform and badge.

"Hey, you're Joel Dean Gregory, ain't you?" a younger voice asked from the back seat. I swung the beam of my dry cell light to pick up the face of Murdoch Monger, Artis' son whom I'd met several times peddling his rotgut at dances.

I said, "How are you Murdoch?"

"Doing real good, Joel Dean," he answered. "You have car trouble? Need a ride into town, just hop in. We're headed to the hanging."

"Shut up, Murdoch," Artis said. He started revving the engine to let the clutch out.

I pulled my pistol and shoved it inside the car, into the face of Artis Monger. I wasn't sure but what a bullet would bounce right off those hard features of his.

"What hanging?" I asked.

"Hell," Murdoch said, "Yawley said you was coming in with the Klan."

"I never heard anything about a hanging," I said.

"He works for the sheriff, Murdoch, you dumb little shit," Griff Monger, the older brother, said from the seat beside Artis. Griff was pudgy where Artis was rangy, but their manners were identical.

To me, Griff said, "Put that gun away. We ain't one of your whiskey runners."

"Just who is the Klan planning on hanging tonight?" I asked.

Nobody spoke.

"I could stand here all night."

"Tell him for crissakes," Murdoch whined. "We're going to miss the whole shebang."

Artis turned and gave me what he probably thought was a smile, but there was absolutely no sign of humor to the man. None.

"Why, we're fixing up a welcome for them boys that killed Shorty Mickelson." he said.

As he spoke he let the clutch out on the Ford and it lurched on down the hill.

In the grove next to the creek and across from the stores, a fire burned. A fire shaped like a cross. When I got closer I could see that it was saplings laced together. You could smell the coal oil they'd used to start the fire.

I knew every car in Camden County, but I didn't know half the ones parked by the grove. Figures draped in white sheets reflected the light of the fire as they milled around.

I wondered again just why we had a Klan in Camden County. I knew from reading papers like the *St. Louis Globe Democrat* that drummers left at Minton's that the Klan was very powerful in towns like St. Louis where large numbers of coloreds were migrating up from the cotton fields in the South. People were scared of being outnumbered and I suppose in their minds that justified dressing up in white sheets and hiding their faces so they could scare the coloreds. And it seemed to be all right, in their cowardly minds, to lynch a colored man ever so often.

But we had no excuse for a Klan in our county. Four of our colored were women and that included Birdie and Nell, the Earnhardt's maid. None of them were going to cause any trouble. Nobody I knew was going to stand by and see something unjust happen to Birdie, and that included Ora. The Klan liked to pick on Jewish people, too, but we didn't have any Jews in our county. Some people accused Yawley of being a Jew, especially after completing a business transaction with him, but I knew that wasn't true because Estelle went to the Methodist Church on occasion.

Yawley must have been doing some powerful talking to get this size mob together. Of course, a hanging would do it.

I was out of the car and unlocking the front door to the jail house when Noah pulled it open in my face.

"Glad you could make it, Joel Dean," he said. "We was beginning to worry you might miss the party."

Ora was sitting at his desk over some papers.

I didn't want to sound too excited. Too urgent. "Ora, I stopped the Monger brothers coming over from Miller County.

They said they were going to take Champ and the others out and hang them."

"They're just talking, Joel Dean," Ora said without looking up. "You been around here long as I have, you'll get used to their boasting."

"I don't know, Ora. I think they mean it."

"They get filled up on that cheap rotgut Yawley passes around, they might *think* they're going to do it. It don't take much to discourage a cowardly skunk."

Noah watched through the window, sucking on a cob pipe, a curl of blue smoke rising from it.

"What do you want me to do?" I asked Ora.

"Go get yourself a cup of coffee," Ora said. "Probably kind of quiet up on the ridge tonight."

In the kitchen I found Addie sitting down with a cup of coffee and a piece of leftover pie. I put my cup down next to hers and pulled up a chair.

"What do you think is going to happen, Addie?"

"Nothing," she said in between chews of the pie. "Yawley has to get his Klan worked up over something every once in a while or they lose interest."

"You mean this has happened before?"

Addie finished her pie before answering. "Every year or two. Last time it was the preacher at the Christian Church saying something they didn't like about some trial down in Tennessee. You know, the one where they're trying to put some schoolteacher in jail for saying people came from monkeys."

"What did they do with the preacher?"

"He got a call from the Lord to preach somewhere else. They don't hurt anybody, they just like to threaten people they know they can scare."

"I don't understand why we have a Klan," I said.

"Oh, Yawley uses them to intimidate people. Used to be a bunch fifty years ago in the county called the Slickers. They were a vigilante group like the Klan. The Slickers hanged a Gowan for stealing railroad ties."

"The Klan ever come against Ora before?"

"They tried," Addie said. She walked to the stove and brought back the granite coffee pot and refilled our cups. "Once they got as far as the jail house. Ora went out and grabbed Yawley by his sheet, turned him around and kicked his butt."

We could both laugh at that.

"Must have been quite a sight," I said.

"Got Yawley's clean sheet all dirty. Those Earnhardts got their pride."

She was looking at me, waiting for some response.

I might as well bring it up. It was plain she wanted to talk about it.

"I've been kind of taken by Estelle," I said.

"Better watch yourself Little Brother," her eyes lit up telling me she had something to say about it. "Estelle's a fighter."

It wasn't what I expected, so I laughed. "Estelle? A fighter?"

"Little Brother, seeing as how I'm all the family you got left, I guess it's my responsibility to tell you something about men and women."

I was still laughing. "I hate to spoil your little brother idea you got, but don't you think it's a little late? I'm twenty-four, now. Be twenty-five in a couple of months."

Addie made a motion in the air with her hand. "I ain't talking about a roll in the hay, Little Brother. You can learn all you need to know about that down at Toby's Pool Hall. I'm talking about something more serious. I'm talking about the fighting men and women do."

I was getting embarrassed—probably because Addie and I had never had this kind of serious talk before—but I hadn't lost the smile. I'd play along and let her be the big sister. Get it out of her system.

"See, Little Brother, men fight the rest of the world to get what

73

they want. Women mostly fight the men."

My smile had faded by then. She *was* being serious.

"Fight?"

"Anyway they can. With whatever God give them to fight with."

"Like Nita?"

"Hell," her hand waved again, this time in disgust. "Nita gave up a long time ago. Whatever anybody wants. That's how she survives, by giving in and taking whatever anybody gives her."

We drank our coffee, looking at each other. Did she have more, or was that it?

"Now you take Estelle," Addie said, finally getting around to where we had started. "People like her, like Yawley, they don't give anything away. That's why they have everything. You can bet they give you something, they expect 300 percent in return. Yawley lives on markup. Calls it profit. Otherwise, they wouldn't have any more than the rest of us."

I knew what she meant. She was sure enough right about Yawley and his fifty dollar bills. But Estelle? She was a young woman looking for life and excitement. And the road to take her into the future. I wanted to help her find it.

"I understand, Addie," I said. "But so far, Estelle's never given me anything but a few kisses. And she's never asked anything of me. I think she doesn't even know yet what she wants in life."

Addie nodded. "When she finds out, watch out."

"While we're on the subject," I said, "though it ain't any of my affair, I've been concerned about you and Ora."

"In what way?"

"I'd like to know my sister's happy."

She drank her coffee. Then, looking at the table, she said, "Don't see me fighting any do you?"

I heard the lock and the door to the office swung in. Noah stood in the opening.

LIMB OF THE JUDAS TREE

"Joel Dean, maybe you ought to come on out. Looks like the party's moving our way."

From the window I could see the mob coming toward the jail house. It was a memorable sight and I could see how it could get men excited and want to take part. Twenty men or more abreast, the burning cross leading, hoisted up on a pole. Anybody could recognize Yawley in the center of the line, in spite of the clean, white sheet and the pointed hood over his head with holes cut out for his eyes.

What did surprise me was that I was sure I recognized Doyle under one of the sheets.

"Want me to go out and talk with them?" Noah looked over at Ora.

Ora thumped his pencil against the desk a few times.

"No," he said, rising from his chair. "I'll go. Bring that shotgun out to let them know this ain't no game. Joel Dean, you lock the door behind us."

Ora stepped out into the night. Nice weather, nice night for a stroll. That's how he did it. Noah moved out of the doorway holding the shotgun in one hand, pointed loosely toward the crowd. After locking the door, I moved to the window, goose bumps all over me.

"Evening boys," Ora said. He cut a chaw off his plug of tobacco. "Anything I can do to help y'all."

It was Yawley who spoke up. "We want those prisoners, Sheriff. We're going to have some old-fashioned American justice here. Dangling from the limb of that Judas tree."

Ora looked up at the tree, then spat on the ground. "Yeah,

expect that would cap off the evening for you boys. But I got a better idea. Go home and sleep on your sheets before I kick your ass."

Someone under a sheet who looked and sounded a lot like Ernest Raines stepped forward and turned to Yawley and said, "I didn't agree to no hanging. A flogging and a cross burning is what we came for. That's all."

Yawley turned on his heel to face the other sheets.

"Y'all don't have the stomach for this, I 'spect you better go on home. We know what kind of justice is needed and we aim to see to it. An eye for an eye. Shorty's dead and somebody's got to pay. Ain't nobody getting off with a flogging."

"Yeah," another hooded figure said from behind Yawley. "We come to see justice, by God."

"You'll see it in due time," Ora said. "Might even feel some of it you don't leave this street."

"We come to make sure," Yawley said. "It's time to put a stop to killing and scaring people from making an honest living. We aim to leave an example hanging from the limb of that tree."

"This is the last time I'm going to say it, boys," Ora said, his voice getting a bit louder. Some edge to it. "Go on home."

"Not this time Sheriff," a gruff voice beside Yawley said. It could have been Artis Monger. He raised a shotgun from under his sheet and pointed it at Ora.

The way I saw it from the window: the men on either side of Yawley pointed a shotgun. Noah stepped forward and raised the one he was holding, then another sheet in the crowd raised and two barrels covered Noah. Ora, without blinking stepped straight at Yawley who retreated a step behind the shotguns.

"Looks to me as if somebody's about to lose his ass," Ora said, barely loud enough for me to hear.

"Ain't going to be me," Yawley said.

Noah said, "Don't worry none about the one on this side, Ora. He blinks and he goes to hell."

76

LIMB OF THE JUDAS TREE

Something had to be done. The whole affair had gone too far. Yawley wasn't bluffing this time. My hands felt clammy. Why didn't Doyle do something. He was just standing like a statue, hiding under that sheet. If it was Doyle.

I wished something would happen. Something so I wouldn't have to go out there.

The key felt cold in my hand—which goddamn way did that lock turn—then the barred front of the gun case swung open. Which one, the 30-30? The Marlin double barrel, sawed off so it would spread all over the street? Something that would make a lot of racket. Scare the hell out of them. Ah, this one. This ought to do it.

I came through the doorway in two quick strides putting me ten feet in front of the jail house, thirty feet from the white sheeted mob. You could see all the hoods turning, all fastened to the same string, could see Ora's head coming around, could see Yawley's eyes bugging out through the cutouts in the hood, could see the shotguns that had been pointed at Ora starting too late to swing around, could hear a voice that sounded like—no, I could swear it was—Doyle's saying in a low voice and drawn out in not much more than a loud breath:

"Gaw-w-w-damn. . ."

And it was just like the Studdard boy had said, tat-tat-tat-tat. . .

. . .chips flying off rocks in the street, dust swirling around the cross, the cross falling, crashing, splintering red coals into the dust, men scrambling, sheets flapping, hoods yanked off so eyes could see the street, falling over each other, cussing, yelling; then the street dark except for the coals that had been the cross, and a light on the ground coming through the open door. And Addie casting a shadow in the middle of it.

Ora said, "Meant to tell you to use it if you needed it." He held out his hand.

I was glad to be rid of it. Made a hell of a racket, but other than that, what did people see in a Thompson submachine gun? I never hit a thing with it except some rocks in the street.

Law Day was the first Tuesday in the Camden County Circuit Court. Once a month all the cases Prosecutor Gideon Norfleet had put together were presented to Circuit Judge Henry Black. Twice Gideon had more than a dozen cases on hand and that was when I was asked to help him with some. On this day, however, I had a client to defend.

Murl Beemeier had driven off from Volly's Shell Station without paying for six gallons of gas. Six gallons of gas was not something you can give away every day and stay in business, so Volly had gone to Murl's place a couple of miles out of town to collect. Murl swore he didn't owe it and had become belligerent, running Volly off with a squirrel rifle. Ora sent me out to serve the warrant. Murl talked Cook Farleigh into posting bond for him with a couple of Poland China boars for collateral. Cook was Linn Creek's sometimes bondsman, insurance salesman and real estate broker.

Murl, all five-foot-four of him including the crown of his hat, complained at length about being railroaded without a lawyer to defend him so I offered my services for $15. The six gallons of gas had only cost 96 cents. Of course, Murl didn't have the cash so I took a note.

Noah was the bailiff for the day, so I helped him escort Buster, Wilbur and Champ to the courthouse next door since I was going anyway. The three of them were being arraigned for shooting Shorty Mickelson.

LIMB OF THE JUDAS TREE

The arraignment hearing was first. Judge Henry Black paid more attention to trying to unstop a crooked stem briar pipe than he did to the evidence Gideon presented. The evidence consisted of the Thompson submachine gun Noah had found. Gideon had brought it into court that morning to impress the judge.

The lawyer for the three accuseds was a worn-shirt-collar type from Lebanon who had gone to court for Champ three years ago. Champ said, "What the hell. Only got three years before. Might as well try the same guy again."

The lawyer tried to tell Judge Henry Black that the three had been drinking at Mamie Crouse's place in Zebra, between Linn Creek and Bagnell, and couldn't possibly have shot Shorty. Only he got Mamie's name wrong, the time wrong and his blunder put the three on the Bagnell road at just the right time to have done the shooting. Judge Henry Black lost patience with the lawyer and ordered the three bound over for jury trial in two weeks.

Murl's hearing was later in the day after a couple of hearings on stolen cows and one on stolen tires. Murl insisted on pleading not guilty even though I knew he was because of what Volly had told me. I advised Murl to plead guilty and Volly would probably go along with my request for leniency.

Judge Henry Black asked Murl if he wanted a jury trial. Told him what the cost would be and how long he would have to wait. Murl said no, he would trust the judge to do it. The judge asked if Murl had any witnesses and I told the judge that he did not. Gideon said he had one, Volly. The judge said all right, they would try the case today. I wasn't prepared for that. In fact, I had been sure Murl would plead guilty, I would ask for leniency and Volly would say fine, he would let Murl pay off the 96 cents at 16 cents a week. That was what I was prepared for.

Gideon put Volly on the stand. Volly said Murl had driven his Chevrolet into his station and Volly had pumped six gallons of gas into the tank. When he went to help another customer, Murl had just driven off. I couldn't think of anything to ask Volly that would help Murl.

When Murl took the stand he said that he had told Volly he wanted two bits worth of gas. If Volly pumped six gallons in the tank, it wasn't Murl's fault. When Volly left to take care of the other customer, Murl left a quarter on the lip of the pump and drove off.

I was flabbergasted. Murl was fabricating the whole thing as he went along. The judge asked Volly how much gas Murl had asked for. Volly said Murl ordered six gallons, very plainly. And Volly said if a quarter was on the lip of the pump, he sure didn't see it.

Murl jumped up and said somebody else stole the quarter.

"Murl, you're making all of this up," I said.

"Am not."

Judge Henry Black asked me if I was being paid to represent Murl. I said he was supposed to pay me $15 but I hadn't seen any of it yet. Furthermore, I said, I didn't want any of it because I didn't want to represent Murl any longer. The judge said, well, you can't just quit in the middle of a trial.

A whole lot more talk took place between Gideon, Volly, Murl, me and the judge. I can't even remember all of it. And it's just as well. I do know that Murl said a lot more than was good for him and the judge ended up sentencing him to thirty days in the county jail plus restitution. About that time, Murl's three month old baby, being held in the front row by Murl's wife, began wailing and making a real fuss. Judge Henry Black frowned and looked at Murl's wife with a "do something" scowl on his face. Murl reached over and took the baby in his arms and it stopped crying immediately.

Without really intending to and not knowing just why I did it, I said to the judge, "The baby really does need his daddy right now, your honor." So the judge suspended the sentence and strung the restitution out for thirty days. Volly jumped to his feet and objected. Gideon calmed him down some before Volly slammed his Shell cap on his head and stalked toward the door.

"Judge," Murl said, cuddling the baby to his chest. "Can you make Volly give me back my quarter?"

After court was over I walked past Volly's station. He was some put out with me.

"Dammit Joel Dean, you kept your mouth shut and Murl woulda been in jail right now where he belongs. He's a liar and a thief."

"I was being paid to defend the man, Volly. I wasn't being paid to keep my mouth shut."

"All right then, you pay me the 96 cents. Take it out of your pay for defending that liar."

"He didn't pay me, Volly. You know Murl. He never will pay me."

"That's your problem. Now give me that 96 cents."

Volly rammed his hand in my pocket and began dragging out my jail house keys, coins, pocket knife and assorted lint balls. I grabbed his hand before he could pull it from my pocket. Lonnie came out of the repair bay.

"What's going on here?" he asked.

"Joel Dean owes me 96 cents for Murl's gas," Volly said. With a big jerk he dislodged his hand from my grip and everything in my pocket came clattering out all over the station's concrete drive.

I could see Volly was embarrassed by his action. He stood looking at the contents of my pocket all over the drive for a moment before kneeling down and picking it all up. He handed it to me.

"I'm sorry, Joel Dean. It's just that I was so damn mad at Murl for going into court and making that story up. And you know what? I think the judge might have halfway believed him."

I smiled. "Had me believing it just for a little bit."

"I started wondering if maybe he *was* right," Volly said, laughing along with me. "But of course, he wasn't."

I counted out 96 cents and handed it to Volly. "I'm buying beer all around. This calls for a celebration."

Volly was puzzled. "What are we celebrating exactly?"

"The way you were objecting, I guess I must have won my first case."

Three o'clock in the afternoon they started putting the platform down in the grove for the dance that night. And it was my night off.

Doyle was put out at supper because they were missing a banjo picker. He was saying, "Cy Rush stuck a rusty fishing hook in his picking finger and it turned to blood poisoning. Damn shame. On account of him, I'm going to have to leave out a lot of my best numbers."

"Cy Rush hand fishes," Noah said.

"Uh huh," Doyle agreed. "And that's how he got the hook stuck in him. Damn fool. He ought to start fishing like the rest of us. Don't catch me sticking my hand down in all that brushy water."

"I pick a little banjo," Champ said.

Doyle was finishing up the last of his vinegar pie Birdie had made.

"You don't look like a banjo picker to me," Doyle said. "Let me see your fingers."

Champ held them over the table, palms up. From where I sat his fingers did look callused on the tips where you fret the strings.

"Maybe you are a banjo picker," Doyle said. "I'll come over and get you about nine o'clock. Crowd ought to be just about ready for what I had in mind by then."

"Suppose it would be all right I had a drink or two?" Champ asked as he hand combed his hair back in place. "Playing that banjo on a hot, sticky night calls for refreshment."

Doyle looked at Ora. "Don't see why not. You Ora?"

Ora was looking down the length of the table, listening to them. He nodded. "See you get him back in here by midnight. That's when my shift starts and I want to get some sleep. And remember that bunch that wants to string him up will be around."

"Won't anything happen," Doyle said. "I always carry my pistol in my guitar case."

"What about us?" Wilbur asked.

Doyle looked the little guy over like he had every time Wilbur had spoken to him.

"What about you?" Doyle asked.

"We get to go to the dance? Buster and me?"

"What d'ya play?" Doyle asked.

"I can dance," Wilbur said, smiling at his own joke.

"That's nice," Doyle told him. "I'll leave the window open so you can hear the music. You can dance with Buster in your cell."

Yawley announced it was a going away party. Estelle, he said, was leaving for Stephens College in a few weeks.

I said, "I like your dress."

Estelle looked at her simple little blue frock with high collar, flat bodice, and made a face.

"Daddy's idea," she said. "How am I supposed to Charleston in this? It needs to be tighter at the knees. Say, do you Charleston?"

I said no, but when the pencil line eyebrows came together, I offered to try.

The old people started the evening. They danced the old dances. Doyle and two fiddlers played for them while they did the Fox trot, Waltz and Two Step. I watched Estelle dancing with Yawley. At nine Doyle left to fetch Champ and then things started moving.

About ten couples were gyrating through the Charleston and the platform was getting crowded. We took a break between dances and drank Ernest's whiskey. Estelle drank too much. By the end of the second dance I had it figured out, and I started warming up to the crowd who would yell at us and clap. The contest had started. No more breaks. The last couple standing were the winners. It didn't take long before the platform went from elbow to elbow with couples from all over the county doing all kinds of steps to just Lonnie and a girl from up on the Glaize and two other couples. And us.

Doyle motioned for Champ to follow him as he picked it up a little. The fiddlers dropped out. Champ followed along with Doyle. Doyle got after it a little more and Champ was right with him, hitting every lick. Another couple dropped out, but I had the feeling I could dance till morning.

Estelle was drunk.

"Dance," she kept saying. "Dance."

So I danced and as I came by Doyle and Champ I said, "Slow it down. Slow it down for crissakes. Can't you see we can't keep up your beat?"

They didn't listen to me; they were listening too hard for the other one to stop. Neither of them did.

Doyle wasn't playing the Charleston anymore. It was music I'd never heard before. Champ played right along with him. Then Doyle put some really different licks on his strings, but Champ matched him, frailing and whamming on the banjo strings, staying right with Doyle. The last two couples dropped out, falling to the grass and wiping the sweat from their faces. Lonnie tipped up a bottle.

Estelle's feet barely touched the boards. Blurred objects to my eyes. By now she had shed the top of her little blue frock and all that was left was a straight gown to her knees with bare shoulders and two skinny straps keeping the whole thing decent. I looked up at the crowd, at Estelle holding my arm, at my feet, but they were separate from the rest of me, moving on their own.

Doyle was doing things learned from the colored pickers in East St. Louis maybe because none of it had ever been heard in Camden County before. Champ never faltered, coming right in with Doyle. The crowd first looked stunned, then started appreciating it and finally became exuberant, stomping and clapping and yelling. Doyle looked up at Champ's face and I saw them both grin before I got spun away. We weren't doing any particular step. We were just moving.

Doyle picked up the tempo on his East St. Louis jazz and I began to slacken. I lost the beat entirely and fell off the platform into Ernest Raines. He held me up, blinked his eyes rapidly, gave me his jar of smooth whiskey and I drank it.

I reached out for Estelle and grabbed her arm, but she twisted away from me saying, "Come on. Come on and dance or leave me alone."

She actually danced faster as if I'd been a drag to her. Her shoes were off now and her stocking feet were thumping against the boards in perfect beat to the music. The people crowded around, trying to clap to the tune, but they just could not keep up

85

with Doyle and Champ and especially Estelle.

Yawley was saying, "That's enough, Stell. That's enough, Baby. Don't wear yourself out," but she kept going, not missing a step. Doyle was flat out now; he couldn't pick it any faster.

I saw it when she began to slow, knowing she had to stop, but when I looked in her face I could see she wouldn't quit.

I knew then I loved her.

When she fell I was there to catch her before she hit the boards. They clapped for her, and for Doyle and Champ. They thought the players would quit then, but they didn't. Champ looked at Doyle, but Doyle was watching his strings. He tried something different, a new beat. Champ stayed right with him.

Estelle's clothes were wet and her breath was deep and fast. One of the women brought a damp cloth to hold to her face while I held her in my arms. Yawley spoke to her and Estelle opened her eyes and blinked them at him. Yawley patted her hand.

Doyle wouldn't quit and neither would Champ. They went on and on without slowing and the crowd grew tense, knowing they were watching something.

They'd played them all and were starting over, this time up-tempo. *The Irish Jig, Leatherwing Bat, Irish Washer Woman, Cripple Creek, Old Joe Clark, Ida Red, Sally Ann, Cumberland Gap.* Then Doyle got back to the jazz tunes, the banjo right along with him. Doyle's face said he was going to do it. He was going to break the banjo player. But he didn't. He couldn't.

Cords stood out in his neck. Perspiration was coming down his arm, onto his hand, onto the guitar where it ran off in rivulets. Champ's shirt was plastered against him, his hair hanging in his face where he'd toss it out ever now and then.

Then a string broke on the guitar and flew across Doyle's face leaving a scratch with a few drops of blood oozing out. He kept going. Then he lost another string, and another one. Champ had two strings left when Doyle finally broke the last one and nothing was left for him to play. Champ hit two last licks on his only remaining strings, then fell over backwards, sprawling into the dirt with the banjo across his chest.

The duel of strings was over.

A dew had formed so I spread the blanket and laid her on it. I couldn't remember where I'd gotten the blanket, not that it mattered. In the distance the fiddle player was doing a waltz. I kissed her gently on the little rosebud mouth.

"I was doing it wasn't I?" she asked.

"I was proud of you," I said, and kissed her again.

"I gotta get this dress off, Joel Dean. It's strangling me."

I helped her. I took off the band that she had buttoned around her. Her small breasts, freed, popped up like they were filling with air. She was warm and sticky from the sweat. I took my shirt off to dry her with, but it too was wet.

"Let's go in," she said. "Cool off."

We walked into the Niangua until she was up to her chin. We stood and kissed. When the heat had left her body and she started shivering, I picked her up and carried her back to the blanket.

She looked up at me, holding me, and said, "I didn't think it would ever happen."

I didn't say anything.

"Let's don't let it end," she whispered to me.

The fiddles had stopped playing and it was daylight before we did.

Everything was going at half speed because of the night before. Ora was in Jefferson City and Noah was out trying to quieten a domestic squabble that had carried over from the dance. Doyle was still on suspension.

I should have noticed Wilbur's state of agitation—because of the trial coming up, maybe—but I was still reliving last night, hoping for another one just like it. Addie said grace in Ora's place. I didn't hear her words nor what Wilbur was saying.

If I'd been paying attention, if I hadn't been thinking about last night on the bank of the Niangua, it never would have happened. And Ora's record of never having a jailbreak would have been intact.

"Where's the sheriff?" Wilbur wanted to know. His eyes were fixed on Ora's empty chair.

I sat alone across from the prisoners. When I heard Wilbur's voice, higher than usual, excited, I reached to where my holster hung from my hip off the edge of the chair and undid the flap.

"Wouldn't mind having a beer with my meal," Wilbur said. "How about you, Buster? You want a beer?"

Buster Workman just looked at us, rubbing the stubble on his jaw, his small eyes unreadable.

"How about it nigger gal? Bring us a couple of beers here." Wilbur laughed a high pitched girlish giggle.

Birdie ignored him, or didn't hear him. She busied herself at the stove, putting bread in, taking bread out of the oven.

"Wilbur," I said, "because I'm a little short-handed today, I'm going to let you off with a warning. You keep popping off and I'll cuff you around this post."

"I got a warning once," Wilbur said, looking straight at me. "In Kansas City from the Dugans. On the North Side. Don't come across Sixth Street, they said." Again he laughed the girlish laugh.

He waited, but no one would ask what happened. Buster ate noisily, looking into his plate and Champ watched Wilbur with a smile on his face.

Wilbur punched Buster in the ribs with his elbow. Buster halted the fork midway to his mouth, slowly turning his head to regard Wilbur.

"Want to know what happened, Buster?" Wilbur asked. Buster only stared, the fork still suspended in air.

"I caught six of them up on Reservoir Hill one night in a big old LaSalle. Shoulda seen the look on their faces when I came up on them and opened up with the Tommy gun. Tat-tat-tat-tat." Wilbur held the imaginary gun out in front of him, pointed at me. He laughed the silly laugh.

"Shut up, Wilbur," Champ said, watching Addie who was watching him.

"Just a little entertainment," Wilbur said, giggling.

Birdie brought a fresh loaf of bread to the table and set it in the middle.

"I'm still waiting for that beer, black girl," Wilbur said.

"Shut yo' mouth you white trash you," Birdie said.

"Had me a black gal once," Wilbur said. "Down on Cherry Street. Funny thing about them black gals. You look down in that black crotch of theirs and you see this big red gash . . ."

"Wilbur, I've had enough of you," I said. I stood up with my hand on the butt of my pistol. "Come around here and park yourself in this chair." I pushed one of the empty chairs up to face the support post.

"I'll just stay here," Wilbur said, his eyes all lit up, his tongue running around inside his mouth and over his lips. Again and again.

I pulled the .45 caliber Colt Peacemaker from the holster and thumbed the hammer back.

"You can if you'd rather," I said. "But in about five seconds, Buster's going to be carrying you up to Doc Hardesty's."

Everyone watched me. Champ grinned at Wilbur. I put the handcuffs in the seat of the chair and motioned to Wilbur with the barrel of the .45.

"What is this, the little red schoolhouse?" Wilbur asked. "Am I supposed to put my nose in a circle on the blackboard or something?"

"Three seconds," I said.

He waited two seconds.

"What do you think, Buster?" Wilbur's laugh was forced.

Buster continued to eat, his features revealing nothing.

"What the hell," Wilbur said, getting out of the chair. "Buster, sneak me in a sandwich in your pocket, will you?"

As Wilbur came around the table, I heard a commotion in the office on the other side of the locked door.

Noah said, "Now get your goddamn ass inside or I'm going to blow it off."

We all heard the voices through the door, then something heavy scraping across the floor. Then a yell.

"Noah?" I shouted. I heard nothing except the noise of something turning over. I looked at Addie and she was standing.

I was turning the lock on the door when Addie yelled. I couldn't stop. The door came open and I saw Noah on the floor with a man on top of him, hammering with his fist. Addie screamed as I turned back to Wilbur and saw the chair moving through the air with Wilbur on the other end of it. It crashed against me and I felt the edge of the door bending my ribs out of shape. I got hit again and again with a shoulder, like it was a football game. I saw Buster slither past me into the office. As I was raising the hand with the pistol in it, Wilbur slapped it away and my fingers loosened on the grip. Birdie screamed.

I looked for Addie, pain jabbing in my side again. I lost my feet, felt the floor under my hand and then saw the ceiling.

Someone was still yelling, perhaps it was me. On my elbows now, I began to look around for my pistol. I fell on my face and tried to get up. Now was not the time to give in. I pushed up and knew it was me yelling that time.

Champ was standing in the doorway, ready to run out. Then he stopped. His face was friendly, starting to smile. I followed his eyes and saw Addie holding my gun.

"They're going to hang me, Addie," Champ said, his voice soft and easy. "I didn't do it, Addie. I swear I didn't do it."

"Addie . . ." I tried to ask for my gun, holding my hand out toward her. I was having trouble getting any more words out. I fell back on the floor.

"Don't do it, Champ," Addie's voice jarred me back to reality. "Don't do it. I'll have to shoot. They hurt Joel Dean . . ."

"I ain't going to hurt anyone, Addie. I never hurt anybody in my life. You know that . . ."

"Don't do it, Champ . . ."

"I got to, Addie. I'd rather have you shoot me than to have them hang me for something I didn't do."

I saw him go through the door and I waited for the shot. And waited. And waited.

"Dammit, Addie, shoot him . . ." I tried to get up.

Addie was standing, watching me, the gun in her hand. Then she let the gun fall to the floor and sat down in her chair.

"Lay still," Doc Hardesty said.

I was lying on Addie's bed, barely remembering her helping me get there. Doc was winding tape around my body and every turn he made gave me a twitch in the side.

"Noah?"

"Noah's all right," Doc said. "Bloody nose. Cut under one eye. Better off than you are."

"What is it?"

"Cracked rib, probably. Don't think it's a complete break. Hope there's no splinters. Let Addie run you up to Jefferson City and get an x-ray."

He fished around in his bag and came out with a hypodermic needle and began to load it.

"What's that?" I asked. I realized then what he had in mind for me.

"No, Doc," I said. As I moved I had to clench my teeth to keep from crying out. I swung my legs over the edge of the bed and that was about all I was going to accomplish.

"You need this . . ."

I stopped Doc with my hand. "Just leave me some pills or something, Doc. I got to get after those prisoners."

"You think they're around here? You think they're just standing in the street waiting for you?"

"I'll find them."

"And then what? you can't even stand up."

I showed him I could, but it was an effort I wished I hadn't made.

"Where's Addie?" I asked.

"Office I guess. Last time I saw her."

I headed that way.

"Joel Dean, you're a pure damn fool," Doc said behind me.

He was right about that.

Ora got right to the point when he came through the door.

"Where's the last place they was seen?"

"I reckon I was the last to see them," Noah said. "Running right out that door."

"You ask around town?"

"Nobody's seen them," I answered. "They haven't stolen a car or any weapons yet that we know about."

Ora dug through his desk until he found the government map of Camden County. He spread it open.

"How'd it happen both doors were unlocked at the same time?" Ora asked, looking back and forth between me and Noah.

"Plumb damn carelessness," Noah said. "I brung old Titus in, drunk as a lord, smelling to high heaven. He didn't have any fight left in him till he seen where he was. He just went berserk."

"I heard Noah yelling and went to the door to help him," I said. "Got it unlocked when they jumped me. Addie yelled, but I didn't get around in time. When I opened the door and saw the other one open, I knew I'd made a bad mistake."

"Um." Ora said. He looked at the map again, tracing the roads out of town. "How's come they didn't get your gun?"

I looked over at Addie. She was waiting for me to tell him. Expecting it, I thought.

"They knocked it away. I was kind of out of it for a minute, but I saw Addie pick it up. She couldn't shoot."

I looked at her again. Her eyes were on the floor.

"I was in the way," I said. "Things were happening too fast."

Addie looked at me sharply. A reproach for lying.

"Let's get some wires out," Ora said. "Warn the other sheriffs in the counties around us. See if they can spare some men. We'll need some dogs. We'll need Doyle."

"He's gone," Addie said. "I left word at the boarding house."

Ora named off some people in town who weren't with the Klan who would help us. Noah left to talk with them.

"Joel Dean, let's you and me go check the first place Champ's liable to go."

"Where's that?" I asked.

"Nita German's. Might be he wants to settle up with her."

"Who is it?" Nita asked through the door.

"Sheriff Mitchell," Ora said.

A bolt slid back, a lock clicked, Nita stood in the doorway, one hand smoothing her hair. She wore a shiny robe that could have been silk. She saw me and the smile she'd opened the door with faded somewhat.

"Ora, I'm glad to see you . . ."

"Champ Gowan's escaped jail," Ora said.

Watching her eyes I had to wonder if she already knew.

"You ain't seen anything of him have you, Nita?"

"Heavens no," she said. She was still holding onto the door. Ora shoved it out of her hands and it flew wide. Buck Newland, the trucker I'd met on Rifle Ridge, was sitting on her sofa in his undershirt.

"Sheriff Mitchell, this is . . ."

"Buck Newland." The trucker stood up, sticking his hand out. Ora shook it while Buck looked over at me. "This a liquor raid?" He glanced nervously at the table by the sofa, at the fancy decanter sitting on it.

"We're looking for some convicts," I told him. "They jumped me and escaped from jail about two hours ago."

Buck looked at Nita. "Them's the ones you told me about?"

Nita nodded her head.

"Well, now, Sheriff, you don't need to worry none about Nita here. I'll be around anther hour or so. I'll look out for her if they try and come here. I'll be leaving for Mexico after that."

He looked over at me. "Have to be home before dark."

It was the first time I'd ever been in Nita's house. The furnishings tended toward gaudy, but expensive. The sofa was what I'd seen in a magazine called a camelback because of the hump on the back. It was red and black mohair and probably cost more than most sofas I had ever seen. The lampshade was stained glass like a church window and the rug on the floor was Arabian or something like that. Nita saw me going over the room.

"Joel Dean, I guess you haven't been to my house before, now have you?"

My face probably colored a bit.

"She's got a real nice place here, Joel Dean," Buck Newland said, giving me a wink. "You'll have to come back and see more of it."

Ora was anxious to be gone. "You be all right Nita?"

"I . . .I don't know, Ora. You think he might come here?"

"Keep your doors locked," Ora said.

"Well, I do have appointments . . ."

"We'll be going then." Ora touched his hat brim and backed out the door.

"Thanks for coming by, Ora. For worrying about me. Joel Dean, you come back sometime."

I touched the brim of my hat and followed Ora out the door.

"She's some woman," I said to Ora as we walked away. Just to have something to say. Because I was nervous in her presence, I suppose.

Ora looked over at me. "Just how bad did you say you was hurt?"

Midday heat seared my skin as I climbed the hill to the Earnhardt place. The street leveled off and continued on to the Cargrove house and the Norfleets. The air seemed cleaner and cooler up here. As I turned to look down on the town below, a twinge caused my breath to catch and I held my hand over the injured rib. Better than being shot, I thought, which I was sure would have happened if Wilbur had been able to hold onto my pistol.

No one stirred in the streets below. I saw a small group of men in front of the sheriff's office and recognized Ora, standing taller than the rest.

I tapped lightly on the screen door. I hadn't planned on what I would say when she answered. But it was Nell, Birdie's cousin who had been the Earnhardt's housekeeper since Estelle's mother had been killed in a street car accident while visiting in Chicago more than ten years ago.

"Is Estelle home, Nell?"

"Who's askin'?" The question was a routine for her. Nell knew me as well as Birdie did.

"Tell her Deputy Sheriff Gregory is here," I said, playing along with Nell's big city put-on. "Like to ask her some questions . . ."

"Oh, Joel Dean, don't be playing cops and robbers with me."

She came through the archway into the parlor and toward the screen door. It was dark through the screen and I couldn't see her very well until she got to the door.

"It's okay, Nell," she said, and waited until Nell was gone.

She opened the door and stood looking beautiful and fresh as a new blossom. She was wearing a tennis outfit and carrying a racket, though I didn't know of a tennis court between here and Springfield. The skirt was short—scandalously short—and the sweater molded to her form. No boy look this time.

"You hear about the escape?"

"I heard you'd been hurt and I was worried to pieces. I was coming over to see you as soon as I changed. I've had to listen to Daddy all day going on and on about the Klan and how they would have had justice if you hadn't interfered. I don't think Daddy likes you any more, Joel Dean. I don't care. The other day when I was laughing about finding a fifty dollar bill in my little sailor hat, he said, 'Damn that Joel Dean. He's been around Ora Mitchell too long.' How bad you hurt?"

"Cracked rib, maybe."

"Come in. Let me see."

I was still admiring where her outfit wasn't when I stepped inside.

"You're looking at my legs as if you hadn't seen them before," she said. "I powdered them. See."

She held a bare knee and thigh up for me to see. I rubbed my hand on the inside of her thigh.

"I don't think you got hurt too bad," she said.

She pulled the shirttail out of my pants and gasped when she saw all the tape.

"Oh my darling," she said and put her arms around me. "How long do you have to keep it bandaged up like that."

"I don't know. Right now it hurts pretty bad just to move"

"Does it hurt for me to hug you like this?"

"No," I lied.

She stepped back and carefully tucked my shirttail back into my pants.

"Joel Dean, I've changed my mind about going away to Stephens College."

"Why?"

I was elated.

"Well, just because." She took both of my hands in hers. "Because of last night."

"Well, I'm . . . I'm glad," I said.

She dropped my hands. "You're not." Her hands went to cover her eyes. "Joel Dean, I wasn't the first was I?"

"Estelle, what is this? You know how I feel about you . . ."

"You were the first for me. I saved everything for you. But you . . .you haven't saved anything for me, have you?"

"Estelle, come on."

She had her back turned to me. I reached out for her, to turn her around. To kiss away the tears.

But the eyes were clear and bright without a tear, and they sparkled in a way that stirred me. "You think if you don't hurt too much, you'll feel like coming over tonight?" she asked.

By mid-afternoon the hounds arrived. Simon Burchett took a lot of pride in the way his dogs could trail. The big dog was nearly full blood while the two bitches were mostly common hounds with very keen noses.

The big male dog was all business, though he was leisurely in execution. The bitches pulled at their chains, dragging the male dog and Simon—who was portly and near seventy—at a pace faster than either of them cared to go.

Ora and I watched from the doorway as Simon let the dogs work in front of the jail house.

"You people stay back and don't interfere with the dogs," Ora said to the crowd. The onlookers moved and then parted as the male hound found the trail and stayed with it. The bitches worked in circles around him, but always coming back to the scent he was on.

The scent took the dogs around the jail house to the backside, then across the street and in the direction Ora and I had just followed earlier. In a direct line toward Nita German's neat little white bungalow. We went along behind them, me, Ora, Noah and half the town of Linn Creek.

The scent must have been a good one because the bitches were dragging Simon and even the big male was doing some pulling. Simon had his heels dug in and I was afraid the dogs were going to pull him over on his face until they suddenly stopped and he nearly ran them down.

The dogs milled around in a circle twenty yards short of Nita's house, then the male started to howl and bitches began to yip. It became a racket of general proportion before Simon swatted them with his worn old felt hat.

Simon said to Ora, "Damnedest thing, Sheriff. The trail stops right here in the street. They musta got into a car or something. We're dead outta scent."

"Anybody missing a motor car here in town?" Ora asked the crowd.

Some shook their head, others said no. One man shouted out, "Musta been an outta town customer of Nita's," and the crowd's titter became an outright laugh.

Ora turned to me.

"You see a car when we came by here earlier?"

"Just Buck Newland's truck full of furniture squares. They sure didn't steal that."

"Where was that truck from that was hauling that wood? Wasn't it Audrain County?" Ora asked.

"Mexico," I said. "That's in Audrain County. Buster Workman is from Mexico."

Ora nodded his head as he reached the same conclusion I had.

"Wasn't a very long trail, Simon," Ora told the old tracker. "They done their job. I'll see you get paid for it."

Ora dispatched Noah to send a wire to the sheriff of Audrain County with a description of the three fugitives. When we got back to the office Addie had lemonade ready for us.

"Shouldn't be any problem for the sheriff in Audrain County," I said. I sipped the cool liquid and watched Ora ease himself down into his chair. He looked older, now. More lines in his face than I had noticed before.

"Gotta get out of the law business one of these days, Joel Dean. Makes a man old. I ought to be out fishing off the bank of the Osage instead of chasing convicts."

"Ora, I'm sorry as I can be about the escape . . ."

"Don't think about it," he said, cutting me off. "You made a mistake, but an honest one. Noah made one, too, and so did I, leaving you here by yourself to take care of them at dinner time. Don't let it wear on your mind, just remember it for the experience. You're a good hand. You'll be sheriff around here one of these days if you want to be."

I'd never thought about it. And, at the moment, I didn't care to. We drank our lemonade letting a comfortable silence fill the time.

"Sure would like to catch my own prisoners, though," Ora said after awhile. "Instead of leaving it up to some other sheriff. That trucker'll be in Mexico in little more than two hours. Don't think the Chevrolet could catch him now."

"Take an airplane to catch up with them now," I said.

"Don't think Judge Cargrove would look kindly on an airplane in our budget."

"Lonnie says they got one at the millionaire's castle down at Ha Ha Tonka Village."

"What kind of airplane?"

"American Eagle, Lonnie says. Single engine bi-wing, he called it. Or something like that. Claims they been hauling passengers to look at the castle, the lake and the springs that feed it. Lonnie says it can haul two passengers in the front cockpit."

"What two you thinking about?" Ora asked, rising up from his chair, some of the lines fading out of his face.

I looked around and smiled. "Be a new experience."

"Addie can bring the car back," Ora said. He walked to the gun case where he fingered a shotgun.

"If you don't mind, Ora," I said, "I'd kind of like to take this along."

I lifted the Thompson submachine gun out of the rack.

"I just want to stick it in Wilbur's face when he climbs down out of that truck in Mexico."

"I dunno," the man said. "Mexico? Let's see, that's about a hundred miles. Take me an hour and twenty, thirty minutes." He stuck his shaved head, tanned and slick as a Buff Orphington hen's egg, back inside the opening where the airplane's engine was. I was happy to note the cigar butt he chewed on was not lit.

"That mean you'll do it?" I asked.

"Can't," a man in white shirt and tie said. He leaned against the wing watching us with suspicion.

"It's official business," Ora said. "I can see that you'll be compensated for it."

"It ain't that," the man said. "The plane belongs to Mr. Porterfield of Kansas City. It's only experimental. He's planning on going into production, but . . ."

"I might do it and I might not," the man with the shaved head said from under the cowling over the engine.

"You can't," the other said. "You've never flown this plane."

He turned to us. "You see, the pilot is down at the main house. Now if you want to go and talk with him it's possible he'll take you first thing in the morning . . ."

"Be too late," I said. I walked closer to where the man was standing on a stool to work on the engine. "Is it broke down?"

"Adjusting the valves," the man said. He straightened, pointing a wrench at the man in the white shirt. "Piss on Hooks. He ain't in charge. If I want to fly you, I'll fly you."

"And if you wreck the plane?" Hooks whined. "What then? You'll get us both fired, that's what. I'm sorry gentlemen, it just can't be done today. Pay no attention to Coley. He's only a mechanic."

"Only a mechanic?" Coley started down off the stool and Hooks backed along the wing away from him. Coley took the stub of cigar from between his teeth and flung it in the dirt at Hook's feet. "Why, goddamn you, Hooks. I got an investment in this plane, too, you know. I helped design the thing. I rigged the cable . . ." his hand flicked at the steel cable running from under the fuselage to the underside of the top wing. It caught the brim of the hat Hooks was wearing and flipped it from his head.

"Coley, I'm warning you . . ."

"Hooks, I'm going to kick your ass if it's still here in ten seconds," Coley said, advancing on the nervous Hooks.

Hooks took off across the pasture toward the post office we'd passed coming in. Coley leaned his head back and laughed.

"Bookkeepers," he said, spitting on the ground. He turned his shaved head and laugh-filled eyes toward us. "You ready?"

He wiped the grease from his hands.

Ora said, "You sure you can fly this thing?"

"With my eyes shut," Coley said, the laugh still hanging around his mouth. "You ain't getting cold feet are you, Sheriff?"

Ora's eyes became slits. "If I'm going to be sitting up there in the air, I want to be sure the man who's flying knows how."

Ora cut off a chaw and offered the plug to Coley who looked at it.

"Got any cigars?" he asked.

Ora shook his head. Coley reached in his pocket and took out a Roi Tan and peeled the wrapper, bit the end off and lit it up. Squinting through a cloud of blue smoke, he said, "You want to get to Mexico before that truck does, we better get at it."

Addie walked forward from the Chevrolet. "Ora, just let the sheriff in Mexico arrest them. You can drive up tomorrow and bring them back."

"I'm plumb curious about this machine, now," Ora said. He looked it over from tail to propellor. "I think this man can fly it."

Addie took hold of his arm, gently. "Don't do it, Ora. Don't risk your life just because I made a mistake."

Ora kept looking at the airplane. "Thing's will work out as they're supposed to."

"It wasn't you, Addie, it was me made the mistake," I said. "Don't worry about the airplane."

She just looked at me.

"What did that Mr. Hooks mean it was experimental," I asked Coley. "Does that mean it's unproven?"

Coley clinched the Roi Tan between his teeth and turned on me.

"I helped build this baby and there ain't nothing unproven about it. When Porterfield goes into production next year, I get a piece of it. And let me tell you, Coley Goodman don't take a piece

103

of anything that's unproven."

"So we don't have a problem?"

"Just one," Coley said, staring across the pasture at a row of cedar trees. "Those trees."

"Trees?"

"They're a little too close to those in back of us," Coley said, turning to point to another row behind us.

I didn't get it. "Which means?"

"Which means, the sonofabitch of a pilot as Hooks calls him shouldn't have set the plane down here. We're a little short of takeoff space. This ain't where he usually lands, but he got scared when he heard the valves hammering and panicked."

Now I thought that would do it for Ora, but he didn't seem disturbed. He waited for Coley to explain, but he didn't.

"Help me put this cowling back on, will you, Sport?" Coley asked, looking at me. I helped him pick up the hammered aluminum piece and set it over the top of the engine. He fastened it in place.

"Climb aboard," Coley said to Ora. "Sport," meaning me, "you're going to have to pull me through."

"What about the trees?"

"Don't worry, I've got a plan," Coley said around the Roi Tan.

"So do I," I said. "Cut down the trees."

Coley laughed that big laugh of his and it somehow reassured me.

"Cut down the trees," he said, shaking his head, the laugh coming from deep down. "Sport, you're a goddamn gasser, you are. Don't worry."

He pointed at the engine.

"OX-5," he said, which didn't mean anything to me.

"OX-5," he said again. "Curtis. Hundred horsepower. You want something proven, Sport, that's it. The OX-5 is flying all over the sky. Best damn engine made. Don't worry."

Ora was getting settled in the front cockpit, fluffing things around like a bird on a nest. He held the Thompson alongside, pointing skyward. Coley reached into the rear cockpit and pulled out a pack and threw it on the ground. Looked a lot like a parachute to me.

Coley shook his head. "One chicken shit pilot," he said.

It was a relief to me. I didn't want to be flying in an airplane without a parachute if the pilot had one.

Coley found a leather helmet with goggles, ripped the goggles off and tossed the helmet on top of the parachute. He put the goggles on over his shaved head, and with the cigar jutting out of his mouth, I didn't see how the American Eagle could dare not perform.

"After I'm in the cockpit, I'll make sure the magneto is off," Coley said. He gave instructions with his hands as well as his mouth. "When I yell, 'switch off,' you turn the prop through four revolutions and stop it with the blade horizontal to the ground. When I say, 'contact,' you put all your weight on that prop and yank it toward the ground. And when you do, you better step back or there'll be two of you."

That sounded easy enough. I waited for my instructions from Coley and did as he said. The mighty OX-5 he was so proud of rumbled, sputtered twice, then exploded with a belch of blue smoke in a puff that engulfed the whole plane.

I kept plenty of distance between me and the spinning propellor, but now I was having second thoughts about getting inside this thing with Ora. I mean, what did I really know about this shaved head, loudmouth? That is, other than the fact he had never even flown this plane. Had he ever flown any plane?

And, for that matter, what did I know about the American Eagle. Experimental, Hooks had said. Well, I sure wasn't experimental. I mean, there was only going to be one of me. I go down in flames with the American Eagle, they make a few design changes and they got another American Eagle. But there wasn't ever going to be any more Joel Dean Gregorys.

LIMB OF THE JUDAS TREE

Coley yelled, "Get in, Sport, we ain't got all day."

Ora watched me and I swear to God if he hadn't already been sitting in that seat, I would never have gotten inside that contraption. But the truth of the matter was, we were chasing after convicts I'd been careless enough to let escape, so I didn't have any choice, really. None whatsoever.

Ora held out his hand and I managed to get in and get settled beside him. Coley yelled at us over the sound of the OX-5 which was beginning to smooth out.

"The belts are supposed to hold you in. Better fasten them."

The engine picked up speed and we were in motion. Coley brought us around and headed downwind until we were doing twenty or thirty miles per hour by my guess. It didn't seem fast enough to get us off the ground and the line of cedars was coming up fast. I realized then that we were going to go right through those cedars and I ducked my head. I felt the plane wheeling around without slowing and I peeked out at the wing tip and saw the cedar trees being brushed aside.

The OX-5 roared and a sudden rush of air started streaming over the windscreen in front of us and my back was pinned to the seat with such force I could never have gotten out of that thing. Up ahead I saw the other line of cedar trees coming at us with uncommon velocity. All I had time for was to thank God I'd made love to Estelle before I died.

The earth dropped away from us and so did my stomach. We were shooting through the air with no possible means of braking. I saw the thick growth of cedars coming at us and my thoughts just went to hell. I wanted to close my eyes, I wanted to jump, I wanted to get underneath that damn plane and help push it higher, but what could I do except sit and watch the onrush of the trees. I heard the tip of the cedars brushing against the bottom of the wing, then we were past, climbing higher and the air from the headwind and the prop blew hard over the windscreen and into our faces. I glanced back and down at the ground and saw a figure that had to be Addie leaning against the open door of the Chevrolet.

I looked at Ora and smiled, but he had a strange look on his face.

"Be damned," he shouted in my ear. "Swallowed my chaw."

Coley circled the huge estate which had belonged to the family of a Kansas City millionaire named Snyder. We rode horseback here as kids to look at the big limestone castle and to listen to the strange brogue of the stonemasons who came from Scotland to build it. The castle was one of the few things around that had brought the outside world into our world.

The plane circled over Ha Ha Tonka spring, a spout of clear water gushing right out of a vertical cliff. Though I had seen it many times before, seeing it like a bird sees it was something. Really something.

Coley dipped the wings and we got a clear view of the lake a thousand yards below us with the foaming water flowing from the spring. I understood for the first time why so many people were disturbed when one man bought all of that and made it his personal property. It looked like something too spiritual to be owned by man.

The castle loomed in the distance, a great structure of perfect stones, perfectly laid. Coley put the nose of the silver Eagle toward the ground and we buzzed over the five story structure no more than fifty or sixty feet above the slate roof. The nose of the plane went upward and I felt the sensation of soaring. Over my shoulder I looked at the out-of-place mansion sitting atop the crag that everybody around here knew as Deer Leap Hill.

Coley came in line with the Osage and I could see where the Niangua emptied into it and imagined I could see the spot where Estelle and I had lain in love last night after the hot and sweaty dance.

Over our valley we glided, and like a hawk must do searching for prey, I looked for landmarks, but was slow at picking them up. I saw the courthouse, the jail, Yawley and Estelle's house up the hill and I strained, hoping to spot her lounging on the front porch. Then, just as quickly as we'd gotten to the spot above the town, the town was behind us. Ora and I were silent as we passed along the Bagnell road, both of us trying to see everything we could and not being able to recognize it until it was gone. Down under us is—was— Glaize City. I see Bagnell coming, no, going under our tail. On the left is Eldon, going out of sight behind us. After awhile, the capitol dome loomed ahead of us on the right horizon. Coley flipped the right tips of the wings over and we started down. I turned to look at him and saw a little boy's mischievousness behind his goggles.

He flew us within a few feet of the trees surrounding the capitol, and then turned a wing toward the dome—too close to suit me—and righted us before dropping down over the bluff to skim the waters of the Missouri River. Giving us our money's worth.

To the left, the sun had set below the horizon leaving golden tinged clouds and a reddened sky below them. It was the oddest sight of all, watching the sun set from the sky.

A few minutes farther on, Coley punched me from behind with a stick. When I turned, he pointed the stick ahead and off to the right. I read his lips enough to know the town of Mexico was just ahead.

Ora, watching the highway below, motioned to me. I leaned over him and saw what looked like Buck Newland's truck moving along below us, then falling to the rear. I looked at Ora and he gave me a rare smile.

Coley came in low over the town and people on the ground shook their fists at us. He flew around the edge of the city, then turned and went back. I felt the stick punching me again and he pointed off to the left. As we flew over I read the sign on the front of a large, brick building: AUDRAIN COUNTY FURNITURE WORKS. The name that was painted on Buck Newland's truck. I showed it to Ora.

Coley circled the building again. In the rear I saw three trucks like Buck's loading and unloading. A pasture stretched out behind with a half dozen Guernsey cows and one goat grazing there. I heard the drone of the OX-5 slowing and felt the Eagle coming down. Watch out cows, here comes Coley.

We bounced twice then we were down. A full line of hedge trees came fast at us and I wondered if Coley was going to stop in time. When he did, the goat would have had a hard time getting between the plane and the hedge trees.

"Get out and pull me back," Coley yelled. Ora and I climbed out of the cockpit, went to the tail and pulled the plane backward until the tail was actually under the limbs in the hedge.

"I'm leaving," he yelled. "Be dark soon."

"I'll send you a voucher," Ora yelled at him, but Coley gripped the cigar between his teeth and waved his hand.

The OX-5 roared and the American Eagle started the length of the pasture with the Guernseys scattering. The goat stood his ground and decided to charge. Coley lifted off just ahead of the goat and the animal looked around, bewildered.

Coley circled, dipped his wings and waved a hand from the cockpit. Then he was gone. Ora watched silently until the American Eagle was out of sight.

"I think I'll get me one of them things," he said. "Never had such a good time."

Buck Newland pulled the truck into the loading area and parked. He got out, stretched, and took off his felt hat, then wiped his brow on a shirt sleeve. With a hitch of his pants he came toward the back door of the building where we stood. He barely noticed us.

"Hello Buck," I said and he turned for a second look.

"Hell, ain't you . . .how'd you get here . . .?"

He looked around for a car.

"You're running kind of late, Buck," I said. "We've been waiting on you."

"You must have drove mighty damn fast," Buck said. "I never did see you go by."

"Didn't," I said. I pointed to the sky. "Went over you."

He looked up, then back to us, puzzled.

"Eagle," I said.

"Oh," as if he understood, but you could tell he didn't.

"Mind if we take the passengers off your hands?" Ora asked.

"Passengers?"

"Those three escapees," I explained. "They're in the back of your truck."

He looked at his truck. "Hell you say. What makes you think that?"

"All right to pull that tarp off?" Ora asked. He was already untying the ropes that held the big canvas sheet in place.

"Well, yeah, but nobody's underneath . . ."

"They're not armed," I said. "Nothing to worry about."

Buck stood watching us untie all the ropes.

He said, "I never knew anything about this."

110

"We know," Ora told him. "Give us a hand with this tarpaulin, will you?"

With the ropes untied, Buck and Ora started peeling the cover off. I thumbed the safety off on the Thompson, just in case.

The three heads came up over the sideboards and Buck just stared at them with nothing to say.

"We're obliged for the ride," Champ said, not having seen me yet.

When their feet were on the ground, Buck said, "Sheriff's looking for you boys."

"Now you ain't going to tell him are you?" Wilbur asked, advancing toward Buck.

Buck gave ground. "Don't have to."

"What do you mean?" Wilbur asked. He pushed Buster in Buck's direction.

"Wilbur, you ran off without a please or thank you," I said from where I was standing at the front of the truck. They whirled and stared open mouthed at me. "And you forgot your tommy gun."

Ora came up behind me. "Hello boys. Now that you've seen Mexico I suppose you're ready to come on back with us."

Champ had that grin going again. "You probably won't believe us, Ora, but we were planning on coming back just as soon as Buster said hello to his family."

I was driving a Chevrolet about like Ora's that the sheriff of Audrain County had arranged for us to borrow from a dealer who wanted it delivered to Jefferson City anyway, and Ora was sitting up front by me with the Thompson between his knees, not sleeping, I'm sure, but staring into the moonless night broken only by our headlights, and thinking I guess about what changes he might have to make to his system at the jail house. Champ and the others were in the back cuffed together with Wilbur cuffed to a rod across the seat back.

"Jesus Christ," he'd said, "what if we have a wreck and I can't get out?"

We crossed the Missouri, drove through Jefferson City, then rolled over the hills until it leveled out past Eldon. It was near midnight when we came to Glaize City and saw a light in the small store by the highway that the Monger brothers owned. I pulled in because I didn't want to take any chances of running out of gas. I couldn't figure why the store was still open, but I thought we might as well take advantage of it.

Artis was sitting inside watching the highway like he was expecting someone. He made his way out of the building, letting the screen door slam behind him. He stood maybe six feet back from the car—not recognizing us yet—sucking on a match stick waiting to be spoken to.

"Need a couple dollars worth of gas, Artis," I said, but he made no motion toward us or any kind of sign that he'd heard me. "Better check that motor oil, too, seeing that this car don't belong to us."

When he screwed the cap off the gas tank on top of the engine, he looked through the windshield and I'm sure recognized the culprits in the back seat who the Klan had been ready to hang that night. He said nothing to us until he'd put the gas in the tank, then he came around to the other side of the car where Ora was sitting.

"You going to be letting up on my whiskey suppliers now you've caught Shorty's killers?" he asked.

"Whiskey running's against the law, Artis. I get paid to uphold the law," Ora said, holding two dollar bills out the window toward Artis.

"Whiskey running ain't any business of the law," Artis said, his voice unusually low for a big man, but with a rough edge to it.

"United States Congress and the President have different ideas about that," Ora said, still holding the dollar bills out the window.

"Sheriff Barker here in Miller County don't meddle with a man's business," Artis said. "He's welcome here anytime he wants. Anything he needs I got in the store he can have. That's the kind of neighbor I can be.

"You'll go broke you do that for everybody," Ora said.

Artis raised the cowling to check the oil. Ora handed me the Thompson to hold and opened his door, walked over to the open cowling where Artis stood and leaned against it with one hand. I wasn't sure what Ora was going to do, but I kept the Thompson ready just in case.

Artis took the money from Ora and went back inside the small building. When he came back, he had an adjustable wrench in his hand. I heard Ora say something about checking the oil line.

"I need that whiskey I been getting over in your county," Artis said to Ora.

"Where you get your whiskey is your business," Ora said. "Seeing it don't leave Camden County is my business."

Artis ducked his head under the raised cowling over the engine. He spent a full minute or two checking the oil, then came out from under the cowling. Ora put his head under the cowling to check to see Artis had tightened the oil line, I guess. He asked Artis for the wrench, then backed out from under the cowling after a minute. Artis slammed it down, fastened it, and stepped away from the car.

I started the engine and left Artis standing with that dark stare of his following us into the night.

We crossed the Glaize bridge and started up the steep set of hills that led to Rifle Ridge. Almost home. The engine sputtered twice like it didn't want to pull the hill so I slipped in the clutch and pulled the Chevrolet over to the side of the road.

"What's wrong with her?" Ora asked.

"I don't know," I said. "But I don't think it's ever going to make it to the top of Rifle Ridge."

I looked at the fuel gauge and I couldn't believe it, but it read empty.

"Can't figure this," I said, "but we're out of gas."

"You sure Artis put gas in?" Ora asked.

"I saw him. We must have sprung a leak or something. What was wrong under the hood?"

"Noticed oil dripping a little," Ora said. "That wouldn't have anything to do with the fuel."

"I'll take a look," I said.

Ora said, "Champ, you were complaining about needing to take a leak. Now's your chance."

"Thanks Ora," Champ said.

Ora handed me the Thompson. "Maybe you better hold this."

While I got out to look at the engine, Ora uncuffed Champ and let him out the back door.

With the Thompson and a flashlight in one hand, I raised the cowling over the engine, shined the light inside and saw fuel dripping from a fitting. I reached in, tightened the fitting with my finger and thumb until the drip stopped. I pulled on the accelerator connection and the engine roared, backfired once, smoothed out some, then died.

114

As I started to back out from under the cowling, a bright light shined on me from behind and something crashed into the back of my head. I tried turning to see what had hit me, but I lost the strength in my legs and the last thing I remembered was banging my chin on the fender on my way to the ground.

It was close to morning; the sky was getting light. I woke several times, the pain crashing, then ebbing, and crashing and ebbing again. Just like the wash from a power boat.

The only thought I could hang onto was the thought of Estelle. The little rosebud mouth—who was it she reminded me of? Oh, yeah. The picture I'd seen of some moving picture star. Mona Deering I think her name was.

I was sitting on Yawley's big front porch with the movie star beside me, then she was lying on the river bank naked and here came Yawley. The light was in my eyes again, back to where it was when I had blacked out or something hit me. I couldn't decide which.

It was near daylight, I did know that. Maybe that was the light. I was crawling along the river bank looking for Estelle, I guess. Why else would I be close to a river? I found her but she was dressed in man's clothing, hiding her breasts.

But it wasn't Mona Deering. It wasn't Estelle. I knew somehow it was Ora. And he was covered with blood.

I never remembered much else except I lay there with my hand on him for a long time. And I was bawling; I remember that. I guess I was still bawling when they found us.

PART TWO
THE ESCAPE

"Hell, he ain't much more'n a boy."

It sounded like Yawley talking, but it wasn't Yawley I wanted to be dreaming about. I was thinking more about his daughter.

Then it sounded like Judge Cargrove and I sure enough didn't have any desire to be dreaming about the judge.

"People won't stand for Doyle Savoy as sheriff of Camden county." The voice was Agnes St. Cloud's, but not the vision in my dream. Agnes was the leader of the three women on the city council.

Agnes again: "Just remember about the vote of the women in Camden County."

Then I thought I heard Gideon Norfleet talking about how old Noah was, and Yawley pipes up and says we sure enough don't want somebody in here telling us how we could make our living. About then I started getting aggravated about the whole idea of dreaming. I mean, if a man can't have who he wants in his dream, then why bother dreaming at all?

Now there are a lot of ways to wake up from being unconscious for most of a day, and all of them are good, considering the alternative. The way I woke up may have been the best way anyone could hope for.

"Hi, Joel Dean," Estelle said, and the little rosebud mouth kissed me, feeling so cool on my lips.

I took a moment to gather my thoughts, trying to remember, trying to place myself. I recognized Addie's bed. I asked Estelle the most dreaded question in my mind.

"Is Ora dead?"

Tears just seemed to pop out of her eyes and they started running down that sweet little face of hers. She didn't have to answer.

"Last night?" I asked. She nodded, her lips pulled tight, but still trembling.

"I've got to get up," I said. As I tried to move my feet over to the edge, my stomach said, no you don't, so I let myself fall back on the pillow.

"Just stay quiet, Joel Dean," Estelle said. "You've got to lay still. Doc Hardesty says you've had a nasty crack on the head."

I didn't have to be told that.

"I'm so glad you're alive," she said. More tears. More kisses. It suited me if she wanted to keep on showing how glad she was.

I slept, woke up once and she wasn't there, went back to sleep and woke up again and she was.

She told me about everyone being in to take a look at me, including Yawley and the judge. Maybe I hadn't been dreaming after all.

I couldn't put it off any longer. I had to force my mind to think about Ora and how he might have died. And, worst of all—the very lowest point in my life since my ma died—I had to force myself to think about why he had been killed.

I could talk about it now. I wanted to talk about it. I asked Estelle if she would listen to me.

"It was because of me," I told her, then had to place a finger across that little rosebud mouth to keep it quiet.

"I let him down. I was lax and that's how Wilbur and Buster jumped me and got away. And I failed him because we had to stop alongside the road and somehow they took the gun away from him.

"Don't blame yourself, Joel Dean," she said. "You did everything you could . . ."

120

"That's just it, I didn't. I could have prevented it. I could have helped him. But I didn't. He was a big man, Estelle. The biggest man this town will likely ever see. And the best. Won't anybody ever replace him."

"Maybe you will," she said, and it sounded like a joke when she said it. But she was serious.

"Not me, Estelle. Not me. Not anybody."

"Then let's run away. Let's go someplace like Chicago or New York. I'm tired of Linn Creek and nothing but hills and trees and ticks and mosquitos. And being called hillbillies. You know that's what they say about us from the Ozarks when you go to St. Louis. They say we're ignorant and lazy and ugly and everything insulting they can think of saying. I dress as nice as anybody there, and I pull out a bundle of money to pay the bill for the hotel and you know what they do? They look at the register and see I'm from Linn Creek, Missouri, and they just say, 'Isn't that down in the Ozarks?' When I say it is, they just sort of grin like I was about the lowest form of life they ever looked on.

"Let's go, Joel Dean. There's nothing holding either one of us here anymore."

"What about Yawley? What about your daddy?"

"He doesn't need me, he needs a son. I wanted him to need me, but he just wants to send me off to college. Get rid of me."

"Running away with you, Estelle, is just about the most tantalizing temptation I could think of right now."

"Good." She straightened up from her chair. "We'll do it then. Just as soon as you're ready to travel."

"One thing I have to do first, Estelle."

"What's that, Joel Dean?"

"Find the ones who shot Ora and make them pay."

I said I was strong enough to do it and I wanted to do it, so I did it. I was one of six who carried the body of the best man I ever knew and lowered it into the ground. Addie cried and I damn near did, for just an instant, but there really weren't any tears left inside. I was sorry Ora was dead, sorry for myself, sorry for Addie, but most of all I was sorry for all the people in our county because they weren't ever going to have a sheriff that good again.

But greater than the sorrow was my pride at having known and worked for him, and the determination that I would find the ones responsible for his death.

We walked down off the knoll where the cemetery was located and I offered my arm to Addie.

"Addie, I want you to know I thought a lot of Ora. He was almost like my own pa and a brother combined."

"Thanks, Little Brother. He was a good man."

I waited until we were out of hearing of the others.

"I mean to go after them, Addie. If I have to, I'll give up my badge, but I don't plan on letting anything interfere with catching them who did it."

"Pretty big job," she said.

"I'll do it. What about you?"

"Ora had some money put away. Not much, but I won't starve. Who knows, maybe I can get a job in the kitchen with the new sheriff if he ain't married."

"I'll see to it you won't ever need anything," I said.

"Thanks, Little Brother. I know you mean well."

We didn't say anything else until she asked, "Who did it."

"Could have been someone else other than those three. But likely not. It was probably that damn little cowardly braggart,

122

Wilbur. I saw a light, I remember that, and it could have been the lights of another car. I don't know for sure."

"Could be," she said. "And that could be why they didn't take the car you were driving."

"The reason they didn't take that car was because a fuel line was busted. No, probably the light I saw was the hand torch Ora had. I know who to look for."

"Do you know where?"

"They're here in the county hiding out in the hills."

"Then you'll have to find them before Yawley's Klan does," she said.

"I can do that."

"What'll you do with them?"

"One thing I won't do."

"What's that?"

"Bring them back here."

I answered the knock on the door. It was Judge Cargrove, Yawley and Gideon.

"Glad to see you up and about, Joel Dean," the judge said. Gideon expressed his concerns about my well being, also.

Yawley said, "Addie here?"

I invited them into the sheriff's office, then escorted them on into the kitchen. They each sat politely at the kitchen table, holding their hats. Yawley was fidgety. They rose stiffly together when Addie came into the room.

"Addie, there just ain't anything I can say that would bring him back," the judge said. "If there was, I'd be saying it over and over."

Addie expressed her thanks and shook the judge's hand.

"Bertha asked if there was anything she could do," Gideon said. Addie shook her head.

"Agnes St. Cloud offered to help out," Addie said. "You tell Bertha it means a lot to me that she asked."

Gideon nodded.

They stood around, not taking their seats, looking awkwardly at each other. Addie offered coffee, but they declined.

"Why don't you boys be seated," she said, taking a seat herself.

Yawley stepped forward. "Reason we came by, Addie . . ." but the judge didn't like being upstaged and he shouldered himself in front of Yawley.

"The election's not till next April, Addie," the judge said. "We were thinking of appointing somebody until then to take Ora's place. Not that anyone could, but the county does have to have a sheriff."

"Of course," Addie said.

The judge turned to look at the other two, and this time Yawley shrunk away, preferring to have the judge or someone else tell Addie whatever it was they had come to tell her.

Gideon stepped forward.

"It's unusual, Addie, but you have to understand. There just wasn't anyone in this county who was more thought of than Ora. The people want to see whoever did it punished. And they ain't going to accept just anybody stepping in as sheriff, even if it is just a few months."

Addie nodded. "So, who have you decided on?" Her voice was calm and friendly. Make it easier for them to tell her she was being evicted.

"Addie, we were wondering," the judge started out, then faltered. "That is, would it be . . .could you, uh . . ."

Yawley said, "Addie, we've just appointed you to be sheriff."

"Well, it ain't going to be like having Ora," Noah said. He turned the fruit jar up and took a long drink of Ernest Raines' best. Ernest had come by after the funeral and left two jars behind instead of a cake or a pie.

The whole town had come by the jail house kitchen bringing every kind of food. Before they left, everyone had plenty to eat. Addie was plumb worn out and retired immediately after the last person was gone out the door. I took a few leftovers up to the prisoners who had to eat in their cells that night. We just had two, a drunk and a boy about twenty not quite right in the head who had thrown a rock through Yawley's store window for not letting him have a licorice stick on account.

Noah and Doyle and me were having a kind of deputy's meeting I guess you could call it. I wanted to feel them out about Addie being sheriff and they wanted to kind of feel me out and see what Addie might do after she started wearing the badge.

Doyle said, "Addie never took a shine to me. Maybe I was too forward, but it's just my way. She's one of the finest women I've ever run across, but now with Ora gone, it wouldn't be proper for me to let on like I thought that. What do you think, Joel Dean?"

"I think things ain't going to be any different with her," I said. "I believe she'll do what she thinks Ora would do. The rest of us will do the same. We just won't have Ora there if anything goes wrong."

"I wonder what Ernest uses in his mash," Noah said, holding the fruit jar to the light as if he could see the ingredients through the glass.

"What are we going to do about stopping the runners, now?" Doyle asked.

"I hope you ain't planning on making any more runs for Yawley," I said.

"Don't hold that night against me, Joel Dean. I'm sorry if I interrupted anything"—a big smile broke out on his face—"and I would never have drove for Yawley if Ora had told me you were shutting things down."

"It's a crime to tell somebody who can make whiskey this good he has to stop," Noah said, helping himself to another sample.

"Yawley thinks Addie won't try and stop the runners," I said.

"You think she will?" Doyle asked.

"Soon as we bring Champ and those other two in, she's going to go right on doing whatever Ora was doing."

"Damn shame," Noah muttered, holding Ernest's whiskey up to the light again and looking at it through the fruit jar glass.

"Speaking of Champ, wasn't Addie right sweet on him at one time?" Doyle asked.

"Long time ago," I said. "Before she married Ora."

"So you reckon she's over Champ by now?"

"What I reckon is that she'll do her job if that's what you're asking," I said.

"I suppose Addie will do all right," Doyle said like he'd been studying on it. "At least till April."

Noah turned his head away from the whiskey for a minute and said, "You think Addie will file for office come April?"

"I couldn't say," I said. "Something like this comes up, takes some time for people to decide on a thing like that."

"Are you filing in April, Doyle?" Noah asked.

"Don't know," Doyle replied. "Right now I just want to get along with Addie for a few more months.

"There ain't but two ways to get along with a woman," Noah said.

Doyle looked at him sharply. "What are they?"

"Nobody knows either one of them," Noah said, threw back his head and laughed a bit too loudly, then had himself another drink of Ernest Raines' fine, smooth whiskey.

It was rare to find Yawley behind the counter in his own general store, but there he was. I handed him the list.

"These look like supplies for a trek in the wilderness, Joel Dean," he said. "Canned food, dried fruit, coffee, bacon. You sure the sheriff wants these supplies to feed prisoners at the jail?"

"No, she don't," I said. "It's for the expedition that's going out to hunt for the killers."

"Expedition?" Yawley shouted. "What the hell you talking about?"

"To hunt the killers," I said again. "Somebody's got to bring them in. Can't go shooting the sheriff of this county and expect people to just forget about it."

"Ain't nobody forgetting," Yawley said. "They'll be taken care of. Who you say is going on this expedition?"

"Me. Addie. Doyle."

"Hell," he said, dropping the list and making off out the door.

"What about the supplies?" I called after him.

"You won't be needing them," he said.

I knew better. Somebody was taking my sister for granted and it just wasn't going to work. I helped myself to the supplies and left the list where Yawley could find it to figure up what we owed him.

When I got to the jail house, there was Yawley, the judge and

Gideon. They were drinking coffee at the table and trying to be polite to Addie.

"Who's going to watch the jail?" Yawley asked.

"Noah," Addie said. "And I've deputized the Wayne brothers, Ellis and Dave. They will be available to help out till we get back with the prisoners."

"It's dangerous out there, Addie," Judge Cargrove said. "This is serious business, hunting three killers who are apt to kill you on sight. The State already has a dozen men out there and they've sealed off all the roads. Sheriff Barker has a half dozen cars looking along all the roads in the county and over in Miller County. Those killers ain't going to get away."

"We know the risk," Addie said. "If we weren't willing to accept it, we wouldn't have taken the job. Joel Dean thinks they took off through the woods. I'll get some dogs and we'll find out."

"But, Addie," Gideon said, "It just wouldn't be proper. I mean here you are a woman—and a single one now, keep that in mind—leading a group of men on a hunt. I mean, how would that look?"

"Agnes St. Cloud said she was proud of me and she's sure the rest of the county will be, too, when we bring the killers back for trial."

The judge and Gideon looked at each other, baffled as to what to do about the unexpected predicament they had placed themselves in. Yawley, however was not to be silenced about Addie's expedition. He jumped to his feet and shook a finger at Addie.

"Now see here, Addie. We didn't appoint you sheriff so's you could go running all over the county trying to arrest murderers."

You see old Simon Burchett scratching his head and looking at the ground and you wonder if this wasn't just a waste of time.

"I don't know," the old man said, yanking on the chains to the two bitches. "Going on the second day, that's quite a spell. Trail's bound to be cold."

"Just a start," I said impatiently. "Just tell us which way they took off when they left here."

Simon drug the two bitches and the ugly male, with skin hanging in folds under his chin, over to the spot where I'd looked into that bright light and felt all hell breaking loose around me.

"Take your time," Addie said. She was ignoring my urge to get on with it. She held the reins to her walking horse, trying to show how calm she could be in a time of crisis. But I knew her too well.

Doyle lounged in the saddle of the mare that Gideon had let him borrow. He rolled and lit a cigarette, blowing the smoke out into the wind to let it carry off into the thicket of dogwoods bordering the road.

"You mean you ain't never found a trail two days old?" I asked Simon. If he couldn't detect my dissatisfaction he was blind, deaf and dumb.

"Didn't say that," Simon shot back. "What I said was, you bring me here the morning after it happened and I'll not just find your trail, in two hours old Drum here'll have his nose up their ass."

"Uh huh," I said. "How long you been tracking, Simon?"

"I tracked thirty years before you was even a gleam in your pappy's eye," he said. "If there's a trail here, they'll find it."

"Never fail. Is that right?"

"Joel Dean, leave the man alone you want something done," Addie said. "Cut him a little slack there so his dogs can get to working."

"He don't bother me none, m'am," Simon said, then added, "Sheriff," after hesitating. "Why one time I tracked a stolen steer and the man what stole it had already butchered it and his kids had it for breakfast. Damned if old Drum here didn't track them kids right to the schoolhouse. Yes sir, we ain't bothered none by the likes of him."

Doyle laughed at Simon's story. That didn't go along with soothing my feelings any.

I was riding Katrina, Ora's mare, and she was skittish; not used to my hands on the reins. I had spent all the time I wanted to at this spot on the road which held grim reminders for me. I threaded the mare through the growth, picked up a game trail and came out at the top of the ridge. From there I listened to the dogs and Simon threshing about in the underbrush.

Farther up the ridge I spotted a glade and rode there to let Katrina munch on some of the long grass while I pondered my status under my sister, the sheriff.

You wanted to be sheriff, is that it?

Not me. Let somebody else have the responsibility.

Then, why the resentment.

There's no resentment.

Bullshit. This is yourself you're talking to. To thine own self be true. Remember that one?

Okay. Maybe I resent it because she's a woman.

That's more like it. Now think about why they wanted Addie for sheriff.

So they could tell her what to do.

And what are you going to do about that?

Me? What am I going to do about it? Why should I do something about it?

Well, for one thing, she's your sister. For another, you're a deputy sheriff with some responsibility. And there's Ora . . .

I don't want to think about Ora. I'm too young for sheriff, Yawley said so. I'll do what I'm told. Nothing more.

You'll do more. You'll do what you have to do to bring Champ and the others in. You'll do it because Ora might still be alive if. . .

Shut up. Shut up. I ain't listening to any more of this. The dogs found the trail. I gotta go.

Drum's bloodhound stock put him on the trail first, then the bitches started bellowing right on his heels. By the time I caught up with them, Simon had mounted his mule and turned the dogs loose.

"You sure it's them or just a rabbit?" I asked as I rode up to join the others.

"It's them, it's them," Simon said. He jabbed his heels into the mule's ribs and yelled at him, whipping the reins from right to left on the mule's neck.

Doyle found amusement in something going on.

"I don't think it's them," I said. "This trail's leading away from town, away from the highway. They'd head for Bagnell, for the railhead."

"Shut up, Joel Dean," Addie said, riding out into the lead. I nudged Katrina and we shot ahead of the mule in time for me to catch a branch in my face that Addie had deflected.

"Watch those branches," I called out out to her.

"Watch them yourself," she yelled back.

LIMB OF THE JUDAS TREE

Before we got to the top of the ridge the dogs had split up and were now following two trails.

"Told you it was a rabbit," I said to Simon as his old mule plodded up to us.

"Appears to me they split up," Simon said.

"Appears to me there was two rabbits," I snapped back at him.

About then old Drum came back to where the four of us were standing our mounts. He sniffed in circles and finally took off after the two bitches on their trail.

"Looks like old Drum is backing and filling," I said. "He don't know where the hell he's going."

"Sonny, why don't you go over there and set down. Do some whittling or something to fill your mind while the professionals do the tracking," Simon said, a bite in his voice.

"Listen, old man." I wheeled Katrina around to face him. "I knew this was a bad idea. Those flea bitten mutts couldn't find a bone hanging off their collar."

Simon slid off the back of his mule and advanced toward me.

"Young fellow, you can call me any name you want. I'm an old man, like you say, and I ain't got any fight left in me to try and change ignorant people's minds. But as long as I'm alive, ain't no man going to bad mouth my dogs."

He came at me swinging the metal chains that had been fastened to his two bitches. I ducked and heard them whistle over my head. Katrina heard them too, and she reared her front legs, then twisted her back quarters and I caught a limb on my shoulder. The ground came up to hit me hard and there was Simon coming toward me, those damn chains singing in the air.

"Simon," Addie said. She rode between us making me roll away from the hoofs of her horse. "Pay no attention to him. Now tend to those dogs before they do scare up a rabbit."

Simon pulled in his chains, looking at me all the time. My head hurt and my ribs hurt, and I knew how badly I had hurt him, but I just didn't give a damn at the moment. If he was going to track, let him get at it. If he couldn't do it, he damn well better stay out of my way.

"Simmer down, Joel Dean or I'll send you back to take Noah's place," Addie said.

"Like hell you will. You ain't the one. I was the one. Me."

I got up and brushed off my clothes. "I was the one," I said again, unable to get it out of my mind. "It was me."

She didn't say anything for awhile. Then, "You don't have to feel that way."

"I do, though."

"But you don't need to."

"How do you know what I need to feel? It's there, in my mind. Tell me how to erase that."

"You take all the blame on yourself, you're a fool."

I slapped my hat against my jeans, knocking off leaves and dry grass. I said, "Not a fool. No, no. Not a fool. A fool would feel nothing. A fool would say it just happened."

"It did. It just happened. That's all."

"It didn't just happen," I blurted out. "Nothing just happens. A tree doesn't just fall in the woods with no wind, no lightning. A man isn't just shot."

"Then go ahead, feel it. Live in hell." She turned her mare away from me.

"I've been living there since it happened."

"And finding them? That's going to erase it from your mind?"

"Of course not. Nothing will ever do that. But they have to be found. They have to be killed."

"Not by you, Joel Dean," she said. "You don't have to kill them."

"Yeah. By me."

"Then you are a fool. I don't need some fool thinking he can just go around shooting people. I need you to do your job. When we catch up with them, we'll arrest them. And we'll take them back for trial. If you're not willing to do that, go on back to town."

She spun her mare around in a complete circle, then rode off in a gallop after Simon.

The dogs were all on the same track and were baying from the top of the next ridge.

Doyle came riding up with the reins to Katrina in his hands. As he handed them over he said, "New bosses take some getting used to."

I didn't want to turn and look at him because I knew he would have that damn smile on his face.

I got on Katrina and to show I was in full control of myself, I waved for him to go on ahead of me down the path.

"Thing to do, Joel Dean, is to just let her burn herself out. Then you and me can get down to looking seriously for them three."

"Doyle, you don't know her well enough yet, so I'll explain something to you. My sister never gives up. And she never forgets. I never seen her quit at anything and she won't quit this tracking expedition until we've caught up with Champ Gowan."

Doyle said, "Then the question is, what's she going to do when she catches up with him?"

It was good, I decided, that the dogs were tracking back and forth, back and forth, from ridge to ridge, sometimes losing, sometimes finding the trail. I needed time to settle down, to compose myself. I was going to be calm, I told myself, from here on out. Until we found the three who had killed Ora. No more outbursts. No more adolescent behavior.

I tried rolling and smoking one of Doyle's cigarettes, but that had no calming effect on me. So I stripped the saddle off Katrina, rubbed her down, then resaddled her and rode leisurely after the others. I caught them at Glaize Creek when the dusk was just beginning.

"Trail runs right into the creek," Doyle said, pointing.

"Where's it come out?" I asked him.

"Hasn't yet."

We watched as Simon brought the dogs back toward us from the other side of the creek.

"It's no use," he said to Addie. "I don't figure they failed," he glanced over at me, "It's just been too long. Two days? Normal dogs have a time smelling them after three hours. Then when they hit the water . . ."

"The dogs did fine," Addie told him as she dismounted. "We'll camp here for the night. Doyle, bring that pack horse over here and unload the gear."

Doyle led the horse forward, but did not dismount.

"You know where they're headed don't you?" He looked at Addie.

"Do you?"

"The railroad at Stoutland. He ain't dumb. He knows they've got to get out of the county and out of the state as fast as they can."

"I don't think so," Addie said. "I think they're still out there."

"We're spending time and time's on their side. I figure they got to Stoutland today sometime. They hopped a freight and probably headed for the yard in Springfield."

"What makes you so sure?" she asked.

"That's what I'd do," Doyle said. "They do that and they're out of the state tomorrow. We'll never get them."

"If you're right, there wouldn't be anything we could do about it now."

"I could ride back into town, wire the police and the railroad in Springfield. They could search the trains in the yard."

"And you could have a night on the town, couldn't you? Instead of spending it out here in the woods, you could be drinking and dancing and living it up."

"Is that what you think?"

"Why wouldn't I?" Addie asked. "That's all you've done since you come here. Making music and drinking and trying to get in bed with every woman in town."

Doyle's easy smile showed how unruffled he was by Addie's accusations. "I admit to participating in all those pleasurable activities you mentioned Addie. But I still do my job as good as any man. Or woman."

"Question that's always bothered me and troubled Ora some is just exactly who you doing your job for? Yawley? The judge? I know how the two of them forced you on Ora. That gave Yawley protection for his bootlegging and him and the judge had somebody from the Klan inside the jail house."

"Dastardly charges, Addie," Doyle said, looking up from the cigarette he was rolling to grin at her. "Good thing I like you and know you don't really mean it."

"I mean it all right. I'll tell you something else, Doyle. I ain't going to be pushed around like they thought I would. Good old Addie. She can go right on cooking and cleaning and we'll even let her wear the sheriff's badge till spring then we can get who we want in there. Probably Doyle Savoy. People will forget about Ora by then and they'll elect whoever the judge and Yawley tells them to."

"You sound bitter, Addie," Doyle said through a cloud of blue smoke. "No need to be. Things'll work out."

"Sure they will. All I gotta do is keep on being the sheriff's wife like I been and come next spring maybe they'll let me have a job in the kitchen at the jail house."

"Come next spring you'll be an attractive widow woman, Addie. Men'll come calling."

"Is that so? Does that include you, Doyle? After they make

you sheriff will you want to marry me? You better, Doyle. Then just like your other wife, I can go back to work where you found me. In the kitchen at the jail house. Save you having to hire somebody. I'm sure the judge'll point that out to you."

"Hard to say what'll happen come spring, Addie. Town thought a lot of Ora. They think a lot of you. You'll be all right."

"Oh, sure I will. 'Morning Miz Mitchell. How's the sheriff? Well, I don't know about that order, Miz Mitchell. I'll have to have the sheriff's signature on it.' Oh, yeah, they thought a lot of me as the sheriff's wife. But come spring, I'm nobody. I ain't even got a house to live in. All I got is a few hundred dollars that Ora saved up from the measly pay the county gave him for getting shot arresting the people who was trying to steal Yawley Earnhardt's whiskey."

"No need to look at it that way."

"Ain't there? Well, you can tell Yawley and the judge I got some surprises in store for them before spring gets here."

"That may not set too well with them," Doyle said. "No need to get them riled up. Just smile and talk nice to them and go ahead and do what you want to do anyway."

"I'm tired of smiling and talking nice to them," Addie said. She came over and took the reins of the pack horse from Doyle.

"Go on, Doyle. Go on back to town. Play your guitar, drink your whiskey and chase the women. Wouldn't want you to have to spend a night in the woods. We might come across that bad ass Wilbur tomorrow. You always manage to miss out on all the shooting."

"Got that right," Doyle said, the old Doyle Savoy grin lighting up his face. "I'll get those wires off then I'll wait around for the answer saying they captured them. You'll be saying thank you."

Addie started untying the load off the packhorse.

"Take Simon and the dogs with you, we won't need them anymore. Me and Joel Dean will find the convicts tomorrow."

"Tell me which way you're heading so I can find you."

"You won't need to," Addie said. "You're fired."

The stars were holes in the sky through which some could see and some could not. And some could see through sometimes and sometimes not.

"Addie, I wonder if we're making a mistake," I said while trying desperately to see through the holes up there.

Not answering, I got to thinking she was asleep already. When she did speak, it was a voice I hadn't heard in a long time. A voice from across the loft in a cabin on a dirt-poor farm that only had fourteen acres of cleared bottom land. Land that flooded out six out of every seven years.

"My first mistake was being born at all. The second was being born a girl. I ain't improved my record any since."

"I think that sneaky Wilbur's out there with that Thompson in his hand, just waiting to cut loose on us. I found out his true nature when I turned my back on him for two seconds. I thought, 'Aw, he ain't going to do nothing.' Then, Whap! he lets me have it with a chair in the ribs."

"He gets back in jail, I can't wait to cook some poison mushrooms for him," Addie said.

"Maybe Doyle's right. Maybe all Champ wants is to get out of this state."

Addie the sheriff said, "He's out there."

I waited for time to pass, for sleep to come, but it didn't.

"You think Champ killed Ora?" I asked.

She was slow in answering. "All three of them were in on it together, probably. Champ wouldn't be the one to pull the trigger, but in the eyes of the law, that don't matter."

The one thing you remember at a time like this is what you don't want to remember: That fight where Addie got her nose broken for rights to Champ Gowan.

It was quiet again with only the tree bugs singing and the frogs croaking along Glaize Creek. I figured Addie sure enough had gone to sleep this time. But then I heard her faintly, sounding like she was crying or maybe laughing.

"Addie?"

She was laughing, making it louder, and she says, "One time the Afternoon Literary Tea started inviting me to their socials once a month. I guess because they thought they should, being the sheriff's wife and all. So I went and set by myself month after month, nodding politely when on some rare occasion someone would say something to me. Finally, I decided it was my turn to be the hostess, so I invited them all to the jail house for tea."

Addie was overcome with her remembrance. When she had settled down some, she went on with the telling of it.

"Shoulda seen Agnes St. Cloud and Bertha Norfleet and the rest of them when Ora marched the prisoners in and set them down at the table with the cream of Linn Creek's society. I will say, though, the prisoners were all well behaved. Some of them even lifted their little fingers in the air when they drank their tea.

"But I don't think the women of Linn Creek really felt like it was an uplifting experience. They plumb forgot to notify me when it was time for their next meeting."

I was having trouble seeing Agnes St. Cloud sitting at the same table with convicts.

"Well, anyway," Addie said, "I wasn't alone in town in not being invited to anymore teas. There was Nita and Bertha and Nell. None of us ever got invited again. I suppose we should have started our own tea."

"Us Gregorys were never great socializers," I said.

"You're doing all right with Estelle."

"Me and her make up our own society."

Addie said, "Hope you like tea."

I didn't. But, I didn't like bust-flattening smocks either. Or little sailor hats. I tried to concentrate on the tennis dress, but something was in the way and I couldn't hold the thought long enough to comfort me.

I had something else to say to Addie.

"The one thing I think of, Addie, when I think about Ora dying, is that it's the end of one part of my life. I won't ever be the same again. It's the end of one part of your life, too."

Silence.

You ever notice how one bullfrog seems to lead the chorus in the night? He'll tell the rest, Hrommpp, hrommpp. And they'll come in with their best imitation—some pitifully weak—and it'll go on all up and down the creek until the old bullfrog has taken in another load of air. Hrommpp. Hrommpp.

"I shoulda loved him more," Addie spoke up, right after the old bullfrog. "He deserved it. Anybody to blame, it was me."

Her voice was small and weak, for her, and I could tell she was getting ready to sleep. But I had one more question to ask her in the dark when we didn't have to face each other. A question I had no right to ask, I suppose, yet I had to know.

"Addie, you ever get over Champ Gowan?"

I thought she wasn't going to answer. She didn't have to, brother or no brother. I was out of line for asking.

"Probably not," she finally said, so quiet I hardly heard her over the Hrommpp. Hrommpp. "It's complicated, Little Brother."

In 1910 Grandpa Gregory rode a railroad tie to the bottom of the Osage, straddling it like it was a horse, they say. He never came up. A holding boom broke and five thousand cut and branded railway ties got loose and swept him and six others away along with them. Shortly after, I saw his face through one of those holes in the sky for the first time. I was five years old, but I will never forget it.

His face was as hard as a tie, and long and slim like one. He'd cut ties for forty years, getting so he resembled one. I remember his voice had been so deep and soft it made a young boy want to get closer. I remember his tales about rafting the ties, but then, it could have been my father's retelling of them because five years old is pretty young to recall much except a face and a voice.

One raft I kept seeing from memory was one in the river at Linn Creek after all the rafts had come down the Niangua, three-four hundred ties at a time, then around the bend of the Osage into the holding boom. They joined a four-thousand-tie raft that was a half mile long. I do remember seeing Grandpa Gregory along with some other men guiding the raft down the Osage. A white oak strip—nailed in a wrong spot by a man too drunk to be doing it—came loose in a current too swift for them to have been in the water, and the raft broke apart. Three men had died and Grandpa Gregory nearly did before they fished him out of the water.

"Take more'n a tie raft to kill a Gregory," Pa told us Grandpa Gregory said.

But it didn't. Tie rafts killed two Gregorys. It was when Pa's foot slipped on the slick mud at the banking at Roach on the Niangua that he got some kind of internal injuries when the ties in the raft fell on him. And he never recovered.

When I came back from Springfield, I'd studied for the bar exam at night and looked for work in the daytime. I talked with the Hobart Lee Tie and Timber Company about a job but the tie operation was dead.

A likely reason I'm still alive, I guess.

I did cut strips and nail together a few rafts that first summer back, but they were no more than two-three hundred size. Then the operation ceased and, like Ernest Raines had said, there were mighty few ways left to make a living anymore on the Osage.

No reason for me to be thinking all this while I looked at the stars, waiting to fall asleep. But it beat thinking about killing three men.

Only God knows what will happen.

A cabin stood in the center of the clearing. From it's condition and from the absence of stumps around it, it could have been there fifty years. Several fresh hand-hewn shingles showed the owner had prepared early for winter. Four posts supported the porch roof. As a testament to its builder there was no sag between them.

A man sat on the edge of the porch; a woman stood behind him. From the looks of them they could have been there as long as the cabin.

You see an old man like that—an old woman, too—and you think they'd be glad to see somebody out here in the middle of nowhere without even a road coming by the house. You'd think they would get up off the porch and walk out to greet you. You'd think that. Unless you'd lived around here all your life. Unless you knew how close-mouthed they were in the Ozarks. Unless you'd been gone long enough to forget.

"Howdy," I said. The old man nodded.

"I'm Sheriff Mitchell," Addie told them after getting off her horse. Though she was dressed in a pair of men's rough jeans, one of Ora's chambray shirts and a wide brimmed hat, the fact that she was a woman was obvious to anyone.

"We're looking for three men who are wanted for murder," she said. "Thought you might have seen them."

They might have been waiting for each other or who knows what before answering. The old man was whittling, making it look like it was a contract job the attention he was giving it. The old woman stared right through us.

"Last time you came by you was a man," the old man finally said, his gray, close cropped beard hardly moving with his lips. He was sparsely built, but you could see the strength in his shoulders in spite of his age.

"My husband was sheriff until three days ago when he was shot and killed by three cowards," Addie said.

"You stepping in to take his place?" the old woman asked. She wore a scarf tied over her head and a polka dot, dark colored dress. Her chin was as firm looking as the old man's. It was difficult, in fact, to tell which of them might be the stronger.

"My sister Addie," I said, stepping forward. "The judge wanted her to hold the office until spring elections."

"Right smart job for a woman," the old woman said. "Suppose you could do it, though."

"You ain't looking for stills?" the old man asked, rising to his feet. He was taller than he'd looked sitting there.

"I have no interest in stills," Addie said. "But I wouldn't mind a dipper of cold water."

A half log ran horizontal across two of the support posts. A galvanized bucket sat on the flat of it, a granite ware dipper floating in the water.

The old man stared at the bucket for several seconds like he was trying to make up his mind about something.

"Help yourself," he said, pointing at the bucket.

143

"Much obliged," Addie said.

While she was drinking the old woman said, "You're really the sheriff, then? Hard to figure."

Addie finished with the dipper and passed it to me. She dug in her shirt pocket and brought out the badge. The old man and old woman stared at it.

I dug my badge out for them, too.

"Joel Dean Gregory," I said. "Deputy sheriff."

The old man scrutinized his whittling.

"Knew a Tom Gregory once. Died when the holding boom busted."

"My grandfather," I told them.

The old man nodded his head, but he didn't say anything.

I added, "That's been seventeen years."

"Nineteen ten," he said. "I was there. I dove for him and the others. No use. They was all good men."

It was my turn to nod. I looked at Addie like it was time for us to be on our way. Addie waited like, let's see if these old people invite us in or turn us away or if they're going to tell us anything. The old woman looked at Addie's badge again and said, "Might's well stay for a bite to eat. We was just fixing to sit down. They's plenty."

"Obliged," Addie said again.

I unsaddled the horses and let them rest and cool off from the climbing they'd been doing since we'd broken camp on The Glaize that morning.

We sat down to a jar of home canned beef with some dumplings and gravy and some late garden vegetables cooked fresh. They ate well, this old man and woman. She'd learned how to cook in her years, and there was no doubting it when she dipped up the apple cobbler.

While we ate, I told them about Ora getting killed. I said we weren't sure the three men we were after did it, but everything pointed that way. Especially since one of them was a known machine gunner for a mob of criminals in Kansas City.

The old man shook his head and the old woman said it was too bad there was a road to Kansas City. Now all the trash and riff-raff would just get in their motor cars when the police got after them up there and bring their misery down here.

I was inclined to agree with her.

"Ozarks ain't no more," the old man said. "I came here from Tennessee when I was younger'n you are. They was people everywhere over there. Couldn't hardly spit without somebody standing on the spot you was aiming at. Mind, I ain't saying I'm one of them what does, but a man can run a little whiskey around here without somebody coming down on him."

"You deal with Yawley Earnhardt?" I asked, and the man's eyes narrowed down to a line I couldn't see through. "Well, if you do, I just thought I ought to tell you Yawley's been shut down. He lost a driver a few nights back. Shorty Mickelson. Fact is, that was why we'd arrested those three in the first place, for killing Shorty."

"Why'n hell they do that?" the man asked.

"My thought is somebody wanted to shut down the competition."

"What I figured," the man said. "Furriners bound to take over the whiskey trade, too."

The couple didn't own an automobile and hadn't been to Linn Creek but once all year. As we prepared to leave, Addie cautioned them again about the three killers on the loose, and went over the instructions to let the constable in Dog Hollow, a crossroads store about two miles away, know if they saw any sign of strangers.

"Ain't nobody ever comes by here," the old man said.

"You haven't seen anyone, then?" I asked.

The woman said, "Just my nephew. He was by yesterday."

As an afterthought, and to be polite, I said, "Who is your nephew? Maybe I know him."

"Probably do," she said. "He use to live around Linn Creek. Name's Champ Gowan."

I tell you, that was a lesson for us both right there. I mean, suppose we'd told the old couple right off who we were looking for. You think they would have fed us?

We laughed about it on the way to the store at Dog Hollow. We laughed at the luck of it all. We stopped laughing when we saw the twelve cars sitting around the store. One of them was Ora's Chevrolet.

Doyle was still wearing the deputy's badge pinned to his tan shirt. He stepped off the porch of the Dog Hollow store and came toward us, smiling his smile.

"You look rested," Addie said, climbing off her horse. She looked at the badge, but never mentioned it. "You bring enough cars so you'd feel safe out here in the woods?"

"There's been a development," Doyle said. Behind him a dozen men came down off the porch, all of them armed, all of them grim faced. Yawley was one of them.

"Well, you authorized to tell me about it or Yawley say to let him do the talking?" Addie looked over at Yawley.

"Told you, you should have stayed in town, Addie," Yawley said. He marched right up to the front and stood a few feet away from Addie. Yawley looked a tad uncomfortable and I guessed it was because he wasn't used to talking up to a woman.

"There's hell to pay back there, now," he said.

Addie waited.

Doyle said, "Truck driver name of Buck Newland says his truck is missing. So is Nita. The truck was parked in front of her place. When Buck got back from eating dinner at Minton's it was gone."

I said, "Whoever took the truck would have had to drive it down Main Street."

"Right past my store," Yawley said. He raised a finger toward Addie, then let it drop to his side. "I coulda been killed, Addie. They coulda come in my store, stole the supplies they wanted and shot me down." He looked over at me. "Coulda shot Estelle, too. Or kidnapped her."

My heart skipped. "Is she all right?"

"No thanks to the law," Yawley said. "We can't go on depending on luck to protect people, Addie. We got to have some law in town."

Addie looked at Doyle. "Truck must have come right by the courthouse, too. And the jail."

"I saw it," Doyle said. "I've seen it about twice a week for the last month. It goes down to Nita's house where it stays a while and then goes on."

"Same truck they hitched a ride in to Mexico," I said. "Guess they like old Buck's truck." I looked at Addie. "Wouldn't be any reason for anyone to be suspicious of it."

"So what happened to the truck?" Addie asked.

"Nobody knows," Yawley said. "They're waiting around out there to kill somebody else. Those three have got to be caught."

"Reason I'm here," Addie said. "They came through here yesterday."

"They know Champ in the store," Doyle said. "He came in, talked awhile, then asked for a ride into Linn Creek."

"And the other two?" Addie asked.

"Didn't say. You can bet though, they was around hiding in the bushes," Doyle said.

"What are you doing about the truck?" I asked Doyle. He turned quickly to me, his smile fading, and Yawley along with the others turned toward me also. I knew by that I had spoken too sharply. My anger was getting off the leash again. Anger at Simon for wasting time with his dogs, anger at spending the day riding around in the brush when we could have driven Ora's Chevrolet down here to the Dog Hollow store and been waiting for Champ after he walked over from having a nice meal with his aunt and uncle.

"Waiting on orders," Doyle answered. "Sheriff Barker from Miller County is out on the roads with three cars and we've got a dozen cars here waiting for orders."

He looked at Addie. "Sheriff Barker has kind of put himself in charge."

Addie snorted. She kneeled down in the dusty road and with her finger began drawing the county roads.

"Let's put somebody here," she jabbed the dirt with a fingertip, drawing a line across the road she'd just made. "And another one here," another jab, "and one at the toll bridge and one at the ferry. Somebody ought to drive over by Ha Ha Tonka and put up a barricade there. And be sure everyone remembers these three have that Thompson they took off Joel Dean."

Doyle stared at Addie's crude map in the dirt for a few seconds, hands on hips, then asked, "What about the main roads? Up on Rifle Ridge and Lebanon road?"

"If you haven't had sense enough to put somebody watching them already, then do it," Addie said. "Then get somebody to take these horses into town. We'll be driving Ora's Chevrolet."

"There's something else, Addie," Yawley said. He was speaking gingerly and that flew up a flag. When Yawley comes at you with humble talk, watch out.

Addie looked at him like she knew there was bound to be something else or Yawley wouldn't have driven all the way out here. She waited until Doyle returned to the group of men who had accompanied him from Linn Creek before she asked, "What else?"

"Senator Ragan is down from Jefferson City," Yawley said.

"He's ready to commit the State Militia or whatever you ask for. He says you're the only county official who can request it, that is unless he can determine the county is in imminent danger—which I'm ready to concede it is. What I'd like to see—what the town would like to see, actually—is some strong leadership here. Make it look like we're on top of the situation in Linn Creek. You know what I mean don't you Addie? It'd help the town, reassure the people that is, if you just came right back into town and walked into the courthouse and took over. No fumbling around or acting unsure . . ."

"Or acting like a woman?"

"You know what I mean, Addie. Show Ragan we're not the bunch of hicks he thinks we are. He's already thinking critical of us for appointing you sheriff. He just doesn't understand local politics, being from Jefferson City. Put Doyle in charge of the search, put Joel Dean here in charge of safety in the town and Ragan will bring in anything from the State we need for the search. Otherwise he's going to go back there and tell everyone we don't know what we're doing down here and they had better send someone from the Capitol to take over."

"He'd have to do a bit of juggling of the State Constitution if he did that, wouldn't he?" I asked Yawley.

"Now don't you go getting technical on me, Joel Dean, with all your lawyering," Yawley snapped at me. "You're wearing your deputy hat right now."

"Don't worry about Ragan," Addie told Yawley. "I'll take care of him. Who's entertaining him now, Noah and the judge?"

"Sid Hatch."

"Sid Hatch?" Addie's voice crackled. "They came out of the woodwork for this exercise, didn't they? What's Sid Hatch doing speaking for the county?"

"I asked him," said Yawley. "We needed a leader."

"You got one," Addie said as she walked toward Ora's Chevrolet. "Soon as I get back to town."

"Joel Dean, you round up the town council and have them at the courthouse in fifteen minutes," Addie said as I let her off in front of the jail house. It wasn't until I started driving away that I caught on to what sister Addie was asking. She wanted Agnes St. Cloud and Bertha Norfleet there with her so she wouldn't be the only woman to face the senator and ex-governor in the courthouse. Sort of saying, we got women running the county and the town around here and that's the way it is.

It turned out to be quite a meeting.

When I got back to the courthouse, Addie was there in the court room on the second floor, sitting at the table reserved for the defendants. A stern, self-important man I took to be Senator Ragan—because he wore a suit that hadn't come mailorder—sat in the witness chair. Sid Hatch and Judge Cargrove sat behind the judge's bench. Sharing the high post.

Sid Hatch loved an audience. Most of the adults in town were there, focusing their eyes on Sid as they usually did on those infrequent occasions when he appeared in court. Ex-governor Sid Hatch was a legend already in Linn Creek. Not because of what he'd been, but because of the stories they told about what he'd been.

Sid was old, pushing seventy I would guess. His rare appearances in the Linn Creek courtroom were on cases guaranteed to draw maximum exposure. He was loathe to do the work necessary to handle a case alone. There had been talk a year or so ago that Sid was about to take on a protégé and Gideon Norfleet had put in a word for me. I did some research for Sid, went to his house several times with briefs on what I had looked up at the law library in the courthouse. But Sid Hatch did not see in me what he was looking for—if indeed he had been looking for a protégé. I found out, in what little time I spent with him, that Sid wasn't really interested in the finer points of the law—scorned them, in fact. Sid Hatch was interested in one thing: the jury. Every point I would raise in my brief, he would respond with speculation on how the jury would view such a point in court. He discarded every idea that did not stand the chance of becoming a salient point in a juror's mind.

If I was on trial for my life, I'd hire Sid Hatch.

Another part of the Sid Hatch legend was his fondness for women. Sid had never married, but that didn't mean he slept alone. It has been said that Nita German was a frequent visitor at Sid's mansion. Pity the poor soul who ever tried to take *her* to court.

Sid was all decked out in his usual black suit today with white shirt and black bow tie, a kindly smile on his face and twinkle in his baby blue eyes, his hair a fine glistening silver color, a trifle long on the sides, a bit of a curl in the back. Altogether a rakish and dashing appearance, even for seventy. When Sid Hatch was in the room no one—especially the women—looked at anyone else.

"Addie," Sid was saying, "I can't tell you how proud the town is of you, and how sorry everyone is about Ora. You're doing the finest of jobs, under the circumstances. Whatever you need or require in the way of men or equipment, the State of Missouri stands ready to assist you. Is that not right, Senator Ragan?"

Ragan was being upstaged by an old workhorse turned out to pasture. You could tell the way he held his full lips pressed together that he didn't like it. But this was Sid Hatch's town and the Senator was playing second fiddle, like it or not.

"Absolutely," the senator said. "Sheriff Mitchell, I can have four companies of guardsmen patrolling these woods in twelve hours . . ."

"And Addie, dear, you know you can count on me," Sid said, cutting Ragan off in mid sentence. "I make it a point not to trifle in local politics, but when I'm needed, when I'm wanted, well, you can't keep an old fire horse from following the smoke once in awhile now, can you?"

The crowd chuckled along with Sid. Ragan sat stony-faced in the lonely witness chair.

"Ora had a lot of respect for you Sid," Addie said. "And so do I. Nobody has to worry about Camden County. Not when we have Sid Hatch around."

The townspeople applauded Addie's speech. Danged if she wasn't beginning to sound just like a politician already.

Sid blustered and smiled, pretending to show embarrassment, this man who had conversed with kings and presidents. It took just that long for him to have a hundred potential jurors in the palm of his hand.

I sneaked a look at Senator Ragan, but he had not changed his expression. They say timing is everything in telling a story and in politics. The senator was simply waiting for his time. He wore the look of a man who knew patience. Probably from listening to all those boring speeches in the State Senate.

"From what I can tell, the truck is still in the county someplace," Addie said, addressing the crowd now more than any one individual. "And the three men along with it. All we have to do is flush them out."

"We could start a company of two hundred and eighty men from each side of the county," the senator said. "Work their way toward the center. By nightfall we would have them in custody."

"What would that cost the county?" Addie asked, and you could see that the idea of paying for this operation had never crossed anyone's mind. Judge Cargrove leaned forward from the bench.

"Three to five thousand dollars, I should imagine," the senator said. "Little enough when you consider the danger of having three killers running loose in the county."

"Alleged killers," Sid Hatch pointed out. "Let's see that these men get a fair trial in the eyes of the law."

"Of course," Senator Ragan said.

"We'll give them a fair trial," Yawley Earnhardt stood and shouted from the back of the room. "Then we'll hang them."

The crowd cheered that and several men close to Yawley clapped him on the back.

Addie waited for the cheering and laughing to die down.

"I think we can handle things here ourselves," she said.

For the first time the senator showed a change in expression. He was piqued.

"It wouldn't be a good time to miscalculate your office's ability," he said. "I've been briefed on you and your deputies by Mister Earnhardt and I'm impressed with your staff. They sound well qualified to handle most normal emergencies. But this is understandably beyond a normal emergency. The state has one hundred and fourteen counties and we simply can't allow anyone who shoots even one sheriff in one county to escape justice."

"I aim to see no one does," Addie said. Then, firmly and with her feelings bare around her eyes she added, "For more reasons than one."

Yawley stepped forward from his position in the back of the room.

"Addie, you can't let this situation get out of hand. You decide later on we need the Guard and it'll take several days to get them here. Senator Ragan has placed four companies on alert and can have them here by morning. Let's not dally here, just for false pride . . ."

"I haven't observed any dallying since you appointed her," Agnes St. Cloud said. "It's Sheriff Mitchell's decision to make and I for one know she'll decide what's best for this county. We'll do what we've always done in Linn Creek—what we did for Sid Hatch and what we did for Ora Mitchell for eighteen years—we'll let them make the decisions and we'll back them one hundred percent."

A chorus of Yeas sounded from the crowd, especially the newly franchised women voters. Yawley backed off. Those women voters were his best customers at the store and the mill.

Addie said, "Now I know everybody would like the excitement of the National Guard boys running around town here—especially the young ladies and the schoolboys—but the fact is, this county hasn't had a military operation here since 1865. And we didn't invite that one in. We sent our share of boys to France to help them out when they couldn't handle the Kaiser, but we don't care for Linn Creek to be compared with no France."

Addie had to pause for the chuckles and the applause to die down.

"I'm asking the county court to approve a thousand dollar reward for citizens—not law officers—who provide information leading to the arrest of Champ Gowan, Wilbur Crowder and Buster Workman. The word will spread faster then you can get any National Guard companies in here, and when those three come up for air—and something to eat—somebody's going to see them. We've already got enough people out in the county, with Sheriff Barker's help, that we won't be more than an hour away when they show themselves. And we won't have two hundred and eighty men coming in from all four sides of the county carrying rifles and tramping everybody's garden down. And up in Jefferson City we won't be known as the county that had to call in the Guard because we couldn't take care of ourselves."

Addie would have won the election right then if they'd been casting ballots. You could see Senator Ragan didn't like it a bit and even Sid Hatch had a queer look on his face. As if he'd come here for his usual adulation and to take command of the situation, but damned if some woman didn't end up the center of attraction.

I could see the confusion on Sid's face trying to get a handle on these modern politics. It may have been the first time he'd ever thought of himself as being out of touch.

They filed out of the courtroom, the townspeople and now Addie's supporters along with a dejected Yawley and the upstaged Sid Hatch and Senator Ragan. The three of them had failed in picking up any positive support on this day.

I followed closely behind Addie. She was smiled at and warmly encouraged on her way out the door. Even patted on the back by several. We were nearly back to the sheriff's office in the jail house before she turned to speak to me.

"Now, if only I was an eagle I could fly over the trees and spot that truck before people get fed up with me and ride me out of town on a rail."

And from that I got the best idea I'd had since Ora had been shot.

"Let me see if I've got this straight, Sport," Coley said. "You want me to fly over all that timber and see if you can spot a truck down there and if you do, maybe I'll get a thousand dollars?"

Coley froze on the last word, wrench in hand, teeth clenched around a Roi Tan, lips spread in a smirking grin.

"The thousand dollars is a sure thing—if we spot them," I said. "My sister's the sheriff. You can bank on it."

"Your sister?"

"Yeah, my sister."

"Well, now," Coley unfroze and tapped the wrench against his hand. "I didn't realize this was such a progressive little place you got down here in the sticks. Last time I took a sheriff flying around here, he was a man."

"Those three you flew us to Mexico to capture? They shot and killed him on the way back."

Coley said. "He seemed like a pretty nice old guy. So your sister is going to do the job he couldn't, is that it? Who was she, his wife or something?"

"That's right."

"So those three are armed now and they've already killed the sheriff and wouldn't be against killing more. Or shooting at airplanes in the sky if they thought somebody was spying on them from up there, would they?"

"It would take a pretty good shot."

Coley laughed. He tightened up the fitting he was working on and wiped the oil from the OX-5 engine.

"What about her?" he asked, nodding his shaven head in the direction of Estelle, clad in her tennis getup and holding a little white cloche hat in her hand. She was studying Coley with amazement, trying to derive some knowledge or some experience—if I knew Estelle—from the trip I had talked her into making in her little Jordan roadster.

"She gave me a ride," I said. "She's going back to Linn Creek."

"That was your sister, I take it, who drove you and the sheriff out here the other day," Coley said. I nodded. "Fine looking woman. God didn't provide much for you hillbillies to do down here so he gave you some swell looking women to occupy your time with. I might just get it in my mind to move down here and join you."

Coley stood polishing his wrench with a rag and eyeing Estelle. She eyed him right back, enjoying the attention.

"I'm going along, Joel Dean," Estelle said. "You said it has two seats in front."

"Not this time, Estelle," I said. "Maybe after this is over Coley here would take you and me for a ride."

"Sure," Coley said. "Anytime."

"Today it is, then," Estelle said, advancing toward the American Eagle. "Why I don't hardly feel like I'm of this century if I don't get an airplane ride."

"Honey, you're definitely of this century," Coley said, laughing. "But according to your boyfriend, the Sport here, there's some bad guys down there who are more than likely going to be shooting up at us. We can build more airplanes, but putting something like you together must have taken God awhile."

"You believe in God?" Estelle asked Coley.

"Have to," Coley said, smiling around the Roi Tan. "I'm flying in his territory."

"Then don't you believe God meant for women to be beside their men?"

"It's up to Sport, there, honey."

"It's not up to Sport. It's up to me."

"Let's go then," Coley said. He stepped up on the step and into the rear cockpit.

I said, "Estelle, I'd like to take you, but . . ."

"Good then. Give me a hand up please."

I knew it was a bad idea, but I knew Estelle, too, and how stubborn she could be when she set her mind on something. I would have had to carry her back to the car in order to keep her out of the airplane. She might not speak to me for a week if I did that. I helped her up to the seat in front of Coley, him smiling around the damn cigar all the time and eyeing every inch of Estelle's bare thighs.

I went to the front of the Eagle and began pulling the propeller through without Coley telling me.

The OX-5 started up in a cloud of smoke, then settled down to purr smoothly. Estelle pulled the little hat down tight on her blond head and gave me her grand-sized smile.

I climbed in, and after getting settled and locking the belt over both of us, I decided I liked the feel of her in that front seat beside me. She gave me a peck on the cheek and let out a squeal of delight when the Eagle began speeding down the field. Coley was at the regular field for the takeoff and we gently and smoothly left the earth with Estelle gripping my arm and looking up at me with astonishment on that pretty face. I was glad at that moment that I got to go along with her on her first airplane ride.

Coley punched me with his stick and made a circular motion with his hand which I guess meant he was going to be flying around in circles above the area I wanted to look at. He tilted us so that my weight was against Estelle and she looked at me with those big eyes and I looked right back, the wind riffling through her fringes of hair under the hat, ripe color in her cheeks and complete trust in me showing all over her face. When Coley jabbed me hard with his stick, I didn't have to turn around to know he was telling me to quit looking at Estelle and keep my eyes out for Buck Newland's truck. It was hard to do.

I didn't know if it was because Estelle was sitting beside me or if it was the chase we were on, but I felt an excitement I hadn't felt yesterday. Cutting through the air, silver wings under us, sunlight glistening off spray-painted fabric; it sure beat riding around on Ora's horse through the brush. Or in his Chevrolet, for that matter.

We were in our third circle before I began to pick up on some of the landmarks below us. I recognized some of the creeks and streams and clearings as we passed over them. This time I could see them coming up, had time to remember where we were, and began to search through the trees for Buck's truck. It was big enough and heavy enough they wouldn't have been able to move it far into the woods, if, indeed, they had decided to come this way.

It seemed like a good bet to me that they would be here somewhere. If they had driven the truck down the highway they would have been spotted for sure. If they had taken it off the road, they wouldn't have gotten much farther than here.

I began to spot movement on the ground — rabbits, foxes and squirrels even — scrambling around on the ground and through the trees. But no truck. No people.

Coley laid the American Eagle over on its other side and now Estelle was leaning her weight against me. We began a counterclockwise circle over new territory. We weren't even through a complete circle when Estelle's hand shot in front of my face and she screamed in my ear, "There."

I saw Buck Newland's truck about the same time she yelled. Then Coley's stick punching my back told me he had seen it too. I turned to see him smiling a thousand-dollar smile around the dead cigar.

The truck was sitting alongside a creek that ran but a trickle of water in August. Maybe they couldn't get across because of the rocks or maybe they ran out of gas. There was no one around Buck's truck.

Coley laid the Eagle completely on its side and the wing tips followed the path of the small creek. It shot out of sight under the plane and Coley flopped the craft over quickly onto the other side and my stomach tried to follow along, but it was rebelling. Estelle was under me again and looking as if she thought airplanes were just dandy. Her eyes sparkled with life when she looked at me and I wished I felt as good about the ride now as she did.

The creek bed came in sight again under our wings, twisted along for a quarter of a mile and broadened into a good sized pool behind a natural dam. At the edge of the pool, two people—a man and a woman—stood in the water, dressed as nature intended with no clothes on at all. The man's hand shot upward as we passed over them and I was sure it was Champ Gowan.

Estelle saw them too. She snickered and pointed. Coley was jabbing the heck out of my back with his stick. I turned to see him pointing at the nude swimmers, then up at the sky and down at his wristwatch. The black clouds we'd seen in the west after taking off had nearly caught up to us. I caught a flash of lightning on a horizon that looked black and angry. Coley said in his hand message that we had fifteen minutes left in the sky.

We could be back at the landing field in five minutes easy, and could be at the mansion in another ten or fifteen minutes in Estelle's little coupe. One of the county's 13 telephones was in the mansion which meant Addie and Doyle could be here with fifteen or twenty men in another 30 minutes and say another 30 or 40 minutes we could be in the woods where Buck Newland's truck sat. That gave Champ less than an hour and a half to get out of the area. I was curious about the woman, who she was and what she was doing with Champ, but I was pretty sure it had to be Nita German since she had been missing from her house.

One thing for sure, I had Champ and his friends cornered with no place to run. Coley didn't quite see it that way.

He pointed over the next rise where a long, mostly level clearing came into sight. Coley told me by his motions he was going to set the plane down in the clearing. I started waving my arms with extreme vigor, shouting "No, no, no." Coley paid no attention to me, but kept up his sign language. I gathered he meant to let me off in the clearing and he and Estelle would fly back to the mansion and call the sheriff. It was plain to see from the look on his face that he thought he had just found a thousand dollars and he didn't want it to get away from him. I was still objecting, trying out some signals of my own, when he began coming to earth and I realized there was nothing I could do about it now.

Coley had picked out a smooth strip in the clearing and he set the Eagle down with hardly a jolt. He drove it right to the end of the clearing where he locked up his left brake and began turning it around for takeoff. That was when things went wrong. I heard a snap like a sapling trunk had broken under us. When we tipped over to one side I knew the Eagle was damaged.

Coley was out of the cockpit and on the ground before I could get my safety belt loosened. When I got down I saw that a metal strut bracing one wheel had caught on a protruding rock and was bent backwards nearly folding the wheel under the plane.

Coley cussed the wheel, the rock, the clearing, the woods and was broadening it to include the whole county and all of us hillbillies in it when Estelle climbed down to look at it.

"Can you fix it?" she asked.

"Oh, I can fix it all right, Honey, but not before that storm comes by. Another 30 minutes and I won't be able to take off into that wind."

"What'll we do?" she asked.

"Don't say it Sport," Coley said, looking at me. "I shouldn't have landed here. I just didn't want that thousand dollars to slip away from me. I can buy my own plane when I get it."

"You may have already," I said as I regarded the wounded Eagle.

I've got to say I was real disturbed with Coley about this time. For a moment there, we had Champ and Wilbur and Buster practically behind bars again. Now, we were closer to them, but farther away from capturing them. The thought of being this close to the three who had killed Ora created an excitement I had trouble controlling.

My problem now was what was I going to do with Estelle? I had made two decisions I'd let someone talk me out of. I never would make sheriff this way.

"I killed a man once," Coley said out of nowhere as we walked down a sloping bank away from the glade where the American Eagle sat.

Estelle didn't even look up. She said, "Are there any snakes here? I hate snakes."

Coley laughed, louder than he needed to, but that didn't cause

Estelle to take her eyes off the ground.

"Better have Sport there carry you, then," he said. "There's copperheads, rattlers, blue racers, bull snakes, spreading vipers and maybe a cottonmouth or two around . . ."

"Don't worry, Estelle," I said, interrupting Coley's lies. "There's not likely to be any snakes out in the open here. Besides, there aren't any cottonmouths in the area and if there were, they'd be close to the water. I'll keep my eyes open for you."

Still she didn't look up. The clearing ended a few yards in front of us where a grove of sassafras saplings grew thick as grass. There appeared to be an animal path skirting the edge of the grove and generally heading in the direction where we'd seen Champ and Nita. I took the lead and walked in that direction. Estelle took my hand, slowing me down some because I didn't want her to let go of me.

"He insulted my woman," Coley said after us. I guessed he was still talking about the man he was trying to make us believe he had killed.

"I suppose that made her feel better," Estelle said with the littlest bit of sarcasm.

I guided her around some loose rocks in the animal path, moved her around behind me, still holding onto her hand, and when the path widened, pulled her up beside me. She smiled into my face like, "Guess I told him, huh?"

"She never said," Coley said. "I didn't give her time to talk, all night." He ended up laughing loud and long in a boastful sort of way. I began to regret talking Coley into taking us on the flight, even if we had found Champ.

The Queen Anne's Lace was waist high on both sides of the path. Estelle reached out and plucked a saucer-size bloom from a stem and stuck it in her hair. I smiled at her.

The path took a sudden turn away from where we wanted to go and I stopped.

"Over that way," I pointed. "We'll have to go through these

162

flowers and weeds until we find a way down to the stream where we saw them. Watch out for the beggar's lice. They're thick in there."

Estelle wrinkled up her nose. "Joel Dean, I don't want to walk through those awful weeds. It'll tear my dress right off of me."

"That I'd like to see," Coley said, and laughed some more.

I picked her up in my arms and started off through the thicket of Queen Anne's Lace and buck brush that was as thick as hair on a tom cat. The hillside grew steeper as the growth gave way to loose gravel and shale. I moved down the slope sideways, sticking my leading leg out straight to balance myself and Estelle. The rocks under my front foot started sliding and I landed on the seat of my pants. Estelle grabbed tight around my neck and we slid twenty feet or more until we came to rest against a large cottonwood tree.

I raised Estelle's head. "You okay?"

"That was fun. But you're supposed to do that when there's snow on the ground."

We stood up and I checked myself for injury. The skin on my rear end felt like I'd backed into a grindstone when it was running. I wanted to rub it, but didn't want Estelle to think I wasn't man enough to get her down the hill without getting hurt. I looked around us to see if maybe we were close to the abandoned truck or the stream where Champ and Nita had stood bathing in the nude. The cottonwood tree meant we were close to water, probably the same stream. Looking back to the top of the rise we had just come sliding down, I saw no one.

"Where's Coley?" I asked, talking more to myself than Estelle.

"Who needs him? All he does is fly the plane and brag about the people he's killed. My goodness, you suppose he really killed a man?"

I shrugged.

"You never killed anyone did you, Joel Dean?"

"No."

"I don't believe him. I think he just likes to brag about his women. Is he doing that to impress me, you suppose?"

"Probably."

"Well, we don't need him. There's more reward money for you if he's not along."

"Law enforcement officers don't collect rewards, Estelle. That's our job."

She wrinkled up her cute little nose and stamped her foot on the rocks.

"Well, how fair is that? You mean you do all that work, risk your life and you don't get anything for it?"

"Like I said, that's my job. I get a salary for doing my job."

She sighed, brushed at her hair with one hand and looked off through the trees. "Maybe I could collect the reward then. I'm not a law enforcement officer. Then I could give the money to you."

She was looking prettier every minute and I was starting to forget what I was here for.

About that time the sky turned loose of the rain it had been holding and big drops the size of silver dollars began pelting us. I grabbed Estelle and pulled her close to shed as much rain from her as I could.

"This way," I yelled in her ear and led her through the cottonwoods until we reached the creek. The rain was really coming down now and I couldn't see far enough in either direction to tell if we were close to Buck Newland's truck or not.

Across the creek I could see a big opening in a rock bluff so straight up and tall that nobody was going to climb over. I guessed it was a cave, at least a depression in the rock wall that would give us some protection from the rain.

I put Estelle in my arms again and made a run for the creek. The ankle deep water shocked me, it was that cold. The swift running current told me it was rising with the speed of a frightened deer as the runoff from upstream was rushing our way.

Estelle was light and warm to my body, but by the time I had struggled to the other side of the creek, with the water now knee deep, her weight had become an obstacle to reaching the cave.

Walking out of the water and into the gravel shoals, I stumbled and Estelle jerked her head around to look at me with big eyes, her hair wet and plastered to her forehead with one rivulet of rain running down the side of her nose and draining across the rosebud lips. The thin knit shirt she called a polo shirt was fast to her body outlining her small breasts, her nipples protruding with the certain proof she wore nothing underneath.

She was truly beautiful.

Gravel crunched under my boots and my feet squished water from their tops with every step.

"Maybe you should put me down," Estelle said, noticing my stumbling gait toward the cave opening.

"We're almost there," I said, trying to sound stronger and surer than I actually was. I leaned forward to allow the brim of my hat to shield her face. The rain came harder. Flashes of lightning ripped across the black sky with the crashing sound of thunder sending a ripple up my spine and a shudder through Estelle. I ran the last twenty yards to the opening of the cave.

The gravel was loose where the water coming off the rock face of the wall over the cave tore at the pebbles, lined them up in narrow trenches and rolled them toward the stream. I was close enough now to the mouth of the cave I could see remnants of old campfires scattered on the floor. I dodged a waterfall right at the opening, stumbled, then fell to my knees and elbows. But I saved Estelle.

"Are you all right, Joel Dean?" she asked, concern genuine in her voice.

I kissed her hard on the mouth.

She took my hat off, now soaked and stinking like wet felt does, and ran her hand through my hair. As she got to her feet, I felt the pain in both elbows and figured I had sacrificed some skin there to save harm to Estelle. But I waited until she turned her head before examining them.

The cave opening was fifty yards across, but narrowed to what I guessed to be a lone passage about thirty yards into the cave. The smell of wet smoke and dank air was in my nose. Blackened walls had been scribbled on by travelers spending the night here or by adventurers and explorers. With the walls dark, the sky outside the same as late evening and the floor giving nothing back in the way of reflected light, all I could make out were recent markings. I waited for my eyes to adjust.

"My goodness, a couple could set up housekeeping in here," Estelle said, looking around, but hanging onto my arm.

"See if I can get a fire going so you can get dried out," I said. Lightning afforded the only light so I looked the cave over during the moments of brilliance provided by the electrical show. I spotted a mound on the floor and moved toward it, one arm around Estelle holding her away from the splashes and spray from the cascading water as it hit on the flat, smooth rocks.

"I wonder what happened to our pilot," Estelle said.

"Don't worry about Coley."

I pulled the emergency leather pouch on my belt around to the front and opened it.

"Hope I have some dry matches in here," I said.

No such luck, all the sulfur matches in the pouch were wet.

As we moved around the cave in jerks, our walking and looking timed with the lightning, I noticed that the smell of smoke was stronger in some areas. It was particularly strong near the mound on the floor.

Kneeling by it, I thought I saw the ever-so-slight glimmer of a live coal.

"What is it?" Estelle asked.

"A fire. Not yet cold."

"Who could it have been?" she asked, then realized who it had to be.

I felt her warm body pressed against me.

"Joel Dean, what are we going to do?"

"Just wait for the storm to pass. See that opening there at the back of the cave? That spot that's darker than the rest? Probably that's where they are."

"What if they come out?"

"I don't think Champ's in any hurry to go back to jail. We'll just wait. Coley is bound to show up after awhile. If I remember this area right, we're just downstream from the spring, not far from a large pool. That's where we saw the man and woman."

"What good is Coley going to be? He doesn't have a gun, does he?"

"Won't need one. He's so anxious to get that thousand dollar reward he'll be glad to take you out of here. You can walk over to the mansion. There's a telephone there and he can call Addie if the lines aren't down. I'll stay here and wait for Champ and the others to show themselves. Unless there's another opening, we've got them trapped in there."

"How far is it to the mansion from here?"

"Can't be more than five miles."

"I can't walk five miles," Estelle said, both hands on her hips in defiance. "Not in these little old shoes. Besides, I want to stay here with you."

"Can't chance it, Estelle. They killed Ora, you think they wouldn't do the same to you and me?"

"That's why I want to stay with you. *You're* my protector, not that bragging old pilot."

I was some moved by that, but I wasn't foolish enough to give in.

"And I am yours," she added and, boy, that did make my heart pump faster.

"Let's get that fire going," I said.

Feeling with my hands and searching quickly during the lightning flashes, I found a clump of damp grass and some twigs on the cave floor. I laid the grass over the fading coals and waited. Nothing happened.

"What's wrong?" Estelle wanted to know.

"Grass is too damp," I said.

"Hurry, Joel Dean. I'm wet all the way through to my underpants."

She snuggled up close to me and I could feel her body shivering. I blew gently on the grass, but still nothing. Her shivering got heavier and my own hands were starting to shake from the cold and the damp. I laid one of the damp sulfur matches on the grass and blew again, softly. Over and over until I was becoming exhausted just from the blowing.

"Let me," she said.

She leaned close and I heard her breath blowing softly. In the glare of lightning I saw her little mouth puckered over the grass and then I saw, just as the lightning flash died, a flare of blue, then a sulfurous yellow and the grass burned and glowed.

In the light from the smoldering grass she smiled as pretty as I ever hoped to see.

"I just knew it would work," she said. "I had all my fingers crossed."

"You're my good luck charm," I told her.

I piled on the twigs and from their light, found some larger sticks and soon we had a real fire going that was throwing off some clothes-drying heat and as much light as a coal oil lamp.

We sat close to the fire so our clothes would dry and pretty soon the fire drove the unpleasant smell of wet clothes all over the cave.

"We smell like wet puppies," Estelle said.

"You don't," I told her, lying just the tiniest little bit.

She leaned over the fire and spread her hair so it would dry. When the clothes had enough warmth in them, we huddled together and I wrapped her in my arms. I was tired from the walk to the cave and I was cold and I was still wet. Considering Estelle had probably never spent more than two minutes being uncomfortable in her life, I marveled some at how she was tolerating it.

Estelle said, "Are you going to be a sheriff or a lawyer, Joel Dean?"

"Hadn't thought about it since Ora was shot. Always figured I would just go on being his deputy until I had enough law business to live on. Of course, I always figured Ora would be sheriff for a long time."

"Daddy hires a lawyer in Lebanon," she said. "Maybe I could talk him into switching his business over to you."

"You said he was mad at me."

"Oh, poo. I can get him to do whatever I want."

We sat staring into the fire, Estelle's blond head cradled in my arm. At that moment there was no regret in me for bringing her along.

"Tell me about you when you were a boy, Joel Dean," she said. Her eyelids were drooping from exhaustion and she looked to be minutes away from sleep.

So I told her. I told her about the hard-scrabble farm we lived on just outside of town. I told her how I learned to build a symmetrical haystack when I was ten. And how I used to rake potato bugs off the vine into a can of kerosene when I was five. I told her how Addie had always looked out for me and about the time in the third grade when a bully had pounded my head against the ground and how Addie had flattened him with one punch and proceeded to pound *his* head against the ground.

I told her about the first time I'd ever seen her in a lovely pink dress with lace all over it, standing in front of Yawley's store. How I thought she was the prettiest thing I had ever seen, even in magazines. And Lonnie Harper had said to me, "You better leave her alone you don't want to get into trouble."

She smiled sleepily at that.

169

I told her how I'd looked at all the girls in Springfield and hadn't seen any as pretty as her. So I just came on back to Linn Creek.

"Tell me about you," I said.

She moved so that she was looking into my face. I saw the weariness in her sleep-filled eyes.

"My mother didn't love me," she said.

"I can't believe that. I'm sorry about your mother, being killed in that accident in Chicago and all. And you so young. It must have been difficult."

"My mother was beautiful. Too beautiful, Daddy always said. She wanted to be an actress. That's why she went to Chicago, to see plays and real actresses. She told Daddy once if it hadn't been for me, she would have gone to Hollywood and been in moving pictures."

"That doesn't mean she didn't love you. How could anyone not love you?"

She smiled weakly and closed her eyes. For a moment I thought sleep had overtaken her, but she mumbled words so low I could barely distinguish the words over the sound of the storm outside.

"Nobody loved me but Daddy until you, Joel Dean. I see my mother every night just before I go to sleep. I wait for her to kiss me and tuck me in and say she loves me, but she doesn't. She just stands there in front of the mirror admiring herself."

"Doesn't mean anything," I said. "I see my parents and my Grandpa Gregory almost every night. A preacher once told me the dead are never far away."

"What if she's not dead," she asked.

I stroked her head. "It's out of your hands now. As long as you still see her, she's still alive to you. She loves you. Else you wouldn't be able to see her."

"Or else she's not dead."

"I see Ora at nights, too," I said, making a confession out loud that I meant to keep to myself. "He's dead, but I still see him. Doesn't mean he blames me for him getting killed."

"Then stop blaming yourself," she said. She pulled my face down and kissed me lightly on the mouth. "Goodnight my love."

The smile was still on her rosebud mouth when the rest of her went sound asleep.

I shifted around so I could be more comfortable, but without waking Estelle. I reached another wrist-sized piece of firewood and pitched it into the flames. Sparks flew and the cave grew brighter. Sleep was coming on me, so I reclined, placing my head beside Estelle's on my left arm and closed my eyes, but not before I glanced at the blackness at the rear of the cave. What dark secrets was the cave hiding back there?

I would rest for a few minutes and maybe Coley or Addie or somebody would be here.

When I woke the fire was brighter than when I went to sleep and, as I had hoped, somebody was here. Champ Gowan squatted across the fire from us and the flicker from the flames reflected off his teeth as he grinned.

"Glad you could make it, Joel Dean. So that was you up there in that airplane, huh?"

PART THREE
THE CAPTURE

It was near dark outside, I'd slept that long. Nita was there with Champ, wearing nothing but a petticoat with what looked like Champ's shirt over it. Champ wore a white-ribbed undershirt. I saw right away that he had taken Grandpa Gregory's Colt .45 caliber Peacemaker single action revolver from my holster while I slept and stuck it in his waistband. Some deputy I was.

Estelle woke, rubbed her eyes, and snuggled up to me while I still sat on the floor of the cave.

"Champ's here," I told her.

"Are you going to arrest him?" she mumbled. I didn't answer.

"Where's the other two?" I asked.

Champ shrugged. "Haven't seen them since Ora was shot."

"They're combing every inch of this county looking for you," I said. "Spoke with your aunt and uncle over by Dogtrot yesterday. Why'd you double back to Linn Creek?"

He shrugged again. "I thought about hopping a freight, leaving the state, but this is my home. And I ain't done anything wrong."

I looked up at Nita who looked cold and damp and disheveled. No plastered, made-up look. Nita didn't look as nice in her natural state as Estelle.

"Why'd you bring Nita?"

Another shrug. "Me and Nita, we've been close for a long time."

"Tell me how Ora was killed," I said, looking him straight on.

"Strange thing is, I can't say for sure," he said, a serious look replacing the usual grin. "Ora unlocked my cuffs and I was standing on the edge of the road taking a leak into the ditch when I saw this bright light shining on us. I couldn't just stop and I couldn't turn all the way around so I didn't see anyone or what the light was. I heard a shot and Ora grunted. About that time someone rammed me in the back and I went ass over teakettle down that bank alongside the road with my pecker still hanging out. Must have been thirty feet or so down that bank. It took some doing to get back to the road. When I did, I found Ora lying there dead."

"Where was Buster and Wilbur?"

"Gone. Vanished. I found you laying alongside the car and figured you for dead. I called Buster and Wilbur but there was no answer. No sound. No light. Nothing."

"Uh huh. So what's your take on what happened?"

"Damned if I know. I've been thinking a lot about it and I can't figure it. It's like someone was setting me up."

"Uh huh. Well, listen Champ. How many people in this county you think would believe that story of yours."

"Well, nobody. I guess that's why I need to leave the state, much as I hate to."

Estelle raised her head off my shoulder.

"I'm hungry."

Nita said, trying to be the hostess. "We've got some cans of soup and beans. I could open one and warm it for you."

Estelle looked disappointed. "That's all?"

Nita rubbed the petticoat along her hips with both hands.

"The soup's not bad when you warm it up. I'll just fix a can for both of you."

She dug into a large canvas bag lying by Champ and came out with a can. Champ took it from her and stuck a hunting knife through the top and peeled it open.

"Only one spoon," he said. "When I packed this at Nita's I wasn't expecting company."

"I'm going to have to take you back, Champ," I said.

"We'll see."

Nita said, "Joel Dean, Champ's telling the truth. I know the two of us ain't got enough reputation between us to stuff inside a walnut shell, but he's telling you the truth."

Champ said, "I don't aim to go back to jail, Joel Dean. I couldn't take that. I'd rather you just shoot me."

I looked at Nita. "Why did you turn Champ in?"

She was taken back by that. "Well, I . . ."

"Yeah, Nita. Tell everybody. Just why did you turn me in?"

She turned to Champ. "We've been talking about that, Champ, my goodness. I told you it broke my heart when you took up with that McGuffy girl that time you stole Yawley's new car."

Estelle turned on Champ. "So you're the one stole Daddy's new car. I forgot about that. Boy, he was some disturbed with you."

"I paid for it," Champ said. "Three years in stir."

"And you're the one who killed Shorty Mickelson," Estelle said.

"I didn't kill nobody. I just got out of jail. I didn't know nothing about Yawley's rum running or Shorty Mickelson."

"Who else could have done it?" I asked.

Champ shrugged and turned away. "Somebody's sure trying to set me up is the way I see it."

"One way to look at it," I said.

"The other way is the Gowans are a bunch of thieves and liars and so I must have done it."

"Which way you think a jury in this county is going to look at it?"

"Maybe if I had a good lawyer I could get my trial moved to another county. What do you call that?"

"Change of venue. You got the money for a good lawyer?"

Champ grinned. "Not unless I stole it."

"I think this, Champ Gowan," Estelle said, hands on hips. Being firm. "If you killed the sheriff or Shorty Mickelson, you ought to give yourself up and take your punishment like a man. If you didn't, I think Joel Dean ought to let you go."

"How about it, Joel Dean?" Champ asked, grinning really big. "You going to let me go?"

"Champ, if I was dead sure you killed Ora I'd shoot you myself instead of taking you in."

"This soup is hot," Nita announced.

Champ wrapped the can in a red bandanna as he removed it from the fire and handed it to me. I offered the first bite out the can to Estelle.

Estelle said, "You don't have any china?"

Champ's grin became a laugh. Estelle made a face at him.

As I ate I thought about what I was going to do about Champ. He was either my prisoner or we were his. I wasn't sure which way it truly was.

If Champ had killed Ora, why would he let us live? He could shoot us both, leave us here and it might be years before anyone found us. If he let us live, would that be proof in itself that he wasn't guilty?

I was mindful that the Gowans had the reputation of being the most skillful liars and flim-flam people in the county. It would be wise to be especially skeptical of anything Champ said or did.

Nita was rubbing her petticoat, stroking downward toward her hips with both hands, then bringing one hand up to fuss with her hair which was pretty much a mess at this time. It occurred to me then that Nita was always doing something with her hands when she talked.

When we finished the soup, I checked the time again. Nine thirty. Nita pulled a rough, woolen blanket out of the canvas bag and handed to us.

"We only have two blankets," Nita said. She looked at Champ. "Are we spending the night here in the cave?"

Champ didn't answer her. I thanked Nita and handed the blanket to Estelle. Instead of acting mortified and repulsed by our condition, Estelle acted as if she was actually enjoying it.

"I've never spent a night in a cave before," she said. "It sounds so adventurous."

Champ put some new wood on the fire. Nita took another blanket out of the canvas bag and spread it on the floor of the cave across the fire from where Estelle and I stood.

Sparks jumped into the air as the partly damp wood caused the fire to crackle and flame higher for an instant. Champ looked at me and seemed to read my thoughts.

"I'm a light sleeper, Joel Dean. I'll wake you in the morning."

"I'm a light sleeper myself. I expect I'll hear you when you get up."

He squatted and poked at the fire.

"You always were a stubborn little mule, Joel Dean. I remember you when you were just a pup."

My skinned parts were starting to bother me and, in spite of the sleep I'd had in the afternoon, I was still tired and chilled. Estelle had wrapped herself in the blanket and Nita had reclined on the one she spread across from us. I could have laid down and gone right to sleep again, but I wanted peace of mind while I slept. I needed to know what Champ intended for tomorrow.

"Champ, if you were to give up and come in with me, I have an acquaintance in Jeff City I could persuade to take your case. He'd probably be willing to put payment off for a few years."

Champ grinned. "Would you take me in, Joel Dean, if you knew I was innocent and there was a good chance they'd find me guilty and sentence me to hang?"

"I'd have to. But I'd find a good lawyer to represent you."

"What's Addie think?"

"Same as me. Except for the part about shooting you. She

179

wasn't the one who failed Ora. It was me."

"Me and Addie, we've always been close. Do you resent that?"

"No need to." A thought occurred to me. "Does Addie know about this place?"

He walked around the fire and sat down beside Nita. "We'll have to get out of here before first light."

I heard the gravel crunching when Champ rose the next morning. I checked the watch by the faint glow of the coals in the fire. Five after four. Champ saw me.

"Wake up your girl friend, Joel Dean. Time to get out of here."

Estelle didn't want to wake. I pulled her upright and held her against me.

"I'm so tired and cold, Joel Dean."

"I know, Estelle. But we have to go."

"Are you arresting Champ?"

"He's got the gun. He makes the call."

Nita folded up both blankets and stuffed them back inside the canvas bag. Champ held a dry cell light. He swung the beam around to the dark passage at the rear.

"We'll be going out that way. Addie might be waiting for us the other way."

Nita snapped, "So, Addie *has* been here with you."

"Let it go, Nita," Champ told her. "Addie's the sheriff and I'm the crook, remember? And Ora's dead so you can forget about stealing him from her."

"Well whoever said. . ." Nita protested, but Champ had

turned his back to her and was walking toward the rear of the cave.

When Estelle and I didn't move, he turned back and shined the light in our faces.

"Let's go, Joel Dean."

I had to decide. Would Champ shoot us if I bolted toward the front of the cave and escaped into the dark outside? I didn't think he would, but could I chance it. Alone, that's exactly what I would do, but there was Estelle. There was no way I could escape dragging her along with me.

"Let's go," I said to her and she clung to me, completely trusting my judgment. Maybe somewhere I would get a chance to jump him, take the pistol, and be in charge.

I took the lead with Estelle and Nita behind me and Champ in the rear, shining the light ahead of us and giving directions to me. I tried to remember the turns we took and the different chambers we were in so that I could lead us out if I had to.

I hated caves. Always had. I'd been in a few of them with Lonnie because he was always trying to get me to go along with him snake hunting. Said cave explorers were special people with special gifts. They even had a special name for them. Spelunkers. That name didn't sound so special to me.

Once in a cave about a mile off the road to Roach, Lonnie had stepped into a deep pit and dropped his light and emergency pouch. Before he could yell out a warning to me, I did the same. I was no damned spelunker and I didn't follow his instructions about not coming along too close behind him.

We had followed a passage out of the pit, crawling on our bellies for a hundred yards—with me sure that each time I reached my hand forward I would grab a snake. Lonnie said, don't panic, there's always a way out. Read the signs, he said. Find an air current and follow it. Find a trail of warmer rocks that would lead you out. Listen for different sounds.

I tried to remember all the other tips he had given me, but I hadn't been paying attention. I had very little confidence that I could lead us out of here.

We had been walking for perhaps fifteen minutes, through narrow passages—then through chambers where the bats flew around and Estelle had screamed—when Champ told us to stop. The room we were in seemed enormous with standing stalagmites—or stalactites, I could never remember how Lonnie identified them—showing layers of rainbow colors and flashing metallic flakes in the light of the dry cell lantern Champ swung around.

"Pretty, ain't it?" he asked. "Big, too. This room is about three times bigger than the courthouse."

"You spent time in both of them," I said.

"This place is creepy," from Estelle as she hugged me tighter. "How much farther is it before we get out?"

"Here's what I decided," Champ said, shining the light in my face. "I'm going to surrender to you, Joel Dean. And you're going to be my lawyer."

It was so ridiculous I wanted to laugh.

"Champ, I can't defend you. First off, I'll have to testify against you. No judge would allow me to be your lawyer and be a witness for the prosecution. Second, I'm Gideon Norfleet's assistant. A case like yours, he'd have to have an assistant. It would be a flat out act of betrayal if I refused to just so I could defend you. Third, I don't want to defend you. I'm not convinced you killed Ora, but I'm not convinced you didn't. I know there's some guilt on your part. You were there and if you hadn't escaped in the first place Ora would still be alive."

"I never did anything to be in jail for."

"If I defended you in court, everybody would assume I thought you were innocent. They'd say, 'Well, if Joel Dean is representing Champ, it must mean he knows Champ didn't do it cause he was right there.' And that would be the wrong thing for everybody to think. No, I won't be your lawyer. Completely out of the

182

question."

"Only way I'll go back," Champ said, still holding the light in my face.

"I'm arresting you right now, Champ Gowan, for the murder of Ora Mitchell. You can't be deciding if you'll go back or not."

"Then I'd have to leave you here," he said. "I'll tie both of you to one of these formations. You could get loose after awhile and maybe you'd find your way out of here. Or maybe not. There's hundreds of passages in here and without a light I'm not sure I could find my way out. Anyway, it will give me time to get out of the state. The only way I'll agree to go to trial is if you're my lawyer."

"But the judge won't allow that."

"You could persuade him."

"But I don't want to be your lawyer, Champ. Once you're in jail and the judge says no, I'm out of it."

"I trust you, Joel Dean. You tell me here and now you'll be my lawyer, I know you'll do everything you can. You quit on me, you go back on your word and you'll be a different man than I think you are."

"Just do it, Joel Dean," Estelle said. I could feel her body trembling next to mine. "We can't stay here. They'd never find us. I'm cold and I'm hungry and just look at my skirt and this shirt. And I've already had this underwear on for two days and it's not going to last as long as it takes us to get out of here. I want to go home."

She began to cry into my shirt and I tightened my arm around her.

"Let's just go," Nita whined, holding her arms around herself. "You two men can settle this outside."

"Damn you, Champ," I said, the old bitterness rising in me.

"Joel Dean, I didn't murder Ora. And you're the only chance I got."

Estelle clung to me, still shivering and still crying. I realized then what she had been through and I knew I couldn't ask her to stay here with me in this dark cave without light or heat or food. I really had no choice.

"I promise you this, Champ. I ever come to the conclusion you killed Ora then I quit. And I just might shoot you myself."

Champ handed over the old single action revolver that had been owned by four generations of Gregorys.

"I cleaned it up for you. Had some gravel shoved up the barrel. And I took the liberty to empty the cartridges out."

I checked to be sure, then shoved it back into my holster. When I looked up, he had his hand stretched out into the beam of light. I took his hand, feeling like maybe I was shaking hands with the devil.

It took us another five minutes to reach a passage that showed daylight. We crawled outside on our hands and knees through the brush and briars that grew over the opening. Estelle squealed and cried, then got angry.

"Champ Gowan, I hope they do hang you. Just look at this shirt. Torn to shreds and dirty as sin. You ought to be ashamed of yourself."

"I'm sorry, Estelle," he said. "Joel Dean gets me off, I'm going straight. Get a job. I'll buy you a new shirt."

"This shirt came from Stix Baer and Fuller in St. Louis and cost twelve dollars. I suppose you can afford that?"

"Well, if I can't, Joel Dean can buy you a new one. He'll be a rich and famous lawyer time he gets through with my case."

I said nothing.

Daylight was just breaking in the east and the coolness of the morning after the day of rain felt refreshing. After a night inside a cave, anything outside felt good to me.

"Guess we might as well get going," Champ said. "Hate to admit it but I'm hungry for some of Addie's jail food."

We walked down the hill through a thicket of dogwoods and found an animal trail that ran in the general direction of the road I knew about in this part of the county. We hadn't gone far when four people stepped from behind a big oak into our path. In the low morning light I recognized Noah on one side of Addie and Doyle on the other. Doyle had a shotgun aimed at us.

Yawley came up behind them, saw Estelle and said, "You all right, baby?"

She ran to him and he took her in his arms, smoothing her hair with his hand.

"Damn you Joel Dean. What do you mean kidnapping my daughter and spending the night with her?" Yawley looked mad enough to take a bite out of me.

"This man's my prisoner," I said, and pulled the empty single action Colt from my holster to point at Champ. "I'm taking him in."

But Yawley started yelling and pointing at Champ, "There's that murdering coward. Shoot the sonofabitch."

Addie said, "Good job, Joel Dean. We were beginning to worry about you when you didn't show up last night."

She looked at Champ. "You got nine lives, Champ."

"Figured you for the other opening, Addie," Champ said. "Didn't think you knew about this one."

"I know things you wouldn't believe, Champ," she said. "Joel Dean, your pilot found us last night out on the county road."

Coley came walking toward us from behind the tree.

"Hi ya Sport," he said around a cigar. "Looks like I got me a thousand dollars."

"The owner sees that plane you'll need it," I said.

185

"I'll have that baby flying by noon," Coley said. He turned to Addie. "You got the name right? You know where to send the money?"

"You'll get it," Addie said. "Joel Dean, where's the other two."

"Champ says he lost them where Ora was shot. If that's true, they're probably out of the state by now."

Estelle said, "Daddy, did you bring me some clean underwear?"

But Yawley was busy urging Doyle to shoot Champ.

"If you ain't going to shoot that murderer before he gets away again, Doyle, give me the damn gun. I'll do it myself."

"Be patient, Yawley," Doyle said. "This county deserves a nice juicy murder trial to square losing a man like Ora."

"I expect they'll get one, too," I said. "I'm defending Champ in court."

Minton's dining room never looked as elegant as it did on that first night after we brought Champ Gowan back to jail. Rose wore her Sunday dress of black crepe with an all-white apron over it like you might expect to see in one of the fancy St. Louis hotel dining rooms. Jane McGann, who had been at Minton's longer than any of us, had on her pink muslin dress with delicate orchids printed on it that she wore only on the most special occasions. Uncle Billy Jack Cummins was dressed in his seersucker suit and plaid bow tie. All of the other men, like Lonnie Harper and Volly Newell, wore suits and ties or clean shirts. I had washed up as usual for the evening meal and wore my gray poplin pants and shirt that made up my deputy's uniform, but I began to wish I had changed into something dressier. The only out-of-town guests were two drummers I recognized from Jefferson City.

What was going on here?

The room smelled like the summer bouquet Rose Minton had set in the center of the table; an unexpected treat we didn't get to enjoy but a few times a year. She brought a huge platter of fried chicken to the table—our normal Sunday dinner menu—and handed it to me to begin the serving.

Now that really surprised me. And stirred my suspicions as well.

"Looks like you're the hero tonight, Joel Dean," Volly said. "We want to hear how you captured Champ Gowan and put him back in jail."

"That's right, Joel Dean," Jane McGann said. "Last week you were as down as you could get after Ora was killed. It was like you felt responsible for it."

"You said you were going to get him and you did," Lonnie said. "Now, tell us how you did it."

Everyone was nodding and leaning forward and I felt pretty self conscious. I might be a hero for bringing Champ in, but when they found out I'd agreed to be Champ's attorney, well, that would be a lot different from being a hero.

I helped myself to two pieces of white meat—a treat I usually didn't get a chance at—and held the platter for Oma Thornbush who was sitting on my left.

I told the story of flying in the American Eagle and how the plane got damaged in the landing because Coley was afraid of losing his thousand dollar reward. I told about the storm and everyone nodded their heads because the same storm had hit Linn Creek and blew some shingles and tin sheets off roofs and blew all the rockers over on Minton's front porch.

I told about the cave and how Champ slipped up on Estelle and me as we slept by the fire drying out our clothes and how he took my revolver before I woke up.

"The hero was asleep," I said, trying to make a joke out of it. I could see some disappointment in their faces, but they were figuring, "well, he brought Champ in so it must have turned out okay."

"Those Gowans always been sneaky," Rose said, setting a bowl of cole slaw before me. I helped myself and held the bowl for Oma.

Then I told how Champ had led us through the maze of passages and rooms inside the cave.

"Olin's Cave," Lonnie said. "Been inside there lots of times. You watched all the turns like I taught you, didn't you? So's you could get back out?"

"No, Lonnie, I'm not a spelunker," I said. "I was hopelessly lost. I doubt I could ever have found my way out of there without a light."

"Follow the current of air," Lonnie said. "Remember?"

Then I told them how I shook hands with Champ and agreed to be his lawyer and he gave my revolver back and led us out of the cave.

I looked at surprise and disappointment for sure in their faces now.

Lonnie said, "You agreed to defend Champ Gowan even though you know he killed Ora, just so he'd show you the way out of the cave?"

"I had Estelle's safety to be concerned about," I said, then realized how weak that sounded. "For the moment at least, I am Champ Gowan's attorney. If the judge will allow it, I will represent him in court. If not, I expect I'll be asked by Gideon to help with the prosecution."

"Doesn't sound like you're real convinced Champ Gowan killed Ora," Jane McGann said.

"I don't have any proof that he did. If I am presented with proof, I've already warned Champ that I would probably shoot him myself."

"Last time I saw you, Joel Dean, you were ready to shoot

Champ Gowan and those other two on sight," Volly said. "Now that Estelle's out of the cave and at home safe with Yawley, you don't have to go through with representing him."

"After Ora was shot I sure enough wanted to take it out on somebody. I still feel that way. Only difference, now I want to be sure it's the person who actually did the shooting. Convicting the wrong man wouldn't help any. I'm just not as sure as I was before that Champ did the shooting."

Rose set a huge bowl of mashed potatoes and one of gravy in front of me. While I was taking out the first helping of each, she asked, "What's Gideon Norfleet going to say about this? I thought you were his assistant. I thought when he left the job you were going to take his place. You giving that up?"

"No, Rose, I'm not giving up anything. One way you could look at it is a man came to me, says he's been wrongly accused of murder and would I represent him. That's what lawyers do. We take an oath to see that everyone has a fair chance in court."

Oma Thornbush, whom I had filed several small family estate claims for, said, "Joel Dean, you were the only lawyer I had any use for. Now you're fixing to go and ruin that."

Uncle Billy Jack said, "Ain't no such thing as an innocent Gowan. Champ deserves hanging. Don't matter what it's for."

"Champ deserves a fair trial and fair representation in court, Uncle Billy Jack. That's what I will give him if the judge allows me to represent him. Same as I would do for you or anyone else."

Rose started me with a bowl of green beans seasoned with small, white onions and slices of fatback bacon.

"Joel Dean, you have a future in this town. Everybody likes you. You weren't so young you could probably run for Ora's job and get elected. What you're doing is going to get people down on you."

A lot of small talk broke out around the table. Everybody wanted to have a say about me representing Champ, just that some of them were too polite or lacked the courage to say it to me.

We ate for awhile with me thinking all these people around Rose Minton's table were potential jurors and maybe I should say something that would cause them to have reasonable doubt.

"Does everyone here think Champ Gowan is guilty of murdering Ora? Hold your hand up if you do. I'd be interested in knowing what his chances are."

Everyone but Frank Minton, Rose's teenage son, and the two drummers held their hand up.

"See, what it is, Joel Dean," Lonnie said, "is you told us all right here at this table that Champ Gowan and those other two ex-convicts were the ones who killed Ora. You were there, you convinced us. What was it Champ told you to change your mind?"

I finished off the second piece of breast meat and was chewing it while I considered what Lonnie said.

"What Champ told me is, of course, privileged information. I can only say I have come to have a reasonable doubt."

Jack Rasher, who had lived with his brother until Jack's sister-in-law suggested he move to Minton's if he wasn't going to pick up after himself around the house, said "Seems to me, Joel Dean, when court opens Gideon Norfleet is going to call you to the witness stand and have you tell how there wasn't nobody else around except Champ and those other two when Ora got shot. Then you're going to stand up in Champ's defense and say he didn't do it. Seems to me like Champ's only chance of not being hung is if everybody thinks that if you believe he didn't do it, then he must not have done it."

"Jack, are you asking me did I allow myself to be used by Champ Gowan so that he could get by with killing the best man I ever knew—the best man this town ever knew—without being punished for it? You asking if I would be willing to do that, Jack?"

I guess my words were sharp—sharper than I had intended. Jack Rasher got red in the face and took a sudden interest in his food. Conversation became as still as a church pew on Monday.

A few minutes elapsed in silence before one of the drummers began asking questions about the dam.

"I don't care nothing about no damn dam," Uncle Billy Jack said.

That brought on another period of quiet. When Rose brought a steaming cobbler I knew was cherry by the smell, she set it down in front of Jack Rasher and gave me a hard look across the table.

I pushed back my chair and stood, then excused myself saying I had work at the courthouse. I told Rose I would take my piece of cobbler when I came back, if she was to save it.

"It'll be cold," she snapped.

Like my friends, I thought.

Gideon Norfleet paid the county $10 a month for the use of the prosecutor's office in the courthouse for private cases he handled there. There was no need of keeping two offices, he said. Besides it would only confuse people as most everyone thought of him as the prosecutor first and a private attorney second.

There was a notice on the glass door into his office about a Grange meeting coming up. As I walked through the door, I had an empty feeling inside and it wasn't because I had skipped breakfast just to avoid talking with anyone. Jack Rasher's suspicions were—I was sure—the suspicions of every person in town by now. Maybe even Estelle. But mostly they were my suspicions. I'd made a deal with the devil and I was going to have to pay for it.

Winnie Marston, Gideon's secretary, researcher and investigator, had a friendly smile for me. Bless her.

"Go on in, Joel Dean. He said you'd be here sometime this

morning."

So now I was predictable.

Gideon's office smelled of oiled leather, old wood and stale cigar smoke. I entered cautiously and took a seat in front of his desk in an oak ladder-back chair. The office was barely large enough for Gideon's desk, two guest chairs and a stack of barrister book cabinets full of legal books. Gideon removed his wire-rimmed reading glasses and waited for me to begin.

"You've heard?" I asked.

He nodded.

"We found Champ and Nita from an airplane I hired. The pilot tried to land instead of going back to the mansion and calling Addie. He was afraid he would lose the thousand dollar reward. He damaged the landing gear and the storm was on top of us."

"Heard all that from Addie," he said. "Jibes with the pilot's version. You took Estelle out of the storm into one of the caves, Addie said. One of the sheriff's patrols came across the pilot last night. Sounds like he was real anxious for that thousand dollars."

I waited before going on, to think it all through. To put it in exactly the right words.

"We both fell asleep by the fire. Champ took my revolver, although he never pulled it on us, never threatened us with it. He led us out the other exit because he didn't think Addie would be there. But she was. While we were in the middle of the cave—in a place I would have had a hard time getting out of—he offered to surrender to me if I would be his lawyer. Otherwise, he was going to leave us there."

"But he wouldn't have gotten away, would he?" Gideon asked. "Not with Addie guarding both entrances to the cave. She would have had you and Estelle Earnhardt out before the day was over."

"Probably. I think he would have asked me to be his lawyer anyway."

"But you wouldn't have been blackmailed into it. You wouldn't have to do it to save your life or Estelle's. Isn't that why you accepted?"

"I'm not sure, Gideon. I began to have real doubts that Champ was part of Ora's getting killed. I think I accepted because I was afraid Champ would be convicted without me being sure he did it. We hang Champ and maybe the real killer is still walking around on the street, but nobody cares any longer."

"What makes you think he didn't do it?"

"I just got to know the man. See a different side of him. I don't think Champ's a real solid citizen and a credit to the community, but I have some real doubts about him being a killer."

"What did he say to make you think he didn't kill Ora?"

"Under the circumstances that is privileged information, of course."

Gideon stared hard at me for a long moment like a principal trying to decide whether to expel the student. He pulled a wooden humidor to him around the stacks of legal papers littering his desktop, and pulled out a long cigar. He busied himself clipping off the end, striking the match that filled the air with the smell of sulfur. When the cigar caught, clouds of blue smoke formed a mass around us both and the pleasing odor of the cigar chased the sulfur smell. Gideon removed the cigar from his mouth and blew a thin stream of smoke from one side of his mouth.

"What are you going to tell Judge Black?" he asked.

"I'm going to suggest to the judge that I give a deposition about that night which will remove the necessity of testifying against my client."

"He'll ask me, of course, if I have any objections."

"I know," I said.

"Well, what I'm going to tell him," Gideon said, leaning forward, taking the cigar and pointing it at me, "what I'll say will save you from yourself. I'm going to object."

I nodded. I had expected that.

"This could threaten our relationship, Joel Dean. You've been a good peace officer and you have the makings of a good lawyer. I'm not sure, under the circumstances, that we can continue with you as my assistant prosecutor."

I nodded again. "I would be greatly disappointed, Gideon, if you were to believe me a coward. Offering to serve as Champ's lawyer and save his life just to save my own."

"You need not worry about saving Champ's life. It just isn't going to happen. I'm going to see that boy hung for killing my friend. This town's friend. Your friend. Judge Black will rule against you representing Champ. You did what you thought you had to do. You thought you were taking Estelle Earnhardt to safety. The town will understand that. Yawley understands it. He's already telling people you agreed to be Champ's lawyer just to save his little girl's life."

"We wouldn't have died," I said. "One way or the other we would have gotten out of that cave. I believed that when I accepted. I told you my reason. I was hoping that, as a friend, you would believe me."

"I'm not condemning you, Joel Dean. But you won't be able to help me prosecute this case. When you testify before the jury I want you to be seen as neutral instead of part of the prosecution. But I do think the jury would be wrongly and unduly influenced if you testified, then spoke to them in defense of Champ."

I stood. "Thanks for listening to me, Gideon."

As I left his office I had the feeling of losing another friend.

Judge Henry Black was born on April 9, 1865, the day Robert E. Lee surrendered the Confederate Army to Ulysses S. Grant.

The judge's daddy—having served as a major under General Sterling Price in the Missouri Militia against Grant—never accepted his son because of his unglorious birth date. Young Henry did everything he could to win his father's acceptance—according to legend—but it was common knowledge that when Major Black lay on his deathbed he refused to forgive Henry for having a birth date that Henry had no control over. One rumor had it that the major hadn't been home for two years before Henry was born and what he had against the boy was the fact that the boy had not sprung from the seeds of *his* loins. But Henry always maintained his daddy had been home on a medical rehabilitation for several months in time for him to be Henry's true sire.

Henry Black was now the age his father had been when he died, but the bitterness against his father lingered. I did not particularly like trying cases before him. He was senile, bitter, stubborn and generally ignorant of the law. He had been appointed to his post by Sid Hatch when Sid was governor because the Major had been an ardent and rabid supporter of Sid. Henry was not a rich man and he knew he couldn't live as well on the paltry pension the state would pay him as he was doing on salary. Henry Black would be a judge until he died.

The judge's chamber was a room with three walls. Judge Henry Black sat with his back to one wall leaving visitors with the feeling of being squeezed between the other two. I had tried few cases in my short legal career and had been in the judge's chamber three times before today. I was surprised he even knew my name.

I began by telling him Champ Gowan had asked me to be his attorney, but as I was a chief witness for the prosecution I wasn't sure it would be acceptable to the court.

It was close in the chamber. The air was stale and smelled like strong tobacco and the sweat of men that had been cooped up like a prisoner in one of our cells and never let out into fresh air.

Judge Henry Black looked sternly across his scarred walnut desk at me. He was dressed in his robe, even though no court session was scheduled for today.

"I don't guess they teach court procedure in law schools anymore," he said, working his bushy eyebrows up and down as he spoke. "Of course you can't represent the man you're testifying against. You go on the witness stand swearing to tell the truth, then stand before the jury and deny it? No, no, no. You get some years of experience under your belt, young man, and you won't even think about coming in here with such a ridiculous request. You best just stick to clerking for Gideon Norfleet for another five or ten years until you know something about being an attorney. You ain't had time yet to learn all you need to know."

"But I won't be testifying against my client, your honor. I will only be telling the truth of the circumstances. I didn't see nor hear anything Champ Gowan did that night. It will be up to the prosecutor to prove he killed Ora."

"Even if I was to allow it—and there's not one chance in a billion that I would—Gideon Norfleet wouldn't agree to it. And if I went ahead and let you represent this killer, Gideon Norfleet would have a reason to go straight to the Supreme Court in this state. And he'd be right to do so."

"I can give a deposition, Your Honor, and say what I knew happened. I will not contest any of the facts I give in the deposition. I have come to believe this man did not kill Ora. I believe he has the right to have the attorney of his choice to represent him."

"Oh, hell, boy, I understand why you told him you would be his lawyer. To save the girl. It's all over town. I would have done the same thing. But once I was out of that cave I would have told that blackhearted killer to go to hell. That man's guilty. Gideon Norfleet is going to prove it to a jury of the man's peers and I'm going to sentence him to hang. That's the truth of it."

"I was hoping you'd keep an open mind, Judge, at least until you heard the evidence," I said.

"Evidence be damned; we're going to get rid of that no-good once and for all and that's that. Now you go on back to being a law man until you've learned something about the law. I understand your sister is sweet on this Gowan man so I guess that's where this is coming from. You didn't do such a good job at being deputy sheriff either. I understand you were in charge when that gang broke out of jail and couldn't stop them from killing the sheriff. Your pa and grandpa both got killed trying to make a go of it cutting ties and failed. Seems you Gregorys have a problem doing anything right."

I found myself on my feet thinking evil thoughts about this old man.

"Whenever you're performing the duties of a judge, I'll show respect," my voice said, coming from somewhere that I had no control over. "But you've stepped over the line insulting my father and grandfather who were better men than some who dishonor their position by refusing to step aside long past the time they are capable of doing their job. I do not take insults to my family lightly. When people use the advantage of their position to do so, I think lesser of them. Take care, judge, you don't fall into that category."

I didn't even remember leaving the judge's chamber.

She didn't say so, but I could tell Addie was displeased with something I said after I had asked her, Noah and Doyle to join me in the kitchen after the prisoners ate. During the meal Champ had laughed and joked with everyone, including me, as if he'd just returned home from a vacation. I wondered if he knew, or even cared, that the powers in the county already had him convicted and hanged.

I told Addie and the deputies everything from the beginning, just as I had told Gideon. It was when I got to the part about the judge that Addie's expression hardened.

"You may be correct in what you said to the judge," she said. "But you weren't right to do it. You got to get along in this town, Joel Dean. And that means taking the loose talk Judge Black spews out without backtalking. Gideon, Sid Hatch and Judge Black have all been helping you in your goal to be a good lawyer. Now,. . . now, I don't know where you stand in the county."

"You're sure enough right about that old judge, though," Noah said. "Sometimes when I've been a bailiff over there, he forgets who's on trial and what the crime is. He's going to mess something up bad and somebody's going to have to pay."

"At least you're off the hook on representing Champ," Doyle said. "I never did think that was too good an idea. Don't blame you for what you did, though, agreeing to do it to get Estelle Earnhardt out of that cave. That gal's sweet on you. It's what I would have done. And I would've gone to court for him, too. Because it ain't going to make any difference. Champ is going to hang for this one and that's a fact. I just hope it's not before we can make some music together at a dance."

Addie asked, "Have you told Champ yet you won't be allowed to represent him?"

"No, I haven't. I think I'll hold off for awhile. It's not official yet."

"You mean you haven't filed with the court yet as Champ's attorney?"

"Not yet. The arraignment's not for three days. Something might come up."

"The judge is giving you a way out," Addie said. "Take it. Pushing this any further can only hurt your standing in the community."

"Something you never cared about when you snubbed Sid Hatch and that legislator," I told her.

"I got no future in this town, Joel Dean. But you do. No telling how far you could go. State legislature, maybe. Even Congress. Don't throw all that away."

"What about you, Addie? Are you like everyone else in town? You think Champ killed Ora? You ready to put the noose around his neck?"

"Champ's neck has been in a noose since the day he was born. Just waiting for somebody to kick the box out from under him. Might as well be you."

An unexpected cold front slid in overnight foretelling an early winter ahead and the town awoke in a misty fog that hung thickest over the river with rain-like threads dangling into the water. When the sun came up the fog became a golden veil in the heaviest parts and the moisture drops on the leaves and branches drooping over the river banks glistened like diamonds.

I admired the show of nature as I made my way down Main Street. Volly was wiping a windshield clean on a new Plymouth motorcar, then watched it fog over again. Lonnie had the hood up on one of Yawley's Chevrolet delivery trucks. I called out a greeting to them.

"Missed you at supper last night," Volly yelled at me. I gave him a grin, but it was probably lost in the fog.

At the end of Main Street I took the street that ran up to the Earnhardt's house sitting on a rise a hundred feet or so higher than the town. Up here, there was no fog. Looking down on the town, the misty air obscured it as if it wasn't there. As if the Earnhardts lived alone in this spot on Earth.

I admired the construction and design of the Earnhardt house as I always did. It was a tall two-story with a wide overhanging porch roof across the front and along each side. Dormers marked a third story on the front and sides. Though I had not been farther into the house than the parlor, Birdie told me, by way of Nell, that the house had 14 rooms including two bathrooms with cast-iron tubs made back east somewhere. I vowed to have a house just like this some day.

I climbed the walk that led up to the massive front porch and encountered Estelle kneeling in a flower bed to one side of the walk. She had a pair of shears in one gloved hand and the start of a bouquet in the other. She wore a simple frock—a kind I wasn't aware she owned—and a large, Jane McGann type of floppy-brimmed straw hat. She saw me and her smile was my second sunrise of the day. And here I had worried she might not even be out of bed.

"Joel Dean, what a surprise," she said. She laid the shears on the ground and the glove slid off that hand. She used the hand to push her short, curly blond hair around behind her ear on one side, trying to make herself look prettier. But it was pretty much useless. How do you improve on perfection?

"I look such a mess," she said. "I wasn't expecting anyone."

I reached down to take her hand and pull her to her feet. Two spots of soil showed on the dress where she had kneeled against it.

"You look so outstanding here in the morning sun surrounded by all these beautiful flowers. I don't know if I've ever seen you looking so fine."

"My goodness, you're going to take on so about this old thing I'm wearing I guess I don't need those expensive dresses from St. Louis," she said.

"You look better without them."

She caught my meaning and smiled that real big smile she couldn't control.

"I came out to pull some weeds and thought the flowers looked so neat and fab I just grabbed these scissors and started cutting." She held the bouquet for me to see up close and to smell. "Won't these look gargantuan on the lunch table? Can you stay?"

"I have to go and prepare myself for the arraignment. I'd sure like to, though."

"Oh, poo, you're just like Daddy. I've got an itchy feeling you're always going to be running off somewhere. Leaving me here to pull weeds."

"I thought Nell took care of your garden."

"I decided I needed to know how to take care of things around the house. You know, for after I get married."

I grinned. "You planning on getting married real soon?"

"I might have to."

Now that was a surprise.

"Anyone I know?"

"It's you, of course, you ninny. Some of the women in church think you and I should get married."

"Why are they even concerned about it?"

"Because we spent a night together in that cave."

"Nothing happened."

"They don't know that. They just imagine what could have happened. We spent the night together and to them, that's the same as doing it because we could have."

"Just like they figure Champ killed Ora because he was there and he could have," I said. "What's Yawley think about us getting married?"

"Oh, he's against it. He says I'm going off to Stephens College in Columbia."

"You want to go to college?"

"I don't know. Maybe."

"You want to get married?"

"Is that a proposal, Joel Dean?"

"I guess if I had three wishes, all three of them would be marrying you. I just figured it would be a few years before we did. I don't make enough money to support me, let alone you *and* me. I can't be asking you to be my wife under those circumstances. When my career gets going better, I'll be asking."

"That means Daddy is going to send me off to college then. He says you don't have a future if you represent Champ Gowan in court."

"So if I represent Champ, Yawley won't let you marry me?"

"We could elope."

"The judge won't allow me to represent Champ, but I'm going to fight it. Champ didn't do it. The state will never hang two men for the same crime. Once Champ is found guilty, the one who killed Ora will be free. The thought of that happening eats at me."

"I don't know anything about that, Joel Dean."

"I need somebody to believe in me, Estelle. No one does, not even Addie."

"Then I do. I believe in you and I'll defend you to Daddy. He says you did the right thing in telling Champ you would be his lawyer just to get me out of that cave. But he says you shouldn't do it after we were out."

"What kind of man would I be if I did that?" I asked. "Everybody in town would say Joel Dean Gregory goes back on his word, even if it was to Champ Gowan."

"When are we going to get married then, Joel Dean?"

"The day this trial's over we're going to set a date."

"Then we're engaged?"

"Soon as I can afford a ring."

She flew to me and wrapped her arms around my neck and kissed me hard.

"Ring or no ring, we're going to the moving picture they're having out at the picnic grounds tomorrow night. Mona Deering in *Wayfarer's Daughter*. And I'm telling everybody we're engaged."

Mona Deering was a beautiful woman. Her face was three times normal size on the screen that had been set up next to the grove of Linn trees that bordered the picnic grove. People had been on the picnic grounds all day setting up chairs, the projector and hauling in the piano that Marie Perrin, the church organist at the Baptist Church, would play during the showing of the moving picture.

Admission was ten cents each and I handed over two dimes as Estelle and I entered and took our seats near the front. All the way down the aisle, Estelle spoke and waved at practically everyone. I would have to say that people appeared to be a bit reserved toward me. Something else I noticed: Estelle was getting the rich-daughter treatment, by the women and especially those her own age, as they fawned over her dress and showed real envy at the hair band that circled her hair, her jewelry and the little beaded purse she swung from her hand on a long silver chain. For the first time I wondered what others would be thinking about me being married to Estelle. Would Yawley be expecting me to help run his business? Would I make enough money to meet her extravagant taste?

Joel Dean Gregory, grocery clerk, shoe salesman feed store operator. None of those pictures went along with what I had in mind for my future. But everything would work out. I was sure.

Marie Perrin pounded away on the piano as we waited expectantly for it to get dark enough to begin the movie. The kids ran up and down the aisle, begging their parents for money to buy soda pop out of the cooler set up on the grounds. The sign on the tent that held all the refreshments proclaimed the Methodists to be raising money for a new organ. Which they weren't going to need if the dam went in.

Lonnie and his girl, Bonnie, from near Montreal, sat beside us. Bonnie was a vivacious brunette who "simply adored" everything Estelle wore. Finally the lights went out and a one-reel short starring the Keystone Kops filled the screen. The audience laughed uproariously at them, and was still laughing during the pause to load the main feature.

There was something familiar about the face on the screen. Long lashes, upturned nose, blonde curls and a small, rosebud-like mouth. I glanced over at Estelle and saw her completely engrossed in the feature. I had always thought Estelle particularly gorgeous looking, but now I saw that she was as beautiful as the movie star, Mona Deering. In fact, they looked enough alike to be sisters.

When the movie ended, Estelle was in tears. Mona Deering had suffered at the hands of a slick, oily looking character before she was rescued by the main male character. I didn't consider that she had suffered as many hardships as say, my mother, had in her lifetime, but I guess to Estelle, it was pretty bad because the tears were running freely from her eyes. Bonnie came up with a spare handkerchief and comforted Estelle, sympathizing with her about Mona's plight.

The four of us had an ice cream soda at Parkinson's Drugs and talked about other moving pictures we had seen and books we had read or wanted to read. The mention of Mona Deering caused Estelle to cry again so I switched the subject real quick to who had a new automobile and which model we would like to have. Lonnie and Bonnie both agreed they would settle for a little Jordan roadster like Estelle's, but she said, "Oh, poo. It's black and yellow and I don't have a thing that goes with it."

I kissed Estelle goodnight on Yawley's big front porch and told her how much I had enjoyed the evening and the moving pictures. She teared up again and leaned her head on my chest, saying, "Oh, Joel Dean. It's so sad."

I came close to saying, "It's only a moving picture, Estelle," but I figured it was not the right thing to say at that time. So I held her close and wiped her tears away. If she was going to make a fictional story on the movie screen so real, maybe we just wouldn't be going to very many.

If only I had known the real reason she was crying.

My usual routine when I pulled the graveyard shift at the jail from midnight to nine was to sleep as much as possible until the prisoners woke up at six. I would lean a chair against the outside door so that if anyone came in needing the sheriff they would knock the chair over. But that all changed now with the arraignment coming up in a few days. I stayed awake the entire shift with a set of law books Winnie Marston had let me borrow from Gideon. I read as fast as I could about arraignments and took notes in a spiral binder. I searched past cases for anything having to do with representing someone while giving testimony for the other side. Maybe if I found a case to use as a precedent Judge Henry Black would reconsider. But all I found even remotely related were two cases and they were both weak ones for my situation.

I got the prisoners up at six and marched them to breakfast at seven. Champ was still in a good mood, joking with two colored men Noah had arrested the evening before as they passed through town in a car stolen in Sedalia.

"What made you boys think you could just drive through this town and nobody is going to pay any attention to you?" Champ asked them.

"Was worth getting caught here," one of the men said. He was the taller of the two and was dressed in a green suit with a white shirt and a wide yellow tie. I guessed him to be about 50, but I wasn't schooled in telling the age of colored. He hadn't taken his eyes off Birdie since he came in. "There's some mighty fine stuff in this town."

The younger man and the blacker of the two kept his eyes on his plate, waiting for Birdie to pass the food around. He wore an oversize jacket and worn duckcloth pants.

Birdie brought a platter of eggs from the stove and dipped one on each plate as she walked around the table. When Birdie stopped between the two colored prisoners and placed one egg on each plate, the older man placed his hand on Birdie's backside an inch above her buttocks.

"I could use two of those eggs, fine mama," he said, looking up at Birdie, eyes flashing.

Birdie took the spatula and removed the egg from his plate that she had placed there.

"Case you don't know it, I'm in charge when you're in the kitchen," she said. "Somebody don't show the proper respect in this room, they don't eat."

The man looked and acted astonished. He glanced at me, sitting closest to Addie's empty chair, at the other deputies, then decided I must be in charge as Addie was absent.

"Can she do that?" he asked me.

"She can."

Birdie skipped the man on each trip around the table, serving bacon, biscuits and gravy to each prisoner except the older man. He sat watching her, smiling each time she walked past. There was still a lingering look of disbelief on his face.

Addie came in just as Birdie was pouring the last cup of

coffee for everyone. She was dressed in tan twill army pants and a shirt of the same material. Both the pants and the shirt fit her loosely so they didn't reveal the actual contours of her body. The large silver badge that had looked so small on Ora, hung heavy on her shirt front. I noticed she now wore Ora's holster and belt, but carried a .38 caliber revolver in the rig.

Birdie handed Addie a full plate and filled her coffee cup after she was seated. Addie looked at Champ.

"Judge changed your arraignment date, Champ. Seems they want to get Ora's shooting over before the one on Shorty. You have to be in court at nine this morning."

I said, "I'm not ready."

Addie ignored me. "Joel Dean will take you over," she told Champ.

"No," I said. "I'm off at nine. I have a client due at court at that time. Noah can take him over."

Noah looked back and forth between me and Addie, not knowing which side to come down on.

"Sure," he said, looking at Addie for a clue about whether he said the right thing or not. "I can take him over if you want, Addie."

Addie looked long and hard at me. "All right then," she said at last. "That's the way it will be."

She looked at the colored men. "A car'll be here for you two this morning from Pettis County."

The older man said, "I ain't had anything to eat, sheriff."

Addie looked at Birdie standing by the stove, arms folded. "Give him a slice of burned toast, Birdie, so we can charge Pettis County for a full meal."

LIMB OF THE JUDAS TREE

Motor cars, buggies and a throng of people clogged Main Street as I made my way from the jail to Minton's to change into my one and only pants and suit coat that matched. At first I thought I had my days mixed up and it must be Saturday when the farmers and the hill people came into Linn Creek to do their shopping. But the knot of people before the courthouse and gathering under the redbud tree beside the jail house told me why they were here.

I knew most of them. Walking along the street I called them by name and they responded with a nod or a wave and some with just a stare. It wasn't hard to see I was the object of curiosity by people come to observe Champ Gowan being indicted for the murder of Ora Mitchell.

I stopped to ask Ernest Raines what he was doing in town.

"Come to make sure they hang Champ Gowan for killing Ora," he said, blinking his eyes rapidly. He stared hard at me like he had more to say.

"It's only an arraignment," I told Ernest, making sure the people nearby could hear me. "The most the judge can do today is indict Champ and set a trial date."

Ernest shuffled his feet, looked at the ground and spit a stream of tobacco on a weed beside the road.

"Talk is you're defending Champ. Saying he didn't kill Ora."

"That's true," I said, meeting Ernest's eyes. "If the court will allow it, I will be his attorney. Hanging the wrong man would be something I intend to see doesn't happen."

I moved on to the group standing before the courthouse. Someone must have taken a lot of trouble to let everyone know about the arraignment. Champ had only been notified less than two hours ago. These people had been told before that or they couldn't have gotten here this early. The women were mostly dressed in bonnets and print dresses like the ones they wore on Saturdays. Most of the men wore clean bib overalls with some dressed in belted trousers. Straw hats that were saved for Saturday afternoons and Sunday mornings at church were worn by the men and some of the young boys who played tag in their best Sunday clothes with the mothers admonishing them to stay clean.

The Monger brothers were standing on the top step of the courthouse, right outside the open doors as if they had been waiting there for some time. Ellis Wayne and his brother Dave stood blocking the doorway. They both wore their gray uniform shirts with their deputy badges pinned on. Ora had frequently called the Waynes to act as bailiffs when court was held on days when the other deputies could not go.

Someone touched my arm and I turned to see Estelle, splendidly attired in a baby blue dress that was scandalously short and low in the front. She wore a cute little fabric hat that matched perfectly with her dress.

"I came to support you, Joel Dean," she said. "But, my goodness, how am I going to get inside? The courtroom can't hold all these people."

"You sure look dazzling this morning," I told her and she beamed. "I appreciate your coming. You and Champ are going to be the only ones looking at me with any favor, it seems."

"Daddy's not going to be on your side, that's for sure."

I took her arm and made my way around the courthouse to a back door used by the clerks and county employees. The courthouse had been built in 1880 out of limestone blocks that came up the river from Jefferson City. It was a plain rectangular two-story building with a slate roof that had always leaked. In a hard rainstorm, buckets were scattered all over the second floor under the drips. If a trial took place during one of these storms, the judge would instruct the witnesses and the attorneys to speak up so the jury could hear them over the dripping sounds.

Estelle followed me up the narrow stairway to the circuit clerk's office outside the main courtroom. Nancy Graham stood at the counter inside her office. She had worked under two men who had held the office before her and before being persuaded by Bertha Norfleet to run for the office herself. In the female sweep of offices that occurred, Nancy had won and became her own boss. Everyone figured the office would go to hell and Judge Henry Black had spoken vociferously against her. But Nancy became a better circuit clerk than anyone had before her, now that she didn't have a man interfering with her. She had always been a big help to me as I floundered around in the few cases I had tried in court.

She said, to my request, that she would see to it that Estelle got a front row seat while she admired Estelle's dress. Nancy had always dressed a notch above print dresses.

"You representing Champ?" she asked.

"I'm going to try."

"You haven't filed a motion."

"I'll make it this morning. Orally."

"Judge won't like it."

"I know. He told me."

"Want some advice?"

"From you Nancy? Always."

"Come in as a friend of the court."

"I thought of that, but I gave my word I would be an advocate."

"Good luck," she said and gave me a look that said more. Like, "You're dead."

"Thanks Nancy. I'd like to see the file on this case."

"Sorry, Joel Dean. Much as I'd like to show it to you, I can't. You have to go through Gideon. Strict orders. No one sees the file unless he says so."

I knew that wasn't the way it's supposed to be. But now wasn't the time to argue the point and Nancy wasn't the one to argue it with.

As I left the office, Nancy and Estelle were discussing each other's dresses.

I just couldn't get over the number of people in town. And it didn't end there. At Minton's Boarding House, Rose was all dressed up in a gown I only saw on Sundays.

"Better get dressed, Joel Dean," she said. "Lawyers need to look nice in court."

"I may need your help with my necktie, Rose," I said.

"Better hurry then. I don't want to miss getting a seat. This is no Sunday morning sermon at church where there's plenty of seats."

"What this is about is whether to hang a man or not," I said.

Rose shrugged. "Same people sitting in the pews."

That was some packed house in the courtroom. I had sure never seen that many people in there before. It was as if they expected a hanging right on the spot. Women waved cardboard fans with advertising for Yawley's General Store. Men had removed their hats and every once in a while waved them in their faces trying to create some cooling. The four ceiling fans turned with the paddles stirring currents of air, but there was just too much heat packed inside and more coming in through open windows. People stood two deep against the walls all the way around the courtroom.

I smiled at Estelle sitting on the front bench behind the defense table. Halfway back I spotted Nita German under a gaudy little hat that was an advertisement for her profession.

Judge Henry Black swooped in, his black robe billowing out behind him. His eyes went immediately to me sitting at the defense table with Champ. His bushy eyebrows knitted together over his nose, his lips began to twitch and his face became flaming red. He gaveled the court to order and before we could all be seated, he bellowed out to the prosecutor to call the case before the court.

"The State of Missouri against Champion Gowan," Gideon said. "The charge is murder in the first degree of Camden County Sheriff Ora Mitchell."

Nancy Graham handed Judge Black a folder which he thumbed through like a gust of wind. He looked up at Champ like Champ was a bug he was about to squash.

"And are you the defendant, one Champion Gowan?" the judge asked, about as belligerent as he could be.

Champ, who was slumping in his chair, took his time rising to his feet. I stood with him.

"That's me, Judge," Champ said, wearing a grin.

"And how do you plead?" Judge Black asked.

"The defendant pleads not guilty, your honor," I said.

"Who are you?" from Judge Black.

"I will represent the defendant, your honor. I am Joel Dean Gregory."

The judge made a show of looking through the papers in the folder.

"I don't see a motion in here to have an advocate speak for you," the judge said looking at Champ. "How do you plead?"

"Not guilty, Judge."

"We are here to determine if there is sufficient cause to indict Champion Gowan for the murder of Sheriff Ora Mitchell," the judge said as he slid the folder away from him and slumped back in his chair. "Mr. Prosecutor, present your proof,"

As Gideon was making his way toward the bench, I rose.

"Your Honor, we request the right to see the file on this case and the time to examine the evidence the prosecutor has against the accused."

"Denied," the judge said without leaning forward. "You're about to hear the evidence. Don't interrupt the prosecutor again."

Gideon proceeded to tell the judge about the trip back from Mexico and what happened. He said the State had an eyewitness to everything but the actual shooting. That would be me, of course. He said when he and Deputy Sheriff Doyle Savoy arrived at the scene they found the sheriff dead from a single shot through the heart and Deputy Joel Dean Gregory unconscious. The next day, according to Gideon, he and Deputy Savoy had searched the area in daylight and found Sheriff Mitchell's .45 caliber automatic pistol in the brush nearby.

"Your Honor, the defendant had the motive, the opportunity and the means to commit the murder. We will prove in court he did just that," Gideon said, winding up his presentation.

"Does the defendant have anything to say in his behalf?" Judge Black asked, still slumped in his chair.

"Your Honor," I said as I rose from my chair, "I would like to submit this motion to be entered on record as the attorney to represent the accused."

I walked to the bench and laid a handwritten motion before the judge.

Without leaning forward in his chair or looking at my motion, Judge Black said, "Denied."

"Your reason, Your Honor?"

Now that brought him upright in his chair, jabbing a finger at me.

"Dammit boy, I already gave you the reason. You persist in this foolhardy exercise and I'll find you in contempt of court."

Having my motion denied by the judge was expected by me, but the threat of a contempt charge rattled me.

"Does the defendant have anything to say, I asked?" the judge yelled past me, pointing the end of his gavel at Champ.

Champ rose. "I already said I didn't do it. Just because I was there don't mean I shot him."

"Is that all you have to say?"

"I reckon it is."

"Mr. Prosecutor, do you have anything to say to the defendant's argument?"

"I guess I've already said it, Your Honor," Gideon said.

I rose again. "Your Honor, this defendant is entitled to representation in court . . ."

Judge Black brought the gavel down in repeated raps and his face glowed brightly.

"I told you boy. I told you the last damn time. You're in contempt of this court and I fine you $100."

He stood, bringing his gavel down on the bench as a woodsman would bring an ax down against a log.

"I find this defendant guilty of murder in the first degree and sentence him to hang by the neck until he is dead."

A great hush settled over the old courtroom. I turned to look at Gideon and noticed the crowd inside the courtroom was stunned.

"God help us," Gideon said quietly.

PART FOUR
THE TRIAL

LIMB OF THE JUDAS TREE

Fred Wallace was in jail for butchering a neighbor's calf by moonlight and Frances Billings was in for poisoning ten people. Fred butchered people's livestock for a living, but he usually did it by daylight at their invitation. Frances lived in the Zebra neighborhood where she practiced medicine without any kind of license and treated her patients with herbs and concoctions of her own manufacturing. One of the people she had treated came near death and was brought in the back of a wagon to Linn Creek where Doc Hardesty examined her, made a few tests and rushed her off to Jefferson City to St. Mary's Hospital. Doc then confronted Frances and got the names of the others she had treated with the same herbs and sent them all to the hospital. Then he filed a warrant with Addie for Frances' arrest.

Addie didn't like having a woman in jail since we had to hang a sheet over her toilet and make other arrangements for her privacy.

Fred said how good the bacon was at the breakfast table and told Addie to let him know when she needed more as he could probably get a deal for her. Frances remarked that if you sprinkled the dust from ground-up dewberry blooms on the bacon it would neutralize the fat. Frances with the 230 pound frame looking out for our weight.

Gideon was a guest for breakfast that morning after the arraignment. Birdie piled buttermilk pancakes and blackberry jelly on his plate along with two big, thick slices of side meat.

The first topic for the morning that everyone was anxious to talk about was what the county judges were going to do about the dam. Noah asked Gideon for his prediction on the outcome.

"A lot of people favor it," Gideon said. "The electric company is offering jobs cutting timber and working the dam."

"Is it true if the dam goes in, Linn Creek will be thirty feet under water?" Fred Wallace asked.

"I'm not sure how many feet it will be, but, yes, a dam would put our town under water," Gideon said.

"Well, hell, nobody's going to be for that," Noah said.

"Depends," Doyle offered. "Some people think the electric company will make them rich by buying their property."

"Guess I won't be around to see it," Champ said, smiling as usual. "What with the judge already finding me guilty before the trial begins and sentencing me to hang."

Gideon squirmed, cleared his throat, and shoved the half-eaten pancakes away from him.

"The judge got a little carried away," he said. "It doesn't mean anything. It'll all get straightened out. You're indicted is all and the trial is set for two weeks from yesterday."

I wasn't about to let that pass by. "It does mean something, Gideon. In front of almost every prospective juror in the county that senile old man from the high position on that bench called the accused guilty without a trial. A Directed Verdict with no proof of guilt."

Gideon was pure white in the face and sweating. "I need to talk with you about that, Joel Dean, if you'll stay after breakfast."

"This trial has to be moved to another county and another judge has to be assigned," I said as firmly as I could make it.

Birdie looked at Gideon's plate.

"What's wrong with my hot cakes Mr. Gideon? You used to like them."

Gideon wiped his face with a white handkerchief. "Not feeling so good, Birdie. Been feeling kind of peaked last couple of days. It's the heat, I guess. Nothing to do with your fine hot cakes."

Frances pointed her fork across the table at Gideon. "You got heart trouble, Gideon. I can see it in your face. You need some tea from boiled sassafras root and some powder spread on your chest at night made from groundup pole bean leaves."

"Just an upset stomach, Frances. I'll drop by Doc Hardesty's and pick up some pills."

"You let that old sawbones doctor you and you'll be dead by the end of the year," Frances warned.

"Joel Dean, maybe we could talk out in the office if you're through with your breakfast," Gideon said, trying to act like he never heard Frances' warning.

"Sure," I told him. I forked the last bite into my mouth and picked up my coffee cup to take with me.

"Joel Dean," he began when we had passed through the locked door into the sheriff's office, "We can make a deal on this trial so we can overcome the judge's misstep yesterday."

"What kind of deal?"

"Me and the judge are willing to allow you to represent Champ if you and him will forego any appeal over his mistake."

"Nothing doing, Gideon. There's no way Champ can get a fair trial in this county now, if he ever could have in the first place."

"We're both willing to make concessions as far as your objections on picking the jury."

"That old fool. There's no telling what he'll do. An outburst like that before the jury and we got ourselves a mistrial."

"Which could work in your favor," Gideon argued. "I'll keep close watch on him. I'll refrain from making objections that could set him off. This is the chance you've been asking for, Joel Dean. If you go to the appeals court and get a change of venue and another judge, I guarantee you won't get to represent Champ. And if they turn you down on your appeal . . .well, you know where Judge Black and I stand on the issue."

"So, if I don't appeal the judge's outrageous comments from the bench, I can represent Champ before a jury and a judge who have already decided on his guilt. And if I do appeal, I won't be representing Champ."

"That's about it."

"Doesn't seem fair, Gideon. To Champ or to me."

"Life's like that, Joel Dean."

"Which way you favor?"

Gideon shrugged. "Doesn't matter. Fate has smiled on you, Joel Dean. You can have your wish and represent the defendant in the biggest trial this county's ever had. Or, you're getting another chance to get out of this thing with honor. I don't want to see you get hurt."

"And the contempt charge?"

Gideon waved his hand by way of dismissal. "Already taken care of. There will be no contempt charge. Your record is clean."

"It's not my decision to make, Gideon. Champ will have to decide."

"Either way, Champ's going to hang," Gideon said, staring me in the eyes. "He's guilty and you know it."

I started to say something, but figured, what's the use. Before I got to the door I heard Gideon say, "There's something else, Joel Dean."

I looked at Gideon, but he was avoiding my eyes.

"Bertha . . .well, some of the women in the county, now that they're voting, want to be on juries too."

I knew, from the way he kept looking away that the request had come from Bertha. She put Gideon on the spot and Gideon was trying to shift it over to me.

"Would be different," I said. "What's Judge Black say about it."

Gideon was gruff. "He won't say. That means he'll allow it. You can stop it. There's no provision in the state constitution for women serving on a jury."

"Does the Constitution say women can't serve?" I asked.

"No, of course not. It doesn't say horses can't serve either or hound dogs. It says every able bodied man is subject to be called. You could object and Judge Black could interpret the Constitution as meaning men only."

"And Bertha couldn't hold you to blame."

"She wouldn't hold you to blame, either, Joel Dean. As defense attorney you'd have every right to have a conventional jury."

"Or, it could help my client," I said. I pictured Estelle and Nita German sitting in the jury box. "I'll have to think about it, Gideon."

"You'll have to think fast. Nancy's already sent notices to six women."

A couple of years back Ora arrested this fellow from St. Louis for getting drunk and driving his Ford up the steps to the courthouse. Turns out he was a professional photographer who took pictures for magazines such as *Life* and *Look* and *Saturday Evening Post*. The next morning after he had sobered up in the Camden County jail, drank a gallon of Birdie's coffee and paid his fine, he left, only to come back with all of his camera gear with him. He spent two whole hours shooting pictures of our jail upstairs. Three months later he sent Ora a copy of *PIC* magazine and, sure enough, there were two pages of pictures of our jail cells.

Ever since then I have regarded our jail cells in a different light. The doors are cast iron and weigh about 600 pounds each. Maybe they hadn't been cast with the purpose in mind for which we used them, I don't know. Uncle Billy Jack might know the story behind the cell doors.

I'm always amazed and appreciative of our jail since I realized its artistic value, as I was the morning I came to talk with Champ about his trial. I found him in the cell with Frances sitting on an apple crate turned sideways and playing cards using another crate for a table.

I unlocked the main jail door going into the cell area. We usually left the individual cell doors unlocked so the prisoners could go in and out of each other's cells.

"Champ, I need to talk with you," I said from the door to Frances' cell.

"I'll leave if you want me to," Frances said, starting to get up from her cot.

"It's okay, Frances," Champ said. "I'm going to get hung anyway so I don't have any secrets."

I laid it out for Champ just the way Gideon had for me. He rubbed his chin, moving his head from side to side, then ran his hand through his hair before looking up at me with that grin of his.

"They're looking out for you, Joel Dean. Giving you every chance they can to get out of being my lawyer."

"Take it, Joel Dean," Frances said. "They're of a mind to hang this boy and you can't stop them. Heard that all the way up to Zebra."

"So what'll it be, Champ?" I asked.

"Frances is right, Joel Dean. That old judge proved it. They're going to hang me no matter what. I thought I had a chance if they moved it and the person who testified against me also defended me. But they ain't going to let that happen. So save yourself. I'm a goner anyway we do it."

"I agreed to defend you, Champ, because I don't think you killed Ora. And if you didn't kill him, I wanted to find out who did and make him pay. And I knew why you wanted me as your lawyer. Wasn't any way you thought I was the best lawyer you could get."

"Well, it was a long shot. Guess I should have cut and run when we were in that cave."

"Why didn't you?"

Champ looked down at his cards, flipped them over and laughed out loud.

"Look at that, Frances. Gin."

"You know what they say about being lucky at cards, Champ," Frances said.

"Unlucky at love," Champ said and laughed some more.

He stood up in that lazy way of his and stretched his muscles.

"Joel Dean, you go ahead and file that appeal and get the trial moved. I'm firing you as my lawyer. You got a future, don't waste it on me."

"I'm no quitter, Champ."

"I know that, Joel Dean."

"I decided to stay on. I don't think the appeals court will hear your case. They'd look out for their own. I'm going to tell Gideon he's got a deal."

"You do and they'll hang us both."

"Maybe," I said. "Maybe not."

Kate Minton brought a St. Louis newspaper to church Sunday morning and the preacher read from it. The article was all about the corporation that had been selling shares in the dam and generating plant that was to be built at Bagnell, and how the man who was heading it up was sent to prison for embezzling funds from a Kansas City bank and using it to start the dam project. That put an end to the hydro-electric dream that had some people drooling over the money they thought they were going to get for their land and had others—like Uncle Billy Jack—fuming over the prospects of drowning our town.

The preacher said a lot of people who had invested in the dam had lost their money. He asked the congregation to pray for those people and to give thanks that the dam would not be built and that the town of Linn Creek would not be destroyed to make way for the dam.

"God saved us," a jubilant Uncle Billy Jack kept shouting. The rest of the congregation joined in and there was clapping, shouting, dancing and singing between the pews and in the aisles. The preacher gave up trying to pray and the rest of the service was adjourned to the outdoors, where, down the street, the Baptists and the Methodists had both taken to the street in celebration. Kate invited the whole town to her place to celebrate and she hurried off to prepare something to serve.

The town had not seen a cause for celebration like this since we received word that women's suffrage had passed the Congress and was signed by the President. And then, only half the town was celebrating.

I felt so good I wanted to go see Estelle right away. I saw her down the street with the Methodist congregation and waved to her. She waved back. I watched her take Yawley's arm and walk across the street to Yawley's General Store. I felt a lot less jubilant than I had a moment ago.

At Volly's station, Lonnie and Volly had beaten me there and were sitting in the rocking chairs drinking a couple of Griesedieck Brothers beer that Volly always kept on ice.

"Have a beer, Joel Dean," Volly said. "This calls for a real celebration. My station is saved. The town is saved. Hell, the whole county is saved."

"Half the county's already sold their properties to that corporation for more money than they ever dreamed about," I said. "Now they'll be worrying about how they're going to get the money."

"Well, they can worry all they want," Lonnie said. He drank a long guzzle of beer, pulled the bottle down, drew a forearm across his lips and grinned. "That puts an end to all the speculation about hydro-electric turbines and lakes that stretch all the way to Warsaw. Did you know if that lake had gone in it would have flooded over a hundred caves?"

"And good riddance," Volley said. "Who wants to go in some damn dark and dingy cave full of snakes."

"Amen to that," I said. "Climb around in all the caves you want, Lonnie. I'll stay up here in the sunshine."

Lonnie had another drink of beer, grinned real big and said, "It's a good place to take a girl on a Sunday afternoon."

The joy about the bankruptcy faded fast. A fine mist that

threatened to turn into something serious hovered over us. I took breakfast at Mintons on that day to catch the mood of how the residents felt about a new report we'd read in the *St. Louis Globe Democrat* that the largest electric company in St. Louis had picked up the bankrupt hydro-electric company's permit to build the dam on the Osage in Bagnell and intended to proceed with that company's plans. Uncle Billy Jack was so distraught everyone worried about his well being.

We were all pretty quiet like it was a wake or something. Lonnie didn't have any jokes to tell and Rose appeared about ready to bust into tears. She was so wrought up about the dam she burned her biscuits; the first time I ever knew her to burn anything. No one mentioned it.

When all of us were done eating and sitting around the big mahogany table drinking our second cup of coffee, Volly said, "Seems like Linn Creek and Champ Gowan are in the same boat. Both could end up dying from the decisions made by somebody else."

"Joel Dean has a different take on Champ Gowan from the rest of us," Lonnie said. "What about the dam, Joel Dean? Is there any way to stop it now?"

"It's not a matter of justice like it is with Champ Gowan," I said. "It's a sacrifice. We sacrifice our town so they can build a bigger one in St. Louis. They need electricity to grow. They forgot how to live without it. Over there they call it progress."

"So what can we do?" Lonnie asked again.

"Gideon and the county judges are filing a suit in the State court, but the electric company owns most of the politicians in the state. Have to wait and see if they own the courts, too."

Volly said, "So if the courts rule against us, that's it for Linn Creek, huh?"

"Not necessarily," I said. "Gideon says the State Constitution requires a vote by two-thirds of the people to move the county seat. And there has to be enough people to sign a petition to even bring it up for a vote."

"You working with Gideon on the law suit?" Lonnie asked.

"I'm working to let Champ Gowan live," I said. I got up and shoved my chair under the table. "And if it comes to it, I'll be voting to let my town live."

Uncle Billy Jack said without looking up from his coffee cup, "You do and you'll be a loser twice."

The law suits over the St. Louis company's right to build a dam on the Osage was passed from the State court to the Federal District Court. I figured the jury would be deciding Champ's fate long before the courts decided the fate of our town. The feeling around town was pretty much the same as it always had been since the dam talk started. No one in Linn Creek believed it would ever be built. Still, almost all of us worried about it in the back of our minds.

I volunteered for the late shift at the jail. I had to work on my opening statement so I needed to put the dam out of my mind, or as much so as possible. I sat at Ora's big walnut rolltop desk and looked at a blank sheet of paper for so long I began to see visions there. To break the spell, I sharpened my pencil for the third time and began to write notes:

No proof.

No eyewitness to the shooting.

No record of violence.

It wasn't going well. I knew that I would have to prove Champ didn't kill Ora instead of Gideon proving that he did. There was nothing in the file Gideon had let me take out of the folder that would either incriminate Champ or exonerate him. Thumbing through it I saw a two inch by two inch photograph of vegetation which I assumed had been taken near where Ora had been shot. After studying it for awhile, I was sure an object near the center of the photograph was a gun lying on the ground. Probably Ora's .45 caliber automatic. The photograph had been taken with an Eastman box camera which had a fixed focus of six to eight feet. My statement was in the file as was Doyle's, Gideon's and Champ's. No surprise there. The surprise was the next statement in the file, one from Artis Monger. He and his son Murdoch had been the ones to discover Ora's body and me lying unconscious near by. Artis said they had been on their way to check some trot lines in Glaize Creek. Artis said they never moved anything and after determining Ora was dead and I was not, Artis left Murdoch to watch over me while he drove as fast as he could to Linn Creek and tell the deputy on duty, Doyle Savoy, what he'd found.

Artis' statement didn't strike me right. No one I knew ran their trot lines at night. I mean, why would you go stumbling around in the dark taking your lines in, getting fish off the hooks and putting bait back on in the dark when you could wait a couple of hours and do it in daylight?

And the fuel line, which was all right from Mexico to Artis' filling station, then, strangely, coming loose a few miles down the road. I remembered Artis with his head under the cowling that had been raised. I remember him walking away from the automobile after asking Ora if he was going to let up on the whiskey running now that he'd caught Shorty's killers. He'd walked away from the automobile leaving the cowling up, then he'd come back, but I couldn't recall whether he had stuck his head back under the cowling or not. And I remembered Ora having walked toward the back of the car to look in on the prisoners.

Excitement rushed through me. It could have been Artis. He could have loosened the fuel line, followed us across the Glaize and when we ran out of gas, he could have sneaked up on us in the dark, shined a bright hand torch, then shot Ora, pushed Champ down the bank and clobbered me over the head. After that, the Monger's whiskey would go through from Camden County.

Would a jury believe all that? Maybe not, but it might create some doubt. Reasonable doubt.

I had a defense!

The sun shone brighter and the air was clean and crisp the next morning. The kitchen in the jail house had that good morning smell of frying bacon and brewing coffee. The sunrays beaming through the windows laid big blocks of light on the linoleum floor. I couldn't hide my joy.

"You don't look like you're headed for a funeral," Champ said.

"I figured out last night who killed Ora," I said.

Well, that brought some heads up out of their plates. Addie frowned over her coffee cup and Champ lost his grin for just a moment.

Doyle said, "Just in the nick of time. Boy detective solves crime at last minute. Tell us who did it, junior special operative."

Birdie stood at the stove, hand on her hip staring at me.

"Artis Monger."

Everyone was quiet for a moment while they digested that.

"What led you to believe that?" Addie asked.

"How come the fuel line was fine until we stopped at the Mongers' store for gas? Artis was the only one could have loosened it. He checked the oil with Ora standing there watching him, but when he left—maybe to get a wrench—and came back Ora wasn't watching him and neither was I."

"Why would Artis Monger want Ora dead?" Doyle asked.

"Because Ora was stopping all the whiskey going out of the county. Eddie Simmons and a lot of others were selling to the Mongers, everybody knows that."

"How'd Artis get out there where Ora was killed?" Noah wanted to know.

"Easiest thing in the world. He follows us with the lights off in his automobile. He could see the road and he could see us by our lights."

Champ was rubbing his jaw again like he always did when he was thinking. I had expected him to be grinning even bigger after hearing my theory about the Mongers, but here he was turning philosophical.

"I don't know, Joel Dean," he said. "That's pretty far fetched."

"No more far fetched than the idea of you taking Ora's gun away from him and shooting him," I said. "Anybody knew Ora knows you nor nobody else ain't going to be able to do that. Look, Champ, we've got a difficult job here. Every juror we're going to be able to get, already thinks you're guilty. So instead of them proving you did it, we have to prove you didn't. Without an eyewitness we can't prove anything. So the next best thing is to create doubt in the jurors' minds."

"Speaking of eyewitnesses, what about that little weasel, Wilbur, and his gorilla friend, Buster?" Doyle asked, looking at

Champ. "Common sense tells me one or both of them saw who killed Ora or did it themselves."

Doyle kept his eyes on Champ, waiting to hear his thoughts.

Champ poured some fresh, hot coffee into his saucer, blew on it, then sipped.

"Don't know," he said, looking over the top of the saucer and across the table at Doyle. "It was pretty dark out there."

"Where you reckon they run to?" Doyle asked.

Champ shrugged.

Noah said, "You got pretty well acquainted. Seems to me like you got to have a good idea."

"Kansas City maybe," Champ said.

I asked Addie, "We notify the police in Kansas City?"

"Everywhere," she said.

"We get them back here, we've got a good defense," I said.

"Knowing Wilbur, I'll be hung by then," Champ said.

Picking a jury is like loaning money. Which one will pay you back and which one will welch on you. I had only been involved in selecting a jury one other time and that was working for Gideon. I had studied the Rules of Court Procedure the night before, but that's not the same as experience. Gideon was helpful and Judge Henry Black nodded off several times so I wasn't under a great deal of pressure.

Normally in our court the judge asks each prospective juror called a few elementary questions, but today the judge left that up to the attorneys. Gideon took the lead by asking if the person was related to the defendant, if they owed each other money, their occupation and had they formed an opinion about the defendant's guilt. It was clear early on that Gideon was willing to accept any juror as long as they weren't related to Champ.

By midmorning the heat was building in the courtroom and Gideon and I both agreed to take our jackets off. I had already sweated through my shirt which meant I was going to have to wash it out after court and press it early next morning.

Gideon looked pale and tired and plainly wanted to get the whole process over with. I started out asking each person called if he had been present at the arraignment. My purpose, of course, was to find out to what extent the judge's remarks that day had poisoned the jury pool. The answer was 100 percent.

By noon we had five jurors picked, two of them women. I figured Champ might be better off with the women jurors and so would I. They wouldn't have the experience of being on juries with better lawyers than me arguing cases.

Gideon and I took lunch at the jail where I filled everyone in on the progress.

"Joel Dean, I'm not going to challenge anyone this afternoon," Gideon said. "I've seen the list and there are no relatives on there. Pick anyone you want."

"You sound pretty sure of the outcome of the trial," I said. "I didn't see any evidence that strong."

"We're still working on some things. If any of them develop, I'll let you know."

"What sort of things?"

"Rather not say right now. Probably won't pan out anyway. We've already got all the evidence we need."

Which was to say, they didn't need any evidence. They already had the judge and jury.

LIMB OF THE JUDAS TREE

I okayed six of the first eight people Nancy Graham called after lunch. Gideon never rose out of his chair and the judge actually started snoring at one point. Every person called swore they could be impartial and could render a verdict on the evidence presented in court. I knew they were all ready to convict Champ, but if I excused everyone who had made up their mind, we wouldn't have a jury.

The next person called was Uncle Billy Jack Cummins. I had scanned the list but had failed to notice that he was listed as William. Jury selection had become a one-man process so I asked Uncle Billy Jack all the standard questions. He admitted he had already made up his mind—how could he tell me otherwise—but he believed, for the good of the county that he could render a fair verdict on the evidence presented.

He was dressed splendidly for an old man. The tie was the same plaid bow tie he always wore and the suspenders were the ones he always had under his coat on Sundays, but the shirt was new and so were the pants. He had made a special effort to look like a solid citizen ready to do his duty. I knew how badly he wanted to be on the jury. It would probably be his last opportunity to serve, and if Linn Creek was to end up in the bottom of a lake, Uncle Billy Jack wanted to be part of this one last big murder trial in the old courthouse.

Naturally I could not allow that. He had already told me how he felt about Champ, about all the Gowans. How if Champ wasn't guilty of this crime, he'd done enough to be hung for anyway. How could I possibly get a not-guilty verdict out of a person like that?

I looked into Uncle Billy Jack's eyes and saw all the old men who had lived in this town and thought of all the young men who would never have the chance to grow old here.

"Accepted," I said, and the jury who would decide Champ Gowan's life was in place.

The early fall evening was a trifle cool, especially since Estelle had the top down on her little black and yellow Jordan roadster. I climbed in over the passenger door and Estelle leaned over to kiss me.

"You've been working too hard, Joel Dean," she said. "I'm driving you up to Zebra for a real nice dinner at Mamie Crouse's and a few libations."

"No drinking for me till this trial is over," I told her. "Have to keep my mind unfettered by alcohol."

"Oh, poo," she said. "It'll do you good."

She drove like a swarm of bees was after us, sliding around curves, soaring over hills. My stomach was in no mood for supper when we pulled up in front of a run-down tin roofed barn with a dozen cars parked outside. I'd been in Mamie Crouse's before, but I never felt comfortable around the clientele she served. Though I'd never had proof of it, I understood from Doyle and Lonnie that Mamie was the best cook in three counties.

Mamie was a large woman with sparkling eyes. She wore a frilly gown that must have taken several bolts of good quality cloth to put together. She greeted Estelle too warmly to suit me—indicating Estelle had frequented the place more often than I wanted to think about.

After squeezing Estelle to her ample bosom and kissing her on both cheeks, Mamie fixed her eyes on me as if I was on her personal menu.

"Joel Dean Gregory," she said and squeezed me tightly to her and kissed me smack dab on the mouth. "Why you're ever bit as handsome as Estelle tells me you are. And I hear you're making quite a name for yourself in court these days."

I didn't know what to make of her. She led us through her neat and clean kitchen where the smell of roast pork flavored the air and helped change my mind about something to eat.

Mamie sat us down at one end of a large dining table that appeared to be part of her living quarters. I had never been in this part of Mamie's, in fact, didn't know it existed. At the other end of the table Mamie's daughter Lilac sat talking with an older man. I made him out to be a St. Louis drummer. Rumor had it that Mamie frequently rented Lilac out to rich traveler's and even rented herself out on occasion.

Lilac spoke warmly to Estelle and the two seemed more familiar with each other than I cared to learn about. Lilac knew my name and spoke to me, then introduced us to her companion, a Mr. Jones. I wondered how Mamie and Lilac were able to keep all the Jones who stayed there straight in their mind.

Mamie brought in a gin type drink for all of us, but I declined. She followed up with the supper. The word about her cooking had not been exaggerated. We chatted the length of the table with the other couple as we ate. When Mr. Jones found out we were from Linn Creek, he asked what was going to become of the town.

"I guess we'll know after the courts rule on it," I said.

"According to the *Globe Democrat* in St. Louis the court has already decided. They're not saying for sure, but two days ago eight carloads of lumber and a hundred men unloaded at a little town called Bagnell at the end of a railroad spur."

A big lump came up in my throat and I couldn't swallow.

"I just can't believe that," Estelle said. "It don't matter anyway what the court says. Only the people can vote to move the county seat and people in my town aren't going to vote to send it to the bottom of some lake just so St. Louis can have more electricity."

"The electric company says it's no business of theirs where you have your county offices. They can be thirty feet under water if that's where you want them," Jones said.

Mamie came through the door with four pieces of cream pie that had meringue piled three inches high.

"Mamie," I said, "I'll have that drink now."

There were two cars parked outside besides Estelle's little black and yellow roadster. Murdoch Monger stood next to one of them talking with two men I didn't know. Murdoch was pretty intoxicated, his voice loud and rough with words not meant for a lady's ears. He saw Estelle and me.

"Joel Dean, how the hell are you? I haven't seen you since the night you damn near shot all of us with that Thompson."

"Except the night Ora was shot," I said.

"That? Oh, yeah. Right. Bad. Too damn bad," Murdoch tried to stifle his grin but he was only partly successful.

"Thompsons are hard to control," I said.

"Ain't that the truth. Way I do it, I hold the barrel down on mine cause it always wants to rise up when you're shooting it. Fact is, I put a little short strap around the barrel to hold her down."

I guess that stopped me in my tracks because there I was facing Murdoch.

"Well, now, that's odd," I said. "The one we found in the barn where Champ and them were sleeping had a strap on it just like that."

Murdoch had a queer look on his face when we left.

A good thing happened on the first day of the trial—it turned cool. There were as many people outside the courthouse as there were inside. The windows were slid all the way open and, although the courtroom was on the second floor, clusters of people stood under the windows listening, hoping to hear the trial going on inside.

I pushed myself to be calm, to be professional, to be just like Gideon Norfleet would be, but when I looked inward all I found was me. That was going to have to do. I looked around the courtroom, hoping people could not see the anxiety I felt. They were stacked against the wall, three and four deep, all the way around the room on three sides. Most of the people I knew, some I did not.

A reporter I knew from the *Capital City News* in Jefferson City

City sat on the front row, a ruled tablet on a folded leg, his pocket full of sharpened pencils.

Champ chewed on a matchstick looking as contented as a cow lying in the shade. Who's on trial for his life here, him or me?

Ellis Wayne, the bailiff, called out, "Oyez, oyez, the Circuit Court of Camden County is now in session. Judge Henry Black presiding. All rise."

Judge Henry Black entered ahead of his flowing robe and climbed to his seat atop the bench. He tapped one time with the gavel and called the court to order. He said all the standard words, but I was tuned out, still rehearsing my opening statement. I knew Gideon's would be good. It always was.

Gideon brought himself to his full height, looking regal and official. He began his opening statement in a somber serious tone. "This is not theater," he said. "This is the real thing. We are going to decide on taking a man's life, because he took someone else's life. We are going to scrutinize every fact; we are going to question every witness. We are going to determine if this man had a motive, an opportunity and a means to kill Ora Mitchell and we are going to look at the proof in a very deliberate manner. And only then will we make that awful decision. That this defendant did in fact have the motive, the opportunity and the means to kill Ora Mitchell and the proof, the facts offered up by the State, will convince you that this defendant, Champion Gowan, did indeed commit murder."

Then he sat down and looked over at me.

I felt a trickle of sweat going down the center of my back. I stared at the jury until they became uncomfortable and shifted their eyes away. The audience in the courtroom grew restless waiting for me to begin my statement. Champ glanced over at me and Judge Henry Black leaned forward and picked up his gavel. Gideon turned his head to look at me. The courtroom was as still as a cold morning in the woods.

I rose slowly, straightened my necktie that Rose Minton had

tied so stylishly for me, rubbed the wrinkles out of the front of my suit coat and walked stiffly to the front of the jury box and placed my hands on the railing. And I smiled.

"My name is Joel Dean Gregory. You already know me. I know you. Some of you have said before you came in today that you believe the accused is guilty. That he should hang for the crime he's accused of. You've said that before you've heard one piece of evidence. The prosecutor said this is not theater, but I'm going to engage in theater here today. Theater is the act of suspending belief. You see an actor you know on stage, but when he starts acting, and if he's good, you forget his real name and he becomes the character he's playing. So I'm going to suspend belief and all of you are going to become people I don't know. People who haven't already decided guilt in this case. And I'm going to ask the same of you. Look at the accused as if he is John Doe. Don't look at him as a mischievous kid about town or a young man who has made mistakes in the past. He's John Doe. Did John Doe kill Ora Mitchell or did he not?

"Ora Mitchell was my friend. He was the best man I ever knew. You will hear me testify for the prosecution on what I remember the night my friend was killed. I have to tell you, I feel guilt in my friend's death. I can't convince myself I am not at fault. I should have been able to prevent Ora Mitchell's death. I will not rest; I will not sleep through the night until the person who killed him is caught. But that person is not Champ Gowan. And that's why I'm standing here before you. The prosecutor says the accused is guilty because he had the motive, the opportunity and the means to commit the crime. But not the prosecutor, not you, not anyone can know about the motive. Only the accused knows his state of mind concerning Ora Mitchell. You can guess at it, but is a guess what we want to send people to the gallows with?

"As far as the opportunity and the means to kill Ora Mitchell, I had opportunity and means, also. Should I be put on trial for killing my friend? Others had opportunity and means, too. And we will examine that as the trial goes on.

"If you can think of the accused as John Doe not Champ Gowan, and if you sit back and make the prosecutor prove without doubt that John Doe killed Ora Mitchell, I think you'll do the right thing. I think you'll decide guilt or innocence on what you hear in this courtroom. And I'm confident it won't be proof enough to hang this man."

Completely spent, I found my way back to my chair and sat down, glancing at Gideon as I did. He nodded with approval at me. That meant a lot. Champ leaned over to whisper, "If they'd stop this thing now, they'd have to turn me loose."

But trials are more than opening statements, as we were about to see.

I was the first witness for the prosecution. Gideon extracted the information he needed to prove Champ was a passenger in the motor car we had borrowed in Mexico that night. And that it was when Champ got out of the car that I heard the shot and saw the light before someone hit me over the head.

Gideon was very good at interrogation. I was taking notes in my head all the time I was answering questions. For cross examination we had agreed I would just give a narrative instead of asking myself questions. That was how I got in the information Wilbur Crowder and Buster Workman were also in the car and that I couldn't be sure no one else was there because I couldn't see in the dark. Setting my trap for the Mongers.

I glanced again at Gideon when I finished and he gave me another nod of approval.

Doyle testified about what was found at the scene when he and Gideon arrived there. Gideon particularly emphasized Ora's .45 caliber automatic pistol. Doyle said, yes, they had found the gun about thirty feet from Ora's body in underbrush as the photograph I had seen in the case folder clearly indicated. Doyle said one shell had been discharged in Ora's gun because the clip was one bullet short of full. A spent .45 caliber cartridge shell was found six feet from Ora's body. Doyle testified that he took the gun from the place they had found it after Gideon had snapped a photograph of it, wrapped it in a clean handkerchief and returned with it to Linn Creek.

In cross examination I concentrated on the cartridge shell that had been found close to Ora's body.

"Did the shell come from Ora's pistol?"

"Well, I assume it did."

"Why do you assume that?"

"Because I don't know anyone else in the county who owns a gun like that. It's the official army weapon and they're hard to come by."

"But you can't say positively where the shell came from."

"There's no way of knowing for sure. But if there's fresh horse manure in the corral and only one horse in there, you're bound to have a strong suspicion."

Laughter bubbled up from the people gathered inside the courtroom, like they were trying to stifle it, but just couldn't hold back. The jury squirmed a bit, trying to keep a plain face. I expected Judge Henry Black to gavel the crowd to order, but he was smiling hugely along with the onlookers so finally I turned toward the jury and showed them my smile, enjoying Doyle's joke along with them.

I placed my hands on the railing to the jury box and, facing them—still smiling—asked, "What if you find sheep manure in the corral and no sheep. Would you assume that came from the horse?"

Doyle grinned real big, shifted around in the witness chair and said, "No, I think I know my manure pretty well."

Doyle had the crowd laughing again along with him.

"Now, Deputy Savoy, since you seem to know more about manure than you do cartridge shells, let's continue along that line. Suppose you're walking through a pasture without a fence around it and there's a pile of horse manure a day old and a dead horse close by. Would you be willing to say—with a man's life depending on your answer—that that pile of manure came from that dead horse?"

Gideon came to his feet. "Objection, Your Honor. Immaterial. We're not talking about manure. The subject is a cartridge from the victim's gun. A cartridge that held the bullet that killed Ora Mitchell."

"We don't know either of those allegations to be fact, Your Honor," I said. "The prosecution can't prove that cartridge came from Ora Mitchell's gun. They can't prove Ora Mitchell's gun was fired that night. And they can't prove the accused had anything to do either with the gun or with the cartridge. It is the prosecution's witness who has trouble telling a pile of horse manure from the evidence."

Now I had the crowd and the jury laughing with me. I walked to my chair and sat down, pretending to busy myself with the papers before me. Like in one of the tennis matches I had watched at Drury College, the point was over and I had won it.

Judge Henry Black had an objection from the prosecution to rule on.

"Can the prosecution prove any of the points the defense raises?" he asked.

"My next witness may shed some light on those matters, Your Honor," Gideon said.

"Then the objection is sustained. Let's pitch the horse manure out the window and move on to the next witness," Judge Henry Black said, tapping his gavel lightly on the bench. The crowd tittered and the jury smiled as Judge Henry Black leaned back in his chair, seemingly pleased that he had been able to get in on the humorous exchanges.

I was feeling pretty good about how I'd handled the cartridge shell evidence and Ora's gun. But any smugness or satisfaction I felt had a very short life. Gideon called a man named A. J. Renoe to the stand. A man whose presence on the witness stand would alter the trial in a way no one expected.

I had noticed the name on the witness list and the description as a government expert witness. But in my inexperience I had overlooked Mr. Renoe and shoved it to the back of my mind while I dwelled on just exactly how I was going to get the Mongers on the witness stand.

But now I had this crawly feeling up the back of my neck when the distinguished looking Mr. Renoe took the stand. He was dressed in an expensive blue suit with a vest and wore a very serious look on his face. I knew right away from the manner in which he strode to the witness chair and the self-confident way he took the oath that I had erred seriously in not checking him out and I had the feeling I was about to pay for that mistake.

Renoe was an employee of the Justice Department in a section that was newly formed called the Federal Bureau of Investigation. He was in charge of the Identification Division and described his main responsibility as establishing a means of identifying people from their fingerprints. He stated that the fingerprints of every individual were unique and that no two were the same, not even identical twins. He went on to say that the Federal Bureau of Investigation had the largest collection of fingerprints in the country since forming the division in 1924 by combining the two largest collections of fingerprints and classifying them.

Renoe ticked off the numbers of convictions in courts throughout the country that had been settled by the admission of fingerprints in the court proceedings.

I was completely blind sided. I had vaguely read about fingerprints, the FBI and government operatives in general in the *True Crime* magazines and in the *Grit* newspaper in the Dutchman's Barber Shop. Where this was leading I did not know, but I had a sickly feeling about it in the pit of my stomach.

The jury appeared to be greatly impressed with Mr. Renoe as if he was sharing some new scientific breakthrough with them. I tried to look stoic in case they glanced at me, but I knew the color had completely drained from my face.

First Gideon brought forth Ora's .45 caliber automatic pistol, it's blackness looking ominous in the quiet courtroom. Judge Henry Black allowed its admission as evidence as he did a water glass which Gideon set beside the pistol on the table before the witness. The glass looked exactly like the ones used in the kitchen at the jail house.

Ora's pistol had smudges of chalk like dust on the blued metal while the drinking glass had smudges of lampblack on it. I knew where it was leading and my stomach came right up into my throat and I came close to losing my dinner.

Gideon established the identity of the pistol and told the jury he had personally removed the drinking glass from the table at the jail and that Champ Gowan had drank from it.

Gideon asked Renoe, "Do the prints on that water glass match the prints on the barrel of Sheriff Ora Mitchell's pistol?"

Renoe said, "Yes, they do."

"So you're testifying that the defendant's fingerprints were on the sheriff's gun after finding him shot and killed."

"Yes, that's correct."

"Without a doubt?"

"With no doubt whatsoever. It has been scientifically proven. The fingerprints came from the same person."

"What else did you find on the gun?"

"On the butt of the pistol were several hairs and some skin fragments."

Gideon continued, "And is the presence of the hair and the skin fragments consistent with the head wounds suffered by Deputy Joel Dean Gregory that night to such an extent that the pistol could have been the weapon used to club Deputy Gregory into unconsciousness?"

I found myself on my feet immediately, my face burning at the mention of my name and at the humiliation I felt for being duped on allowing Renoe to get past my notice.

"I object, Your Honor," came out of my mouth, then I searched my brain for some legal reasoning on which to base that objection.

"Basis?" Judge Henry Black asked, appearing to be the most disinterested person in the court.

"Well, I, that is, for a lot of reasons, Your Honor. First off, this man Renoe has never examined my wounds. And it seems to me the prosecutor is leading him. Let the man make up his own mind. And the prosecutor brings in a deputy as an expert on handling evidence and he turns out to be an expert on horse manure. Now he brings in this man Renoe as a fingerprinting expert who he's trying to pass off as a skin expert and a hair expert and he's trying to turn him into an eyewitness to the crime when there was none."

"Sustained," Judge Henry Black said lazily. "Gideon, I'll allow your witnesses' testimony on the skin and the hair if you can offer any scientific proof of their origin, but that's as far as you can go with that."

"I withdraw the question, Your Honor," Gideon said.

Oh, sure. As if the jury hadn't heard it.

Then Judge Henry Black did another favor, surprising me even further. He adjourned for the day and said he would allow cross examination of Renoe tomorrow morning.

I had 18 hours to find a question for him that would make the jury forget that Champ Gowan had his hands on Ora's gun. Might as well be 18 days.

Judge Black let the jury leave before adjourning court. I sat there beside Champ, the sweat running a river down my backbone, mad as hell at him for touching Ora's pistol and began to have my most serious doubt about my client's innocence.

No member of the jury looked at me or at Champ as they filed out. I didn't like what that meant. Out of the corner of my eye I could see Champ sprawled in his chair chewing on a match.

The air inside the courtroom was still and heavy after the crowd left out the back doors and it smelled of sweaty bodies. What had started out as a cool early-fall morning had escalated into a late summer sweltering afternoon. My suit coat and my pants looked as if I'd wrestled alligators in the swamp while wearing them. I would have to put them under the mattress and sleep on them if the wrinkles were to ever come out.

When the courtroom was empty of spectators, I took off my jacket and stood there in my wringing-wet shirt as Gideon came across the well to place a hand on my shoulder.

"You did well today, Joel Dean."

The anger I felt toward him for bringing in Renoe vanished when I turned to look into a face the color of ashes with a sweaty sheen on top.

"Gideon, did you go see Doc Hardesty?" I asked him.

"Not yet."

He took an already soaked handkerchief from a back pocket and mopped his face and neck.

"He can wait until this is over."

"Don't put it off, Gideon," I said. "See Judge Black and have him delay this for a day or two. See Doc Hardesty. Get some rest."

"No, no, I'm fine. I'll be through early in the morning. Can you finish by the end of the day?"

"Probably. Depends on what else you throw at us."

"Good. We can give our closings the next morning and send it to the jury by noon. Shouldn't take them long."

"Go ahead and take Joel Dean's advice, Gideon," Champ said. "I ain't in any hurry."

"I'm fine," Gideon said. He patted me on the back. "You're doing well, Joel Dean. I'm sorry you have to lose this one."

I watched Gideon shuffle out through the back doors, looking like a man twenty years older than a week ago. I truly worried about his well being.

The room began to breathe after the crowd had tromped out. A cooling breeze pushed through the screened windows and soothed my skin under the wet shirt. I pulled on my jacket and looked at Champ who was watching me.

"You thought it went bad, didn't you?" he asked. "About the gun, I mean."

"Did you handle that gun, Champ?"

"Hell, I guess I must have. I sure don't remember doing it."

"You should have told me, Champ. That hurt us. You handled the gun that killed Ora. That removes Wilbur and Buster as suspects and makes it difficult to tie it to the Mongers. When the jury goes into that room to deliberate, they have to explain your handling the gun. That's pretty weak, saying you did it but you forgot."

"Sounds like you don't believe it, Joel Dean."

"It's no longer important what I believe. I worry about what the jury believes. Gideon gives me his approval and pats me on the back, but look what he did to us at the end of the day. Now all those jurors are going to go home and think all night about you

247

handling that gun."

"I wasn't thinking, I'll admit that. Ora was the first dead man I guess I'd seen that wasn't in a casket. I curled up next to a tree and sat there all night without sleeping. Only thing on my mind was would Addie think I did it."

"Guess you can stop worrying about that. She does."

The night was as quiet as a cat on carpet. Up Linn Creek where the oaks whispered softly and the water trickled lightly, a whippoorwill began his lonesome call. I stood on the step before the jail house door looking up into the sky and guessed at the names of the constellations I had known by heart when I was ten. A solitary light bulb burned inside Volly Newell's closed filling station across the street and one glowed faintly through the windows of Yawley's general store. It was just me and the locusts and that old whippoorwill who had business out here tonight.

Addie objected but I had insisted on the night shift again. I had some serious thinking to do. My day in court had been as bad as Noah's on his 40th day in the ark. My situation was hopeless and I felt great despair. But, maybe—like with Noah—the rain was over.

Tomorrow Gideon would end the prosecution's case and I would have to try and get twelve people to believe Champ Gowan never murdered Ora Mitchell when I wasn't sure I believed it any longer myself.

When I walked out the door to stand in the night, I planned to search for some way to put together my defense for Champ. I had tried to concentrate on the Mongers and how I was going to get the jury to believe they could have been on the Glaize road that night and that they could have been the ones who shot Ora. But I couldn't imagine every member of the jury not having a picture in their mind of Champ holding Ora's gun as he stood over his body.

It was hopeless. I had to stop thinking about the trial.

Looking up Main Street I imagined I could see me on Lonnie Harper's new bicycle and I saw me run smack dab into one of the posts in front of Yawley's store while gawking at the cute girl standing there with a lollypop in her mouth. She couldn't have been more than eleven or twelve and though I was 15 already, I had never seen a female as pretty as that one. She didn't dress like the other girls in town. Her dress looked expensive and stylish because, according to Lonnie, Yawley sent her to St. Louis to school and she only came to Linn Creek in the summer.

I had seen her before, but at a distance and never even thought about being brave enough to speak to her. As I lay spread out in the dirt at her feet after flying over the handlebars of Lonnie's bike, she took the lollypop out of her mouth and said, "If you damage my daddy's store, I expect you'll have to pay for it."

I remembered getting up from the ground like a clumsy oaf and dusting myself off. She had leaned down and picked up my tweed cap that was too little for me and held it out. I jammed it on my head and mumbled thanks.

She said, "You're Joel Dean Gregory aren't you?"

When I managed to nod my head she said, "I've been keeping

my eye on you."

I walked on down Main Street looking up at the big old redbud tree that Champ had called the Judas tree. It's branches looked dark against the starry sky and the half-full moon reflected off silvery patches in the bark. The jail house looked drab as did the courthouse, but there was a comfort about them as if they were my home, which I guess they were.

The stores and houses along the street were blocks against the sky and the trees rose above them and spread their limbs over them to shield and protect. Main Street was a street of white limestone gravel bordered by one and two-story structures sitting high on flood-proof concrete curbs and littered with dead branches and milkweed stalks, tobacco wrappers and grocery flyers with an occasional well-aged pile of horse dung that even Doyle Savoy wouldn't be able to trace for lineage.

Down Mercer Street cutting in from the north was Widow Hankin's house that had been purchased by her husband as a wedding present in 1862, just before he went off to fight for the Union at a place called Gettysburg. A place where he remained. In all those years she never remarried. On the porch were the two rockers; one for her, one for him. She rocked there in the evenings with a shawl over her knees and one spread over the vacant rocker.

Across the street lived the Allins, all twelve of them. Harold Allin lost a leg in a tie slide near Bagnell, but he had managed to make a living since for his wife and ten children who were always dressed in clean, threadbare shirts and dresses and wore the look of absolute contentment on their faces.

And down the street were the Cardmans who had lost three children in an accidental drowning in the river. And Boris Schlegleman, the German, who had almost been run out of town in 1918 and who drank heavily and beat his wife on occasion.

My town, its good and its bad.

As I looked at the town, tears began to run down my cheeks.

250

Tears, not because I was going to lose a court case, and tears not for a man who lived his life on the edge and now he was going to have to pay for it, but tears for my town which would be dead before any of us—except maybe Champ—and all that would remain would be the memories as what is became what was.

The greasy smell of cured bacon frying in the pan failed to jolt my brain awake. You don't lie awake until two in the morning and crawl off the cot in the front office at five ready to take on the world.

Birdie laid four slices of bacon on my plate and two eggs sunny side up. The yolks stared at me, daring me, challenging me. I stared back, unable to muster the strength to jab my fork into the yolk and watch the yellow run.

Across the table Champ was munching bacon out of his left hand and scooping up the disgusting looking runny eggs on his fork with his right. He laid the fork down long enough to slurp from his coffee mug. He finished off the bacon, licking the fingers on his left hand and took the glass of water in that hand and drank until the glass was empty. He looked across the table to see me watching.

"Eat up, Joel Dean. We gotta go after that government man today."

"I'll be there," I said. "Right up to the bitter end."

Noah took the prisoners upstairs and left me and Addie sitting at the table. Addie looked at my plate.

"Not getting scared are you?"

"It may sound late in the match, but I've got to come up with a defense for Champ."

"Don't put him on the stand."

"Why not? What do you know that I don't?"

"I know that if the people in that jury see Champ Gowan in the witness chair, they're not going to believe anything he says. Besides, I know Champ. You can never predict what he's going to say."

"May not be necessary to put him on the stand," I said. "But I do need to talk to Birdie."

"You need more than that. You need a shirt that don't look like the dog wore it before you did."

One of the jurors was late and Judge Henry Black kept us waiting for thirty minutes at our tables and in the pews. I asked Nancy Graham if I could examine the glass and the pistol Gideon had entered as prosecution exhibits yesterday. She looked at the judge who nodded and she took them carefully from a small wooden case with a pair of metal tongs. and set them on the table in front of her.

"You can't touch them, Joel Dean," she said. "Might destroy evidence."

Like a kid at a museum, I smiled and I walked around and around the table examining the evidence from all sides. Everyone in the courtroom watched. When finally the court was gaveled into session and the jury seated, I was still circling the evidence and gawking at the glass and the gun. Now, the jury watched me, too.

Judge Henry Black said, "If the defense counsel is ready he can commence to cross examine the prosecution witness."

"A few more minutes, Your Honor. This is my first opportunity to examine these prosecution exhibits close up. I wonder if it might be possible to pass these around to the jury, Your Honor? I'm going to have some detailed questions about these exhibits and the jury needs to see them up close."

"Well, I'm not sure about that," Judge Henry Black said. He looked at Gideon. "Does the prosecution have any objections?"

Gideon said he did not as long as they weren't touched.

Nancy had Ellis Wayne, the bailiff, help her and the exhibits were passed around to the jury members one by one on a board. They looked at the exhibits, but of course they didn't know what it was they were supposed to see.

When I told Judge Henry Black I was ready to begin the cross examination, he called A.J. Renoe to the witness chair and reminded him he was still under oath.

Renoe sat smugly looking out at the court, his broad forehead tanned and his brown hair slicked back. He had on a different suit today, a gray woolen expensive looking piece of clothing, well pressed with creases down the pant legs. The shirt was gleaming white as was the handkerchief that was neatly folded in the breast pocket. The tie was black and tan and red diagonal stripes and was probably silk. Gideon wore an identical tie, the stripes the same as Renoe's.

I said good morning to A.J. Renoe who smiled back at me and returned the greeting. I asked for and received permission from the judge to approach the witness. I stood next to his chair, leaning against the railing beside the chair. By contrast with his attire, I knew my suit, my shirt and my shoes looked downright shabby. But I wagered to myself that most of the men in the jury had a suit at home that looked more like mine than A. J. Renoe's.

I asked Nancy Graham to place the board and the drinking glass on the table beside the witness chair.

"Do you see that print right there, Mr. Renoe?" I asked, pointing with my finger several inches away from the glass.

"Which one, sir?" Mr. Renoe asked. I think he threw in the sir to emphasize the difference in our ages and thus the difference in our experience. I saw several members of the jury smile at the absurdity of a man of his age addressing a young pup like me as sir.

Grandpa Gregory used to say, "The squirrel that climbs the highest has the farthest to fall when you shoot him."

I turned to Champ at the witness table. "Champ, toss that pencil over to me, will you?"

Champ leaned over, picked the pencil up with his left hand, transferred it to his right and tossed it neatly into my hands.

"Now then, Mr. Renoe," I said, pointing with the pencil. "I'm talking about that set of prints right there."

Renoe gave barely a glance at the dusted ridges and whorls darkened with lampblack.

"Yes, I see that particular set of prints rather easily."

"Were those prints made with the left hand or the right hand?" I asked.

"Left hand," Renoe said confidently.

"And they match a print or prints on the victim's pistol?"

"Yes, that's correct."

I asked Nancy Graham to place the board carrying the .45 caliber pistol on the witness's table beside the board that carried the glass.

"Now, Mr. Renoe, would you point out the prints on the pistol that match the prints on the drinking glass."

"Certainly," Renoe said. He extracted a very expensive looking ink pen from his pocket and pointed to a chalk smudge on the flat side of the barrel of the pistol.

"Looking at the location of those fingerprints, would you be able to tell the jury how the defendant was holding that pistol?"

"Certainly."

"Your Honor, if I could borrow Deputy Wayne's revolver for a moment I would like for the jury to see the exact position of the accused's hand on the victim's gun when those prints were made."

Judge Henry Black made a motion with his hand and I took that as an affirmative gesture. Ellis Wayne handed me his revolver and I handed it to Renoe.

"Now, hold that revolver in the position the defendant held the victim's pistol in order to make the prints you just pointed out."

Renoe put Ellis Wayne's revolver in his left hand. He held it with the butt of the revolver pointing up in the air."

"Now, Mr. Renoe, from the position of the prints on that pistol, that would be the way it was being held was it not?"

"Approximately," Renoe said.

"Not held like a hammer that could be used to hit someone over the head with. Because that would reverse the position of the fingers, wouldn't it?"

"Yes, it would."

"So the person who made these prints was not using it as a club to hit me or anyone else over the head when he left those prints. Is that not correct?"

"Objection," Gideon said without rising. "Calls for speculation."

"But he's an expert, Your Honor. Came all the way from Washington D.C. as a favor to an old school chum wearing the same tie. He has the credentials of an expert. Let him answer. What is the prosecution trying to do, impeach his own witness?"

"Overruled," the judge said. "The witness may answer."

"He would not have been using the pistol as a club at the time the prints were made."

"As a matter of fact, the accused is right handed if you noticed when he tossed the pencil to me. If he was going to hit me over the head with that pistol hard enough to knock me unconscious, he would have used his right hand wouldn't he?"

"Objection. Speculation. Leading the witness."

"Overruled," Judge Henry Black said from his almost semi-prone position lying back in his chair.

"Yes," Renoe said, "in my opinion he would have used his right hand."

"But you didn't find any prints from his right hand on the pistol, did you?"

"No complete ones, no."

"No prints of any kind that you could say positively with a man's life at stake that they were made with the right hand."

"No. None."

"And you checked for them, didn't you. The prosecution brought you a coffee cup and eating utensils with the accused's finger prints from his right hand on them, didn't he? He didn't bring them up here for exhibit, but he brought them to you, didn't he?"

"Yes, he did."

"And you checked the barrel where the pistol would be held if it was used as a weapon and checked the smooth metal on the inside of the butt between the butt and the trigger guard and on the trigger and never found the accused's fingerprints did you?"

"Not enough to identify."

"So you have absolutely no proof whatsoever that the accused ever fired that pistol, do you? And you can present this jury with no proof he ever used that pistol to hit anyone over the head with can you?"

"No."

"But there are lots of prints on that gun. Just look at all the chalk dust on there. Did you identify any of those prints?"

"No, I did not."

"Other than the victim's prints, did you try and match those prints with fingerprints belonging to anyone else?"

"No."

"Not with my prints?"

"No."

"Not with Sheriff Addie Mitchell's prints?"

"No."

"Not with the prints of the ex-convicts Buster Workman and Wilbur Crowder whose prints are on file at the state penitentiary?"

"No."

"Not with the prints of Artis Monger who found the body?"

"No."

"So the prosecution came to this courtroom, not to punish the guilty, but to punish the accused without any evidence whatsoever."

My voice had reached a fever pitch and with my last words I turned sharply to face Gideon who was rising, red of face, jabbing his finger at me and forming words that never came out of his mouth. He took two steps away from his table, staggered back, clutched at his throat and crumpled toward the floor.

Champ was out of his chair in a flash and caught Gideon under the arms, easing him down. A murmuring hush went through the crowd as I rushed to kneel beside Gideon. His face was ashen and his eyes stared out at me.

"Somebody get Doc Hardesty," I yelled.

Doc Hardesty was a court onlooker that day. He came rushing forward carrying his black bag. He took a stethoscope from his bag and checked for a heart beat. His fingers searched the side of Gideon's throat for a pulse. After long moments with the crowd now in full fledged jabbering, Doc Hardesty looked up at Bertha who had come running to kneel across Gideon's body from the doctor.

"I'm sorry Bertha," Doc said. "I can't find a pulse."

Bertha Norfleet went chalk white. Tears formed in her eyes as her jaw firmed and she grasped both of her husband's hands in hers. She looked upward as if searching for someone or something. Then she slowly closed her eyes and let the tears flow. She sobbed twice, then bowed over Gideon's body and laid her head upon his chest. The audience was absolutely still and quiet. Outside the open windows, I heard someone asking, "What's going on? What's happening."

The Dutchman, who had closed his barber shop to attend the trial, walked to a window, stuck his head out and said in a very low accent, "It's Gideon Norfleet. By golly he's dead."

I placed my hand on my friend's lifeless arm and closed my eyes. Dear God, what next?

From the creek bank we watched the cold gray light of early morning turn golden. Lonnie Harper, Volly Newell and me. We started doing this the morning after Lonnie's collie had died and we swore we'd do it every time someone or something close to us died. But we hadn't.

This morning I felt like doing something that let out my feelings about Gideon. I'd left Mintons while the moon still ruled the morning sky and after wandering aimlessly around town, found myself here on the river bank when the first line of fire appeared on the ridge to the east. Lonnie and Volly came along later, sat beside me without saying anything and the three of us watched as the great sun ball rose over Rifle Ridge and the fog over the creek began to vanish.

"I think I pushed him too hard at the trial," I said. "The last thing I said about him in court was plain mean."

"Here we go again," Volly said, looking at Lonnie but tilting his head toward me. "Somebody dies and Joel Dean takes the blame."

"What's the last thing you said to Gideon?" I asked Volly.

"I think yesterday I said good morning when he walked by the station."

"He taught me so much," I said. "He made a point yesterday to tell me I'd done good at the trial. Everybody who means anything to me is dying. You boys better watch out."

"We'll watch ourselves," Lonnie said. "Everybody said you were one hell of a lawyer in court yesterday. Said you tied that government man up in knots."

"He came back to help his friend and now that friend is dead," I said. "I don't know how I can face him now. Or Bertha, either. She was there. She heard what I said that caused Gideon to get so upset his heart stopped beating."

"Well, you can check with Doc Hardesty," Volly said, "but I think it takes more than mean words to stop your heart. If that's all it took I'd a been dead twenty times last week. Whew, let me tell you those city people get under your skin in a hurry. Especially those from St. Louis."

"Champ caught Gideon before he even hit the floor. Anybody tell you that?"

They both shook their head.

"He moved so quick you could hardly see him. Caught him under the arms and just eased him down to the floor. That wasn't something you have time to plan. It just happens and what's in your heart comes out. That's what I meant by Champ not being able to just up and shoot somebody."

"You going to get him off?" Lonnie asked.

"I don't know. If it was a tennis match I think prosecution would be facing match point. That is if I don't mess up. But the truth is, of course, the vote was taken before the trial ever started. I expect they'll find him guilty."

"What'll you do then, take over Gideon's job?" Volly asked.

"I don't know. Addie's up for re-election next year, if she runs. In a couple of years the whole government in this county will be moving into the new town they're building. Who knows what's going to happen."

"Maybe the dam won't be so bad," Lonnie said. "Me and Volly's opening up a new station with two mechanic bays."

I stared at the sun as it grew brighter. And hotter.

"He never said anything," I said. "If he'd opened his eyes and said you did good, Joel Dean, then maybe I'd a got some sleep last night."

Volly got up from the river bank and dusted off the seat of his pants. He walked off down the street toward Minton's Boarding House and Lonnie and I fell in behind.

The day we buried Gideon Norfleet started out gray and gloomy with a light rain falling off and on during the morning. Bertha Norfleet asked me to be a pallbearer and told me there were no hard feelings about what I had said to Gideon that morning he died in court. I felt a great relief over that.

"You said what you said because you were defending a man in court, Joel Dean," she said. "And you may have had reason. Everybody was ready to hang that man before the trial ever began. Gideon said it was going to be easier to get a conviction than any trial he'd ever had. He was surprised at how well you did in court and he was proud of you."

"That means a lot to me, Bertha. Gideon helped me more than anyone. I feel lost, now. I don't know exactly how to go on."

"You'll do fine," she had said, patting me on the arm. "I have a feeling Gideon'll be watching you."

I wasn't anxious to go back into court and it didn't appear I would have to for awhile. Judge Henry Black had asked the attorney general's office to assign a new prosecutor, but as far as I knew, that had not been done. I figured several weeks before a new prosecutor could be caught up on the trial and be ready to step in for Gideon. I was glad for the time off. I had a lot of thinking to do.

Mr. A.J. Renoe left town right after the funeral. I guess Judge Henry Black told him it would be all right. The judge never asked me if I had any more questions of Mr. Renoe. I felt as if I should've had more questions for him. I did some heavy thinking trying to decide what questions I should have asked Mr. A.J. Renoe when I'd had the chance.

I was having a hard time with Champ's fingerprints on Ora's pistol. Champ said he didn't remember picking the pistol up, but that was hard to swallow.

So let's say Champ is knocked down the bank on that road just like he said. Let's suppose it was the Mongers who slipped up behind us, knowing the car was going to run out of gasoline because Artis fixed it so it would. Artis shines a bright light on Ora, then shoots him and pushes Champ down the bank. Meanwhile, Murdoch slips up behind me and hits me over the head. Artis' bullet passes through Ora's heart and is lying out there in the woods someplace, or, more likely, at the bottom of Glaize Creek.

Now, Champ says he climbed back up the bank, found Ora dead, me unconscious, and Buster and Wilbur gone. He finds the pistol, either in Ora's holster or maybe on the ground. So he picks it up by the barrel and throws it into the woods.

I don't think so. I think Champ would have kept the gun. After all, he's wanted for killing Shorty Mickelson so whoever sees him is going to shoot on sight. Would someone in that situation be likely to throw a loaded gun away and walk off into the woods?

How would the jury see this? I felt I had put up a decent defense against the allegation that it was Ora's gun that had killed him, against the fingerprints on the gun. But when the jury got behind closed doors, they were going to put all those allegations and facts together and convict Champ unless I could get them to thinking maybe someone else did slip up there and kill Ora.

I was going to need those two weeks I figured I would have before court was in session again to come up with a defense that a jury would believe. But I wasn't to get those two weeks.

The day after we buried Gideon was a Thursday. While I was still eating breakfast, Ellis Wayne came in the jail house and said Judge Henry Black wanted to see me. I immediately assumed the judge had been advised of the prosecutor the attorney general was sending us. I knew whoever he was, he would be an experienced attorney like Gideon which gave him an advantage over me. But I would have one over him because I knew every man and woman on the jury.

The judge was in his robe again and that made me feel somewhat important. Nancy had told me to go on in, the judge was waiting for me, but when I entered the three-sided room, Judge Henry Black was leaned back in his chair holding the Rules of Court open in his hands. I cleared my throat so he would know I was there, but I waited to sit down until he asked me to. Judges don't like lawyers— especially young lawyers — showing initiative. Judge Henry Black read two pages, or at least he had time to, before he looked over the top of the book and motioned to a chair with a nod of his head.

"Sit," he said. He turned the open book around so that I could see it and laid it on the desk before me. "There's the section on replacing the prosecutor during a trial. You best read up on it. I'm continuing court tomorrow morning at nine o'clock."

"So soon? Why so soon?"

"New prosecutor wants to get on with it. He's got one more

witness, then he'll rest his case. After your cross I'll adjourn until Monday. You can get in a fresh start first thing Monday morning. I like to do it that way. Starting off the defense first thing in the morning. Makes it easy for the jury to remember what you tell them. Make it easier for you."

"Who is the new prosecutor?"

"You know him. I persuaded Sid Hatch to finish up the trial for Gideon."

My God. Sid Hatch. The best lawyer ever in Linn Creek, maybe the state. There could only be one thing to bring Sid out of retirement. Being back in the spotlight. Sid knew the jury was going to vote to convict Champ and he wanted in on the glory.

"I'm surprised," I said. "I didn't think Sid would come back into court."

"Doing it as a favor to me. I've known Sid all my life. Best damn lawyer this court will ever see."

"Sort of puts me at a disadvantage," I said. "Me against Sid Hatch. Might as well be the attorney general himself."

"Don't worry about it, Sid'll take care of you. Told me he likes you. You got nothing to be ashamed of except your client. You've acquitted yourself well in court. You'll notice I've been lenient with you. Figured it didn't make much difference what I allowed, everybody knows Champ killed Ora."

I started to say something I couldn't take back, but I held my tongue. The judge was right, he had been lenient and there was no sense getting him riled up. I was going to need all the help I could get against Sid Hatch.

"Who's the witness?" I asked. "There's no one on the witness list."

"Reluctant witness. May testify, may not. But I'm allowing it if she does."

"So it's a woman."

"Nita German. Be in court at nine."

Champ sat on the edge of his cot. The blanket was smoothed out as if he had never slept there. He was fresh shaven and smelled of bay rum.

When I told him about Sid Hatch he made a face.

"That old bastard. He hates the Gowans. He was the prosecutor who sent up my daddy and my granddaddy. If you wonder why he's doing this it's for the chance to send another Gowan to the Big House."

"We're going back to court at nine o'clock tomorrow. Nita is testifying for the prosecution so wear something nice."

Champ made another face. "Nita, huh? Well, that'll be interesting."

"What's she going to say?"

Champ shrugged. "With Nita, you can never tell."

"Why did Nita turn you in that time to Ora?"

Champ shrugged again. "Like she said, she was mad at me for having some other gal with me in Yawley's car. Christ, that was three years in the pen for me. First thing she remembers after three years is that? You can never tell about Nita. Might have been cause she was sweet on Ora. I don't know if he ever took advantage of Nita's services or not."

Champ looked me in the eye. "I do know him and Addie wasn't as close as, say, an average man and wife."

"I don't pry into my sister's affairs," I said. I was surprised that Champ seemed to know what I had only suspected. "Why did you take Nita with you when you stole Buck Newley's truck full of furniture squares?"

"I didn't trust her. If I left her, she probably would have turned me in again. Besides the truck driver was coming back from eating his dinner any minute. I had to get his truck and get out of there."

"What's she going to say? What does she know?"

"Well, she can tell on me for stealing the truck."

"That's all?"

"Like I said, you can never tell about Nita."

Lonnie stood on the blacktop in the station driveway with a bunch of boys crowded around. I walked over to see what was going on. A half dozen copperheads squirmed on the hot blacktop and as they tried to escape to a cooler spot, the boys jumped and yelled and Lonnie cackled at them.

"Kind of dangerous ain't it, Lonnie?" I asked.

"Nah, the snakes are as scared of the kids as the kids are of them," he said. "I'll give a few lessons on how to handle the snakes and they won't be scared at all."

"What are you doing with poisonous snakes, anyway? I'm going to feel kind of leery of coming around here if you're keeping them in the station."

"I got to get them back to their cages and into Dressler's barn before Volly gets back. He put his foot down on my keeping copperheads out back."

The boys yelled again and a couple of them took off down the street, looking back at the snakes who were making their way over to a grassy spot beside the blacktop. Lonnie walked over to the snakes, grabbed them one by one and stuck them into a gunny sack he carried in his other hand. I watched the mouths of the snakes open as he grabbed them and I thought what a crazy person my friend was.

"Answer me this, Lonnie. Why copperheads? What are you going to do with them?"

"Sell them. Five bucks apiece."

"Who's buying copperheads?"

"Bunch of holy rollers over by Roach. They handle poisonous snakes in their church services. Don't ask me why."

"So how much you making off the snakes?"

"Thirty bucks. More'n ol' Volly will take in off gas today. And another twenty off them dam people. I'm fifty bucks ahead. Want to drive up to Jeff tonight? Drink some beer? Chase some girls?"

"I got a girl," I said. "What dam people you talking about?"

"You know, the ones putting in the dam. Or trying to, anyway. There's two of them going around town giving away twenty dollar bills."

"What for?"

"For signing a petition to move the county seat."

"You're voting to move the county seat?"

"Of course not. They don't know that. But I'll take their money. Maybe enough of us take their money, they'll go broke and can't afford to build the dam."

"That's against the law, buying petition signatures," I said. "And I ain't so sure but what it's against the law accepting money for it."

Lonnie held up the gunny sack of copperheads. "You arrest me and I'm taking my pets to jail with me."

He thought that was funny and so did the boys still crowded around.

"Where are these people who are buying signatures?"

Lonnie waved his free arm. "I don't know. They just drove up, bought some gas and offered me twenty dollars. I took it. Somebody was in earlier from Mack's Creek. Said two men had been there yesterday with a bag full of money giving away twenty dollar bills."

I looked up and down Main Street, but didn't see any strangers. "You see them again, let me know."

"You ain't going to make me give the money back are you?" Lonnie asked, grinning real big.

I shook my head and went on down the street. The good mood I'd been in was starting to wear off. I was disturbed about people walking around my town paying our citizens money to vote against Linn Creek, but I had bigger fish to fry. I had a client. And whether the town liked it or not, I had an obligation to defend him.

When I came to the dinner table that night, two well-dressed men looking like city people were already there. They were very polite, saying what wonderful people they had met in town and what a wonderful meal Rose had prepared and what a wonderful place the Ozarks was. They threw the word wonderful around like it was the only word they knew. Or maybe they thought it was the only word we knew. I didn't like their condescending manner at all. Lonnie, down the table from me kept trying to get my attention and when I looked at him he kept nodding his head toward the two men, but my mind was busy with lawyer thoughts and at the moment it would have come as a surprise to me if someone was to remind me I was also a deputy sheriff.

Finally Lonnie says to the men, "So how many signatures did you buy today?" and it finally dawned on me what he was trying to say to me. These were the dam people who had been going around town giving away twenty dollar bills for people's signature.

Both the men looked a little sheepish at Lonnie's question, but one of them, the older of the two, a pudgy man with practically no hair on his head at all and with thick, round spectacles on his reddened face, said, "Why, we're not buying signatures. I'm not sure where you got that idea."

"Maybe it was when you gave me twenty bucks and told me how much better it would be for the whole county when the dam went in," Lonnie said, smiling at them, then at me. "Deputy Sheriff Joel Dean down there was asking me about you."

The men looked at me and I met their gaze. The little one, the younger one with hair, said to me, "Why I think your friend got the wrong idea somehow. It's illegal to buy signatures. One thing we're not going to do is something illegal."

"What was the twenty dollars for?" I asked.

"We're building up good will for when the dam goes in," the fat one said. "We want to be good neighbors."

Uncle Billy Jack was beside himself. "You're dam people?" he practically shouted. "You have the nerve to show yourselves in this town? And then to try and pay people to vote to flood the town? Why damn your souls, you ought to be tarred and feathered."

Everyone was somewhat taken by surprise by Uncle Billy Jack's outburst. Rose, seated at her place at the end of the table, put a hand out to place on Uncle Billy Jack's arm.

"Uncle Billy Jack, these men are guests in my home. Please respect that."

Uncle Billy Jack stood up. He threw his napkin onto the table where it clanged the silverware into his drinking glass and the sound caused all of us to twitch in our chairs.

"I can't be civil to these men, Rose," he said. "I'm asking you to tell them to leave. Right now."

The two men were somewhat in shock. Rose said, "I can't do that, Uncle Billy Jack. I've accepted their money for lodging and food for the night and I can't be disrespectful to them. You can understand that."

"Well, by damn, I can be disrespectful. I am disrespectful.

They are nothing but a bunch of charlatans. They have no right to sit here in the very house they're paying people to vote to send to the bottom of a lake none of us want. They're deceitful and cowards and they ought to be run out of town. I'll not spend a night in the same house where they are."

Uncle Billy Jack scooted his chair back, stiffened his back and marched straight out of the dining room and on out the door of Mulder's into the night.

Rose looked stricken.

The two men looked at each other and I could swear a smile passed between them.

Rose said to the men, "I'm sorry, gentlemen, I didn't know who you were with. I apologize for Uncle Billy Jack's behavior. He's a very gentle man."

The older man said, "Quite all right, Mrs. Minton. We understand. It's going to be difficult for the older citizens to realize how much better off everyone will be once the dam..."

"Perhaps you can explain to Rose how much better off she will be once her house is covered with thirty feet of water," I said.

"Believe it or not, she will be better off," the young one said. "With the money we pay her for her property . . ."

"I'm against the dam," Rose said. "I don't want my house destroyed. I'll not ask you to leave, but please refrain from speaking about the dam anymore while you're in my house."

Jane McGann said, "What are we going to do about Uncle Billy Jack tonight? He can't sleep out in the street."

Volly said, "Maybe I can fix him a place in the station to sleep for one night."

Lonnie said, "Bad idea. I didn't get down to Dresslers with those copperheads, Volly. I left them in a wire cage inside the station for the night."

Volly said, "Dammit, Lonnie, I told you no poisonous snakes at the station . . ."

I said, "I have a solution," and everyone turned toward me. I looked at the two dam people across the table. "You two finish your meal, get your stuff and come with me. We have lodging for you at the jail house."

The fat man said, "Jail house? Does that mean you're arresting us? What are we being charged with?"

"We got laws against disturbing the peace," I said. "We got a city ordinance against registering in a place of lodging under false pretenses. That's just to start with. And bring along that bag full of twenty dollar bills if you have any left. We have laws against procuring signatures for a petition."

The younger one sneered, turned to his older partner and said, "Bunch of hicks."

And I said to everyone at the table. "Sometimes these city slickers are too slick for their own good."

It was getting dark and we hadn't found Uncle Billy Jack. Volly, Lonnie and I had searched the town, but no one had seen him since he'd walked out of Rose's dining room. I began to worry for him, unsure what he might do in his agitated state of mind. Where could he have gone?

"Let's try the churches," Lonnie suggested. "They're never locked. Maybe he curled up in a pew somewhere."

We looked, but no Uncle Billy Jack. As we passed the parsonage of Reverend Clements, the Methodist minister, he came down from his front porch in the dark to see who we were.

"Joel Dean, is that you?" he asked.

"We're out looking for Uncle Billy Jack," I said.

"He's here. Mabel is making a bed for him. He's some put out about something. What's happened?"

I told the minister about the two dam people and what had occurred at Rose's.

"I'm afraid Uncle Billy Jack is going to have a stroke or something the way he carries on about that dam," Rev. Clements said. "We're all concerned about it and worry about what's going to happen to the town, but it's such a life and death thing with him I don't know how he'll take when the dam goes in."

We went inside and persuaded Uncle Billy Jack to come on back to Rose's with us, that he would rest better in his own bed. He needed to be convinced that the two men pushing the dam had been removed from the premises. He patted me on the back when I told him I had taken the two of them to jail and placed them under arrest.

"Joel Dean, you're a fine young man. As a deputy sheriff you're making this town proud and you bring honor to the Gregory name. Both your daddy and your granddaddy were real good men and you're carrying on their name in fine tradition."

A few feet short of Rose's front door Uncle Billy Jack stopped and placed his hand on my arm.

"But I gotta tell you, Joel Dean, as a lawyer you're a great disappointment to me."

You and the rest of the town I thought.

Champ and I walked out of the jail together. He in his new $20 suit the county provided him and me in my ill-fitting five-year-old suit that the county couldn't afford to replace. I had told

Addie there was no need for Noah to go along with me, that Champ wasn't going to run away. Noah said he was changing clothes so he could go watch the trial. Addie said he might as well take Frances Billings with him as she was our only other prisoner. Addie said she planned to attend the trial and I figured Doyle was already there picking out a front row seat.

Again, I was surprised at the number of people in town. I saw some people from Wet Glaize and Chauncey, the old county seat, both of them more than eight miles away. How did they get the word so fast about court taking up again?

On the way across the yard to the courthouse, people spoke to me and to Champ. Some joked and even shook hands with Champ. The attitude of the public had changed since the first day of the trial. I was hoping the jury felt the same way.

We walked up the creaky stairs and down the length of the courtroom to find Sid Hatch leaning on the defense table, a pleasant smile on his face.

"Joel Dean, you can't imagine how pleased I am to be in court with my protégé," he said, then grabbed my right hand with both of his and shook it vigorously. "I hope I've taught you something. I'm sure you'll remember enough to give me a tussle."

I showed a weak smile. "I'll try, Sid. I hope I don't get so scared I run out of the courtroom crying."

"Yes, yes, of course," he said, not hearing me.

Sid was turning away toward Ellis Wayne when Champ said, "Hello, Mr. Hatch."

But Sid ignored Champ and proceeded to tell Ellis how he'd been bailiff when Sid was last in this court, four years ago.

"You reckon he don't like me?" Champ asked.

"He's too busy being Sid Hatch," I said. "One of Sid's rules he taught me: don't ever call the accused by name. Don't make him into a person. Call him de-fend-DANT."

Champ dropped into a chair and slouched back as if he didn't have a care in the world. I looked around at the crowd and saw a lot of the people in the courtroom watching Champ with a smile on their faces. Back in the corner I saw the black beard and dark face of Artis Monger. He too watched Champ, but his shaded eyes burned with intensity. Enough to make you shiver.

Estelle was on the front row again, as she had been throughout the trial. She wore a pale yellow shift with lavender trim and a little hat of the same colors. It was the best way possible to forget the look Artis Monger was sending our way.

I walked over to Estelle and took her hand.

"Thanks for coming," I said. "It's a tonic to my eyes to see you here each day."

"You're doing as good as any St. Louis lawyer, Joel Dean," she said. "Daddy thinks Sid Hatch will wrap you around his little finger, but I said don't be surprised if Joel Dean doesn't do the wrapping. And don't be surprised if the jury doesn't let Champ go free. Daddy said if they do he guessed the Klan would have to hang him themselves."

She laughed at that to indicate Yawley had spoken in jest. I smiled, too.

"I appreciate your support, Estelle, but don't expect the impossible."

Ellis Wayne bellowed out his, "Oyez, oyez, the Circuit Court of Camden County is now in session. The Honorable Judge Henry Black presiding. All rise."

Judge Henry Black almost seemed to fly into court on the wings of his robe. After he gaveled the court to order, I walked toward the defense table. Estelle said to my back, "You're still my hero, Joel Dean."

After Sid Hatch introduced himself for the court record, the crowd broke into applause. Judge Black tapped his gavel lightly and without conviction. He appeared to have no real objection to the adulation for Sid. The judge asked if the defense was ready. I said I was and Estelle and Lonnie Harper behind her applauded. Judge Henry Black smacked the gavel hard and said, "Order in this court."

Sid called for Nita German to take the witness stand. When she followed Bailiff Ellis Wayne through the door behind the judge's bench, the crowd buzzed. Nita wore the brightest of red dresses with extremely lavish lace trim. The judge didn't know what the crowd was murmuring about until he got a look at her gaudy dress. He scowled and touched his gavel as if he had a notion to send her home to change clothes. Sid never reacted.

She told the jury who she was and described her relationship with the "de-fend-DANT" as lifelong friends. She told how she went along with Champ in Buck Newland's truck because she was afraid not to. She claimed under oath to be in fear all the time she was with Champ in the caves until Estelle and I found them.

Sid asked, "Did you ask the de-fend-DANT to take you home?"

"Yes I did."

"Well now, tell the gentlemen of the jury why he said he couldn't take you back to Linn Creek."

I watched the two women in the jury for signs of resentment on their parts for Sid omitting them. Sid would have to get up to date. The women did not seem pleased.

Nita said, "He told me he couldn't go back there because he'd killed a man."

A loud, "Ohhh," rumbled through the courtroom and Judge Henry Black gaveled it into silence. I found myself looking at Champ, but my heart was way up in my throat. Champ chewed away on a matchstick as unconcerned as the birds outside the window.

He looked over at me and said, "See. I told you she'd say anything."

Sid walked toward the jury, facing them, shaking a finger in the air.

"After the de-fend-DANT told you he'd killed Sheriff Mitchell. . ."

"Objection," I practically screamed at the judge. "The accused, Champ Gowan, said no such thing."

"He said he killed a man, the sheriff is dead. Who else could he possibly have meant?" Sid proclaimed.

"Objection sustained, Sid," Judge Black said. "If she meant Sheriff Mitchell, let her say it."

"All right then, let's say it this way," Sid told the jury, facing them, his hands on the railing just like he'd taught me to do. "Sheriff Mitchell has been shot. The de-fend-DANT admits to killing a man. You were sure, of course, he meant the sheriff weren't you?"

Nita said yes. Sid went on to polish this choice bit of testimony as only he could. For fifteen minutes he rambled on to the jury. I could have objected and the judge would probably have upheld me. But I didn't. I was as much under his spell as the jury was, as the judge was, and as the audience was. Sid Hatch at his finest. Just when I hoped he had lost a bit in court, I realized he hadn't. When he was through with Nita, it was as if he had presented a full confession to the jury. It was as if Nita had testified that Champ had told her he had killed Ora Mitchell.

But he hadn't told her that.

I heard the judge say, "Your witness," from somewhere far off from me.

I rose. My palms were sweaty and a trickle ran down my back.

I asked, "Nita, did you see an airplane flying over you the day Estelle and I came to the caves?"

Nita did not move her eyes from mine. "Why, yes. I remember that."

"And Nita, you were standing in a stream when the plane flew over, were you not?"

"Yes I was."

"Naked."

A low noise from the audience and a snicker or two before Sid rose from his chair with a bit of a flair and said, "I'm afraid I'll have to object to the young attorney's line of questioning, your honor. It's not anything I taught him at the time I was mentoring young Gregory, but that is not in line with the prosecution's questioning. So, of course, it can't be allowed."

Sid reseated himself with the same flair with which he'd risen. I could not help but watch his performance.

"Well?" Judge Black was looking at me and I realized I was supposed to answer Sid's charge somehow. I just wished at that time that my mind was working a little quicker.

"Your honor, the prosecution asked about the relationship between the witness and the accused. I believe that relationship needs to be established in more detail in order that the jury can further examine her testimony."

"I'll allow that," Judge Henry Black said.

"Your honor," Sid began, speaking as he would to a child. "I'm quite aware that this young attorney's approach is right out of the text books. Ignore damaging testimony and start a brush fire off to the side to take the jury's mind off of it. But we—you and I — are a little more experienced and sophisticated. We can't allow the vision in the jury's mind of a man admitting to a killing to be blurred by the vision of a beautiful woman with no clothes on."

Judge Black turned to me. "Is this leading to a relationship between this witness and the defendant?"

"Yes, it is, your honor."

"Get on with it then. Objection overruled. But if we don't get there quick, I'm shutting you up."

"Yes, your honor."

"Then we can skip over the state of dress of the witness, your honor," Sid said, not giving in. "It has no bearing and it's only purpose is to titillate and sensationalize."

Judge Black said, "I'll give you two questions to make the state of dress of the witness relevant or you're through. Witness will

LIMB OF THE JUDAS TREE

answer the question."

"Your honor. . ." Sid, still objecting.

"Sit down, Sid. Witness, answer the question."

"I've forgotten the question," Nita said coyly.

"Defense will repeat the question."

I asked again. "Were you and the accused, Champ Gowan, naked in the stream when we passed over you in an airplane?"

"We were bathing."

"You and Champ have been lovers since grade school, haven't you?"

"Well, my goodness, I don't know quite what you mean. . ."

"How many times have you had sexual relations with the accused?"

Sid was out of his chair, jamming his hands in his pockets and walking toward me, shaking his silver-thonged head and smiling.

"Your honor, I know this is amusing and entertaining to the audience who are future potential clients of the defense counsel, but this is not serving any purpose to the jury, this titillation our young friend wants to charm us with. Our generation—yours and mine—never delved into personal matters such as defense counsel is doing when it serves no purpose."

"It establishes the degree and type of relationship and has a direct bearing on the witness' testimony, your honor."

"But the number of times, your honor. . ." Sid punctuated his remark with a disapproving shake of the head.

"I'll settle for the first and last time and the frequency in between, your honor, if an exact number offends the prosecution."

"Enough. Enough," Judge Black said. He cleared his throat and looked at Nita over his wire rimmed spectacles. "Miss German, would you say you and the defendant have had relations over ten times?"

Nita fussed with her hair with a right hand bearing bright red nails and several rings with very large stones in them. "Well, I . . . that is, I guess so, your honor."

277

"Without charge," I said, and the crowd broke into laughter.

Judge Black gaveled loudly until the crowd quieted.

"If you want to hear the rest of this, you'd better keep quiet," he said to the crowd. "Any more of that and I'll clear this court."

"Champ never gave you money or anything else after having relations with you, did he Nita?" I asked.

She turned angry around the eyes so I guess I'd hit a sore spot with her.

"No."

"But you turned him in to Sheriff Mitchell after Shorty Mickelson was killed, after everyone blamed Champ, didn't you?"

"Yes."

"Why did you do that, Nita?"

She stared hard, never taking her eyes from my eyes. "Because he had been out of prison a week and never came to see me. He was with some hussy when he was picked up in Yawley's new car. He never wrote me or sent me anything for three years when he was in prison. I went out to our farm because I figured he would hide out there. He always liked to when somebody was looking for him. I asked him if he was coming to see me. He said he would in due time. When I wasn't busy with my *clients*. He said maybe he would look up Addie Gregory before he got around to me."

"And that made you angry?"

"Yes it did. It made me feel small."

"So you turned him in to Sheriff Mitchell to get back at him."

"He was wanted by the *law*."

"For what?"

"Killing Shorty Mickelson."

"So was that who he meant when he said he'd killed a man?"

"Objection," from Sid. "Defense is putting words in the witness's mouth. She didn't say that."

"The witness testified that the accused said he had killed a *man.* Shorty Mickelson had been killed. Shorty Mickelson is a man. Who else could he possibly have meant?"

"Don't use my own words against me, Joel Dean." Sid turned to me and I noticed his face was getting a bit flushed.

I turned back to Nita.

"Did Champ say he killed Shorty Mickelson?"

"No."

"Did he say he killed Ora Mitchell?"

"No."

"Did he say he killed Buster Workman?"

"No."

"Did he say he killed Wilbur Crowder?"

"No."

"Did he say he killed someone in prison?"

"No."

"Did he say he murdered someone or did he say he killed someone?"

"Killed."

"Didn't say who?"

"No."

"Didn't say when?"

"No."

"Was he telling the truth or was he boasting?"

"I . . . I don't know. . ."

"Your honor, I'm through with this witness."

I caught just the slightest of smiles on one juror's face.

But Sid wasn't through with Nita. He plowed the same ground he'd been over before. Repetition, another thing he had taught me. I let him go, after all, I'd gotten Nita to say what I wanted her to say and it had registered with the jury. At least one of them.

When Sid finally said he was through, that the prosecution rested, Judge Henry Black adjourned the court until Monday. I realized Sid had insisted on having Nita testify on Friday so that the jury would have all weekend to think about her testimony.

Nita passed by the defense table as she left the witness chair. The crowd was filing out of the courtroom, Sid was closing up his big leather briefcase and the judge had already left the bench.

Nita looked at Champ and said, "I owed Sid. If I'd been your wife I wouldn't have had to testify."

As she walked away, Champ muttered low and barely loud enough for me to hear, "Not in this lifetime."

On Saturday night the town held the last dance of the year in Dressler's park across Linn Creek. When Estelle and I got across the creek at the ford everyone used, the plank platform had been set up and the musicians were tuning up. Addie had finally consented to allowing Champ to play for an hour after Doyle asked about it all day Saturday.

There was no dance contest that night; most of the dancers wanted something slow since it was kind of a sad occasion with summer ending and winter coming on. And with the thought that it would likely be the last dance ever in Linn Creek. Doyle and Champ got going pretty good on one Charleston number and Estelle and I danced ourselves out of breath. When Doyle left to take Champ back to jail and just the fiddlers were left to play a slow waltz, Estelle picked her blanket up off the ground and pulled me after her in the direction we had gone that summer night so long ago.

I spread the blanket on the grass beside the Niangua and pulled her down beside me and kissed her lovely mouth. And we didn't stop there. The eyes of the night looked down on us and I imagined that they approved of our love because they seemed even brighter than when we started.

Exhausted, tired and spent, we lay on the blanket and pulled it over us because the autumn night carried a chill breath of air that hinted of winter.

"Oh, Joel Dean. I'm so happy and I'm so sad."

"Sad? Why are you sad?"

"Daddy and I argued tonight."

"About me?"

"Yes. He's so angry at you. Now people in town are saying maybe Champ didn't kill Ora and Daddy's saying it's all your fault."

"I guess I could take that as a compliment. But Yawley'll get over it. Monday Champ will either be back in jail here for another trial for killing Shorty Mickelson or he'll be in Jefferson City waiting to hang."

"No, Daddy will never be over it. He wants Champ to hang and he won't be satisfied until he does."

"I understand how Yawley is upset about his new car three years ago, but Champ paid for that in prison. And Yawley's upset about the Buick and his whiskey. And Shorty, maybe. But I don't think anyone can prove Champ did that. I don't think he did. Sooner or later Yawley will get over it."

"Daddy says I can't marry you. That he'll never permit it and that I have to go to Stephen's College. I got angry and said I would never go."

"I'm kind of glad you're not going. I didn't want you away for months at a time, meeting other men. More handsome and smarter than me. I figured if you went to Stephens you would never want to live in Linn Creek."

"Daddy said I had to tell you tonight that you couldn't see me again."

Estelle began to cry softly and put her head against my chest.

"Does Yawley hate me that much?"

"It's not you, it's Champ."

She was sobbing now and her little body shook. I held her even closer.

"He'll get over it. I'll go and talk with him. He'll come to understand."

"He won't," she said. She looked up into my eyes and the sight of the tears on her pretty face saddened me. "I've got to tell you something, Joel Dean. Something I've never told anyone else. My mother ran off with Champ Gowan's dad."

"Your mother? No, darling Estelle, you've got it wrong. What can you be thinking? Your mother was killed in a train accident when she was visiting in Chicago. You were six. She's buried right up there in the cemetery. Wherever did you get the idea she ran off with Champ's dad?"

"When I was ten, I opened a letter that came to our house without Daddy knowing I saw it. Mother told Daddy that she and Rod Gowan ran off to California. She's an actress. Do you remember the woman in the motion picture we went to see in the park? Mona Dearing? That was her. I know it was her. She looks just like me."

"That's why you cried?"

I felt her head nodding yes on my chest. "Who's in your mother's grave?"

"The casket's empty. Daddy staged the funeral so I would think she was dead and the town wouldn't know she ran off and left him."

"Does Champ know?"

"I don't think so. His dad broke out of jail and came back for my mother. If he told anyone, I guess they would put his father back in jail."

"So we'll just have to run off and get married," I said. "We'll go to California. You can see your mother again."

"No, no, I can't do that, Joel Dean. I can't leave my daddy, it would kill him. My mother abandoned me for a man who wasn't her husband. Daddy stuck by me, loved me, cared for me. I love

282

him. I love you. I don't know what to do."

"Then we'll just get married and Yawley will have to get used to it. He may never get over hating Champ, but I haven't done anything to Yawley. I'll not give *you* up, I know that, I love you too much. I'll give up anything to keep you, but I won't give up you. Not ever."

"That's sweet, Joel Dean. He's got to let us get married. I'll just die if we can't.

"That won't be necessary," I said. "Nobody is going to die."

I was so very sure of that.

At Volly's station, Lonnie and Volly were sitting in the rocking chairs drinking a couple of Griesedieck Brothers beer that Volly always kept on ice.

"Have a beer, Joel Dean," Volly said. "The jury is going to feel bad tomorrow about the dam going in and all. You afraid they may take it out on Champ?"

"Half the jury already sold their properties to that corporation for more money than they ever dreamed about," I said. "I think half that jury is going to be feeling pretty bad and half is going to feel pretty good."

"So how you think it's going to go?" Lonnie asked.

"Yeah, Joel Dean," Volly said. "You have to present a defense tomorrow for Champ. What's it going to be?"

"Well, boys, tomorrow I'm going to name the real killer."

"Yeah?" Lonnie said. "Well, go on, tell us who it is."

"No, you'll have to wait. I can't let it out until I get into court.

Don't want the real killer to know that I know."

Volly laughed. "Joel Dean, if you can do that and make the jury believe it, I'm voting for you for governor. Give us a hint."

"Yeah, Joel Dean, I got two cars to repair tomorrow."

"You'll be there Lonnie. You too, Volly. It'll be something you don't want to miss."

Volly said, looking down the street toward the jail house, "Here comes the sheriff's car. Probably be wanting gas and me closed. Guess I'll have to open up after all."

I saw the Chevrolet coming down the street and pull into the driveway to stop at the pump. Doyle Savoy was at the wheel.

"Volly, I need some gas. Got to go down to Joplin to pick up a prisoner. Probably won't be home until late."

Volly pulled his ring of keys from his pocket and unlocked the padlock on the pump handle. He began rocking the handle back and forth and the red gasoline level rose inside the glass of the pump.

"Who you picking up?" I asked Doyle.

"Buster Workman. You remember that little shit Wilbur Crowder? Well, he got himself killed down there. Tried to fight it out with the cops in Joplin. Buster took one in the arm, but it's not bad. Those damn Joplin cops don't mess around. They just called Addie on the telephone a few minutes ago."

"Weren't those the two galoots in the car when Ora got killed?" Lonnie asked.

"Yeah, that's right," I said. Buster Workman back in Linn Creek. What could it mean as far as the trial was concerned?

Volly put the gasoline hose in the fuel tank filler on top of the hood, released the trigger to let it flow into the tank and looked at me as the red level inside the glass began coming down. "Joel Dean, it looks to me like it's going to be Buster Workman who tells the court tomorrow who really killed Ora."

Doyle said, "Joel Dean, Addie said if I was to see you, to tell you she wants to talk with you at the jail."

PART FIVE
THE VERDICT

I didn't want any more surprises, but when I saw Addie and Champ drinking coffee at the table in the jail house, I had a feeling I was about to get a big one.

"Sit down, Joel Dean," Addie said. "Pour yourself a cup of coffee."

I sat without the coffee. "I hear Buster's been caught," I said.

"Joplin cops got a tip about two men with a tommy gun in a boarding house down there," Addie said. "Little Wilbur tried to shoot his way out, but the cops filled him full of holes. Fourteen to be exact. Buster was hiding under the bed, but he took one in the arm. Just a flesh wound, no bone. Doyle's bringing him back here to stand trial for Shorty's death."

"Buster say anything about who shot Ora?"

"No, but he will," Champ said. "That's what we wanted to talk with you about."

I looked at them. "Both of you?"

LIMB OF THE JUDAS TREE

"We're both responsible," Addie said. "It started like this. . . no, I guess it started a long time ago. Me and Champ have had a thing for each other as long as I can remember. Just when we were set to run off and get married, Pa took sick. Well, you know about the promise I made him. One I wished a thousand times I hadn't made, but I did. And I just couldn't go back on it. Things got bad, you know that. Couldn't pay Pa's hospital bill and the bank was about to take over our home. I told Ora about it—we'd always been friends— and he said he would pay off the loan and the hospital bill if I was to marry him and take care of the jail house. I told him I loved Champ and why me and Champ couldn't get married as long as Pa was alive. Ora said it would be all right. So that's what I did."

"I know all of that," I said.

"Yeah, well, I guess you could say I was a good wife and a faithful one. I took good care of the jail house, feeding the prisoners and putting money back in Ora's pocket. I come to like him more than I ever had, but I never come to love him. I still had Champ on my mind. But that too, had dimmed a little. He was in jail and I was Ora's wife, not his. But when you brought them back to jail, being here in the same building with him, the flame got brighter again. We got together one day when all of you were gone and I did something I had no right to do while I was Ora's wife."

I thought of my love for Estelle and how she was sticking with me when Yawley wanted her to get rid of me. I thought of the sorrow Addie had gone through and I transferred that sorrow to me. I was caught in the same trap Addie had been caught in.

"I understand, Addie," I said. "Love is a stronger emotion than faithfulness. I don't judge you harshly."

"Thanks, Joel Dean, but you haven't heard it all. When Ora got back, Wilbur complained to him about Champ getting such good treatment. Getting to stay downstairs all day. So Ora asked me about it. At first I tried to lie, but I couldn't. It wouldn't have done any good, Ora knew what had happened. So I admitted it.

288

And I told him how sorry I was for what I'd done to him. He just put the gun belt and holster around his waist and put a clip in his pistol and as he went out the door, he said, 'I reckon I'll just have to kill him, then.'"

"That was before the escape?" I asked.

"Two days," Champ said. "On the way back, when we stopped, things happened just the way I told you up to Ora unlocking the cuffs on me. When we stepped over to the bank, Ora said, 'Champ, you been messing with my wife and I can't allow that. Run for it.' He started pulling his pistol out of the holster and when I heard the hammer click back I knew he meant to kill me. Now Ora was ten times stronger than me, but I was quicker. I got hold of the barrel of the gun just as it went off and the bullet went right through Ora's heart. I knew I was in trouble and I couldn't think of what to do, but I guess without thinking—cause I been in enough situations in life—I just grabbed the gun, took about three quick steps and as you were turning around, I got you behind the ear with Ora's big pistol."

"Guess it could have been worse. You could have shot me, too."

"If I'd took time to think, I might have. I unlocked the cuffs on Wilbur and Buster and told them to get. Then I slung the gun away after wiping it off some and I lit out for the woods. I sat by a tree that night and cried. First time since I was about three. I figured my life was over this time for sure."

"Explain the rest of it," I said. "Getting me for your attorney. Telling me all those lies."

"When you showed up in the caves, I figured I'd never get out of there without getting caught. There were only two ways out and I figured somebody knew both of them. If I'd walked out by myself with just Nita, I'd a been shot. You know that. So my best chance was to go out with you. And my best chance in the court was if you were my lawyer. Same man who testifies against you, defends you. If we could have gotten the trial moved to a different county, it might have worked. I didn't figure you to be such a good lawyer, Joel Dean. Way people treat me now, I might have gotten off."

"When you brought Champ back in, we talked," Addie said. "I asked him not to bring it up about Ora trying to shoot him. I didn't think it would do any good anyway. I didn't want the town to know what I'd done. I didn't want the town to know that Ora was ready to shoot an unarmed prisoner because of his own wife."

"But, now, Buster's going to tell the truth," I said.

"And so you have to," Addie said. "I'll testify, then I'll resign. Hell, I don't want to be sheriff, anyway. Let Doyle Savoy have it."

"I almost have Champ off," I said. "Why would I change the plea to self defense and tell all about my sister and all about Ora—the best friend I ever had. Why would I do that?"

"Because, Joel Dean, you honor the truth," Addie said. "You know you have to do it, even though you don't want to. You know you have to get up there and say your sister is adulterous and you have to say a good man, the best man this town's ever seen, was going to do what any husband has the right to do, shoot the man who dishonored his wife. And you have to make that jury think it's not something Champ has to hang for. He was only protecting his life."

"Jury won't buy it," I said. "I'm not sure I want Champ to get off now. I know I can't convince the jury he should."

"They can come back with a lesser sentence," Addie said. "They have the right to do that. A jury can do anything they want to do. Read the law. If Judge Henry Black doesn't tell them that, you get up and you object. You can appeal if he doesn't tell the jury what the law says."

"That's a long shot, Addie. I've done as well in court as I have because I really believed Champ didn't shoot Ora. I was going into court tomorrow prepared to tell the jury it was the Mongers who shot Ora. Now, you're asking me to do something I don't believe in. Champ shot Ora. By his own actions he put himself in the position where Ora had to shoot him to save his honor. That's the way I see it. That's the way the jury will see it."

"It was an injustice for Champ to be in jail in the first place," Addie said. "He didn't kill Shorty Mickelson. If there was justice, he wouldn't have been in jail."

"That's right," Champ said. "I was in Zebra at Mamie Crouse's. Some fellow in Lebanon gave us a ride back to Linn Creek hours after Shorty got shot."

"You can't back out of this trial now, Joel Dean," Addie said. "You got two choices. Go back into court and plead not guilty because of self defense or go on the way you planned. Only that way will be a lie now, and you'll know it. I'm guessing you can't stand there in court and tell something you know is a lie."

I got out of my chair and walked over to the kitchen cabinets and opened the one where Ora always kept a bottle of whiskey. I poured an inch in the bottom of a coffee cup.

"I'm going to sleep on it," I said. "And I'm going to take this bottle to bed with me."

A dim glow of early sun sifted through the lace curtains in my room as I lay awake, staring at the half empty bottle of whiskey beside my bed, wishing I was one of those people who could find refuge and relief inside that bottle. The last time I remembered looking at Grandpa Gregory's watch was at two a.m. It was now seven, an hour past my usual time to start the day. Had I ever been asleep? Portions of a dream came to mind where I was wiping the sweat off Addie's brow as she lay prone on the ground. I didn't much believe in dreams as prognosticators of our lives, but the image of Addie lying on the ground with her eyes staring up at me was haunting. I decided what I had to do today.

I came down the stairs in my crumpled suit and wrinkled shirt to find the dining room empty. The dining room with the red curtains, the little red roses on the wallpaper and the big chandelier. The room where I always felt at ease with my fellow diners. The relaxed way we all talked and the kinship I had always felt with them. But not today. Today I was relieved I had missed breakfast because I was in no mood to converse with anyone.

Rose came in from the kitchen in her apron, a dishtowel over her shoulder, saw me and stopped to look closer.

"You look terrible, Joel Dean. You can't go to court looking like that."

"Guess I look like I feel," I said.

"Frank has a white, full collar shirt that ought to fit you. Might be a little short in the sleeves, but if you keep your jacket on, nobody will notice."

"Thanks, Rose, but I'll be all right."

"You're not leaving my house looking like that," she said firmly. "Sit down there and eat the rest of those biscuits with some jam on them while I find you something to wear today. Why didn't you tell me your shirt needed washing and your suit needed pressing last night?"

"Rose, you have never done my laundry. . ."

"I am today. Now sit and eat. I'll be right back."

I had no appetite, none whatsoever, but when I buttered a still-warm biscuit and spread some fresh blackberry jam on it, I did start to feel different. I went into the kitchen and poured myself a cup of coffee. Rose's kitchen still smelled of bacon and fresh baked biscuits and was friendly and cozy. I stood drinking the coffee and eating the biscuit I'd brought in with me, feeling the warmth of the room. Rose found me there finishing up the coffee. She had a black suit coat and pants over her arm and carried a white shirt and a gray necktie in the other hand.

"I like the feel of your kitchen, this morning, Rose," I said. "It feels like my home, though I don't have one anymore."

"Yes you do," she said. "This is your home as long as you want it to be."

"Today I miss my mother," I said.

She laid a hand on my arm. "Today, I'm your mother."

Without even thinking about it, I hugged her to me. "Things are going to happen today, Rose, that will change the lives of a lot of people that I care about. There hadn't ought to be days like this. People getting out of bed in one life, going back to bed that night and everything different. A different life. A different person."

"Life's like that, Joel Dean. That's why you have to live every day as if it will be your last one. One day Oscar's doing everything for me and the next day he's not even around. Life can change that quick, Joel Dean. And we have to go along with it."

"But today, I'm part of that change. I'm the one going to make it happen. Today, it's like I'm God. I don't want to be God. The responsibilities are too great."

"We don't have a choice. You don't do it, someone else will. You know that, don't you."

"Yeah, I guess you're right."

"Of course I'm right. Now, here, take these up to your room and try them on. The shirt is Frankie's and the rest belonged to my late husband, Oscar. He won't be needing them."

I slipped off my own worn suit coat and tried on the black one Rose had brought. It fit well enough except a little full around the middle.

"Oscar was about your size," Rose said. "Maybe a little heavier around the belt area. He liked my cooking. Here, put this vest on under it and leave the coat unbuttoned. The vest will hide your cinched up pants. Leave your shoes down here while you go up and change and I'll give them a good shine."

I changed into the clothes she brought and viewed myself in the hall mirror upstairs. I looked a whole lot better than I did in my own suit and the black fit my mood today.

Rose tied the necktie for me, slipped the shined shoes on my feet and gave me a kiss on the cheek before I left out the door.

"I know this is a big day for you," she said. "But they're not going to hang you or run you out of town. I'll have a big roast beef dinner on the table tonight when it's all over."

I thanked Rose and stepped out into the street. I was hoping to find that it was like any other day, but it wasn't. Throngs of people filled the walk in front of stores and almost every place along the street was taken by an automobile or a team of horses and a wagon. Down the street in front of the courthouse an even larger group of people stood in line, hoping to get a seat or a standing space inside. I walked in that direction.

I kept a half smile on my face, nodding to people as they spoke. Mostly, everyone was solemn, knowing what was going to be decided inside the courthouse today. But no one knew what I was about to say or do. Not even me.

Inside the courtroom, crowding around the walls were people I recognized as being from other counties. All of them, to the best of my memory, had the reputation of running whiskey or distilling it. Yawley was facing a group of them, talking and gesturing with a lot of energy.

I made my way from the back of the courtroom to the defense table where Champ was waiting. He looked up, expecting me to tell him something I guess. I motioned for him to follow me into the witness room where Addie and Buster were waiting along with Noah. I told them what I expected of them and the testimony I wanted to hear. And I asked if that was the truth of what happened. They agreed it was. Addie started to protest against my plan, but I told her that was how it had to be.

Champ and I returned to the defense table. Champ was silent and so was I.

Sid Hatch was dressed as no one dresses in Linn Creek. The cut of the shirt, the collar style, the blossoming pure silk tie, the fabric of the suit; all would have pegged Sid as an outsider if he hadn't been Sid Hatch. He looked tired this morning and I guessed this was an hour before his usual morning routine started.

I stood to say the defense was ready after Judge Henry Black announced the session was open.

"Your honor," I began, my voice sounding a bit shaky even to me. "We have a change in plea. The accused will plead not guilty by reason of self defense."

Immediately Sid Hatch was on his feet.

"Your honor, I had no prior notice of this change. There can be no possible reason of self defense when a prisoner is in custody of a law officer and kills that law officer."

"Your honor, a new witness, a Raymond L. Workman, known as Buster, is now in custody of the sheriff and is able to testify to what happened the night Sheriff Ora Mitchell was shot."

"I don't know anything about this witness," Sid proclaimed. "I don't have a witness list for the defense at all except the defend-DANT."

"I'm inclined to give Mr. Gregory some latitude here," Judge Black said. "Call your witness."

Buster was sworn in by Nancy. He wore a pair of clean twill pants Noah had bought at the general store for him that morning and a nickle-gray shirt he had fastened at the neck. The bandage on his wound was under the shirt, but Addie had fixed a sling for him. Buster's face was its usual reddened tint and closely shaven. His normally close cropped reddish hair was in need of cutting, covering the collar of his shirt.

I asked Buster to tell the jury what he had heard and seen the night Ora was killed beginning with Ora unlocking Champ's cuffs and letting him outside the automobile.

"Well, Champ, he unbuttoned his pants and started to take a leak. . .uh, I mean started to. . . you know, relieve himself. The sheriff says, 'Champ, you been messing with my wife and I can't have that,' and he started pulling his pistol out of his holster. I seen him point it at Champ and I seen Champ jump through the air and grab the pistol and I heard it go off. The sheriff he slumped down to the ground and Champ was left there holding the pistol. He looked down at the sheriff like he didn't understand what had happened. Then, quick as a flash, Champ, he jumped over the sheriff and I seen him swinging the pistol at the deputy—Joel Dean, that's you, I guess. The deputy—you— was hid behind the hood of that car so I didn't actually see him hit you, but I reckon that's what happened. Then Champ come back over to the sheriff and he felt around on his wrist and on his throat, then he went through his pockets and brought the keys over and unlocked me and Wilbur and said the sheriff was dead and we better get out of there before the deputy—that's you—came to."

"So you and Wilbur ran away through the woods?"

"Damn right. . . I mean, 'scuse me judge. Yeah, we sure did. Wilbur, he wanted that tommy gun so he took it. Champ said, 'No, no guns, get the hell out of here', but Wilbur wasn't giving up no tommy gun. We left and that's all I know. All I saw."

Sid tried to shake Buster's story, but he was trying it on the wrong guy. Buster refused to change anything he said. Sid couldn't get him to say Champ snarled at the sheriff, that he yelled at him or that he came back and kicked him in the side. Buster was resolute, even asking Sid at one point why he was trying to put words in his mouth.

When Sid announced he was through with Buster as a witness, I stood and told the court that the defense rested. Sid was on his feet again.

"The witness list says the de-fend-DANT would testify. The defense brings in a witness not on the list and he doesn't bring in the witness on the list. Your honor, I move we strike the testimony of the last witness and I move the request for a change in plea be denied."

Judge Black said, "Is that what the defendant wants? A plea of not guilty because of self defense?"

Champ took the match out of his mouth and slowly rose to his feet. "The last witness told the truth, your honor. And so that's my plea. Yes sir."

"Then the plea is self defense," Judge Black said. Sid jumped to his feet, but didn't speak. "The motion is denied. The jury is instructed that the testimony of the last witness is allowed along with the prosecution's cross examination. Is the prosecution and the defense ready for closing statements?"

Sid said, "Your honor. . ."

Judge Black raised his gavel.

Sid said, "Ready, your honor."

I said, "The defense is ready, your honor."

So it began. The battle of words for a man's life. Sid was good. He strayed from the facts a few times—to which I voiced objection—but most of his closing was a lesson for any lawyer. I can't begin to adequately describe how he played the jury with words well chosen, with facial maneuvers and body moves that I tried to remember, but couldn't. Mostly I sat and marveled at a man so skillful. Mostly what he told the jury was that the defend-DANT placed himself in the hands of the law by his own actions and he was therefore bound by law, both written and unwritten, to the consequences thereof. That Ora was only exercising his duty as a law officer, a husband and a man and that Champ broke those laws when he interfered with Ora and sent the bullet into him instead of himself.

I asked for a recess and got it after Sid finished. I wanted as much space and time between my presentation and Sid's as I could get.

Champ and I joined Addie, Buster and Noah in the witness

room. Noah wanted to know how it was going.

"I listened to part of Sid's closing argument," Noah said. "He's worth buying a ticket to."

Champ said, "The old bastard's good ain't he? Probably good enough to get me hanged."

Addie asked how the jury took Buster's testimony.

"Skeptical," I said. "I didn't much like the look on their faces. I think they were thinking, 'why did Joel Dean lie to us all last week, then come in with this story.'"

Champ said, "Looky here, Joel Dean, I'm sorry for forcing this on you and for lying to you. I felt terrible about Ora and didn't think there was any use for everybody to know what really happened between him and me. I guess us Gowans have a way of making trouble even when we ain't trying to."

"You know why Yawley's so against you don't you?" I asked.

"I know," Champ said. "Do you?"

"Estelle told me."

Champ nodded and shifted the matchstick to the other side of his mouth.

Addie asked, "What are you going to say, Joel Dean?"

"Just the truth. Like you told me to."

"Ladies and Gentlemen of the jury. This case is about a man's life. Should we take his life for trying to protect it? Maybe he should face some punishment, but his life? That's the most penalty you can hand out. You can't order him burned alive. You can't order him dropped into a can of boiling oil. There are no degrees of the death penalty in this state. There is only one. Death. The ultimate penalty for crimes so heinous we cannot allow a person back into any society, even prison.

"I read about this mad killer back east someplace in the *Police Gazette* down at the Dutchman's Barber Shop. This man chopped off the head of his wife with a corn knife and then did the same with his three small children. And his punishment? Death by hanging. Did Champ Gowan commit a crime as awful as that? Does he deserve the same punishment?

"I came to court today to tell you the truth. You are fortunate in that you know the truth, the whole truth and nothing but the truth. Many juries have to weigh testimony, decide who told the truth and make a decision based on what they *believe* was the truth. In this case, you now know the truth. What you have to decide is did Champ Gowan have the right to save his own life when the sheriff tried to shoot him for reasons only his. No less a person than Justice Oliver Wendell Holmes said, 'You can't expect rationality in the face of an uplifted knife.' When someone points a gun at you and you think they are about to shoot you, you react. Just as Champ Gowan did.

"The life of our town hangs by a thread. Powerful forces in St. Louis and at the capitol want to flood us out so they can have cheap electricity. Let Linn Creek live with honor. Above water or below water. Don't make the wrong decision here today. Don't hang a man for trying to save his life.

"Thank you for being here. For accepting this awesome responsibility. Thank you for being patient with me. May God be with you when you make your decision."

The old attic room in the courthouse was dusty and strung

with cobwebs. I dusted off a spot on the floor and Estelle and I sat there in front of the window and ate the meat and bread Birdie sent over from the kitchen in the jail. Three stories below, farmers and town folk mingled and stirred about.

"How long will the jury be out, Joel Dean?" Estelle asked.

"The longer the better," I said.

"I feel good about it. You looked so keen in your new black suit standing up there before them. And your speech was most exhilarating. I think the people in the jury liked it. What do you think?"

"During the trial it's good to try and read the jury, but afterwards it's best not to. Saves disappointment."

"For once, the other attorney looked better than Sid Hatch. I don't think Sid liked the way you looked today or the way you turned everything around that he said. His speech wasn't near as good as yours. He sounded and looked like a bitter old man."

"That old man has plenty of smarts left in him. The jury listened to him, you can bet on that."

Estelle finished the few bites she had taken from Birdie's basket. She stretched out full length on the attic floor, turned her head and smiled over at me.

"I think you're going to be a real important lawyer, Joel Dean. I think people are going to listen to you. You're going to end up rich and famous like Sid Hatch."

"I know one thing. I'm going to have the prettiest wife in this state or any other."

"You say the keenest things, Joel Dean. After we're married and you're a rich and famous lawyer, we're going to travel all over the world. I always wanted to travel. Paris and London. All those places. Wouldn't it be keen to fly like a bird? Have you ever wanted to fly like a bird. Like we were that day in the airplane, only without an airplane?"

"Sure I would. We're up here with the pigeons right now."

"You told me all about what happened. I mean, between

Addie and Champ and Ora. How come you didn't put Addie on the stand? And Champ?"

"I had this dream last night. It was like Addie was dead and all I could do was to wipe the sweat off her forehead. So I felt I had to save her. If I put her on the stand, Sid Hatch would have savaged her. 'How many other men you lay in bed with besides the de-fend-DANT?' And he would have done the same with Champ. He tried to do it with Buster but Buster didn't know anything. He didn't know what Addie and Champ had done."

"You love your sister?"

"Yes, I do."

"I've always wished I had a sister."

"You'll have one after we're married."

"Did you know Daddy was rich? I got a peek at his papers. He's worth almost a million dollars."

"What's he going to do with it?"

"He bought all the land for several miles up Linn Creek. Past where the dam waters are going to be. He's going to start a new town. He's going to own all the stores, the bank, everything. Then he's going to rent them out."

"He would be in competition with the town the government and the dam company say they're going to build west of Linn Creek."

"He thinks people will want to live in his town. He's going to call it Linn Creek, just like this one."

"Good luck to him. I'm afraid this time Yawley's bucking some powerful forces. Speaking of Yawley, I see him down there in the street with all those Klan members of his."

"He just wants to scare people. He wanted to scare the judge and the jury. I heard him talking to some men on the porch this morning."

I folded up the coat of my hand-me-down suit and Estelle and I used it as a pillow.

"See if I can get in a short nap," I said, putting my arm around her. "I didn't get much sleep last night."

You won't be getting much after we're married, either," she said.

Nancy found us both lying there asleep when she came up the stairs.

"Wake up, Joel Dean," she said. "The judge is calling the jury back in."

Judge Henry Black asked the foreman of the jury if they had reached a verdict.

The foreman, who owned a blacksmith shop in Linn Creek, said, "No, your honor we have not."

"What's the vote?"

"Nine to three for conviction of first degree murder, your honor"

"I'm going to order you to go back in that chamber and come to a verdict. I don't intend to rule a mistrial. I'll keep you there until you reach a verdict you can all agree on. I've given you lots of latitude. Everybody's worked hard out here to put this trial on. We've lost a prosecutor during this trial. We're not going to do this all over again with a new jury. You have a duty to the state and to the people of this community. Now go back and do your duty."

"We'll try," the foreman said. "But everybody's position is pretty locked in."

"Unlock it," the judge said. "That's *your* duty."

As the jury filed out, three of them looked at Champ and me. The two women and Uncle Billy Jack. Imagine that, Uncle Billy Jack.

At seven o'clock that evening, Judge Black called the jury back into court. The vote this time was six for conviction of second degree murder and six for acquittal. The people in the courthouse were becoming anxious and the Klan members looked surly and talked among themselves in loud, angry tones.

"Go on home, then," the judge said to the jury. "But I don't want you talking to anybody about this trial. And I mean nobody. Not your wives or husbands. Nobody. The court has the power to convict people of tampering if you do. I want you back here at seven o'clock tomorrow morning. You *will* give this court a verdict. Court's adjourned until seven a.m. tomorrow."

Night came early on this summer-like fall day. The sun set over the trees beyond the Osage, lighting up the colored tints the leaves were taking and nothing seemed wrong in the world. I wanted to get away from the crowd of people who were stopping me in the street and asking how I thought the jury was going. Estelle and I walked across the ford on Linn Creek to the baseball field that lay by Dressler's picnic grounds. We were all alone in the twilight as two kids went trotting toward home and supper, dragging their baseball bats in the dust behind them.

"It's a good sign isn't it?" Estelle asked. "The vote getting bigger for acquittal, I mean."

"Yeah, it's looking good. I think Champ's out of danger of hanging and that's good. I don't look on him the same as I did before I knew he caused Ora's death. But I didn't want him to hang. A few more years in prison, maybe."

"Will Addie wait for him?"

I shrugged. "Who knows. She's going to resign as sheriff. Doyle Savoy will get the job. He's in love with Addie, too. Maybe she'll stay on to take care of the jail and who knows what would come of that."

We walked, holding hands, through the picnic grounds, past the worn place in the grass where the platform for dancing had been placed. The sound of the frogs in the creek and the crickets in the fields were joined by the whippoorwill and an owl deep in the woods.

"We could walk to our special place down by the Niangua," Estelle said, looking so perky and beautiful in the moonlight.

"I'd like that," I said.

The goldenrods and the Queen Anne's Lace sparkled in the rays from the moon, lighting our path.

"We'll have a regular road worn through here if we don't hurry up and get married," I said.

"We won't need to come here much longer," she said. "This is all about over. The town is saved. Champ is saved. I'm not scared anymore. Daddy will see what a good lawyer you've become. He'll want me to be married to someone important."

"I'll always come here to this spot," I said. "It's the happiest place on earth for me."

"You do say the keenest things, Joel Dean."

A calm and welcome peace descended upon me. What a relief to have the trial over. Tomorrow, or another day, I would have to think about what I wanted to do with my life. I wasn't too sure about being a lawyer any longer. And I didn't know exactly what influence the loss of our town would have in me. Being a prosecutor or a lawyer might not be what I wanted. You hold the power of life and death in your hands and I'm not sure that was to my liking. I squeezed the small hand that was inside my own, thinking life was not too bad after all. I would go back inside Rose's dining room feeling a thousand percent better than I had this morning.

But calm and peace do not last. Like promises and vows, they are made to be broken.

A muffled explosion disturbed the night. It came rolling across the creek and through the meadow like thunder in the sky.

I jerked to a stop. "A gunshot," I said. Then I turned and began running back toward town as fast as I could, leaving Estelle behind.

"The damn Klan," I said, over and over. "The damn Klan."

I raced down the street as fast as my legs would carry me. People stood around in front of the stores across from the jail watching the mass of white sheeted figures under the big redbud tree. In the doorway of the jail house two men in white sheets stood, holding shotguns. Doyle Savoy was sitting on the ground, leaning against the wall holding his right arm that was bloody and red.

LIMB OF THE JUDAS TREE

Someone threw a rope over the large limb of the Judas tree and shouts of "Hang him, hang him," roared through the night. One Klan member had Noah's arms pinned behind his back. Then I saw Addie, struggling with two Klan members and right behind her was Champ being held by four men. There must have been twenty of them altogether. The lead figure, of course, was Yawley. He held the noose in his hand and others were tying off the end of the rope that had been thrown over the limb. A large wooden crate stood under the limb.

"Drag him over here," the unmistakable voice of Yawley bellowed out. "The damn court ain't going to hang him, by God, we'll see justice done."

Addie slung the man holding her right arm across her leg and as he sprawled in the dust, she pulled the pistol from her holster and pointed it right at Yawley.

"Turn him loose, Yawley or I'll kill you," Addie shouted.

"Take care of her," Yawley yelled. "Somebody shoot her. She's the one caused it. Laying with trash."

Addie raised her revolver and shot into the air. "Next one's at you, Yawley. Turn him loose."

"By God, ain't nobody going to shoot her?" Yawley yelled. He grabbed the shotgun a Klan member next to him was holding and swung it around to point right straight at Addie.

Out of breath, staggering, falling forward I yelled, "Noooo," just as the other Klan member holding Addie slapped her hand holding the revolver. Yawley's shotgun went off and Addie's shot went into the ground. She crumpled into a heap on the ground, a big red splotch spreading on the front of her shirt.

I was on my knees holding her head when Champ came sliding through the dirt beside her, his hands tied behind his back.

"Don't die for me, Addie," he said. "I ain't worth it."

Addie looked up at me, tears now in her eyes. "Save him, Joel Dean. Save Champ."

One of the Klan members dropped the noose over Champ's

306

head and pulled him upright.

"Get on with it," Yawley yelled out. "Hang the bastard."

Addie was dead. I saw it in her eyes. I took my hand and wiped the sweat from her forehead and kissed her. Just like in the dream. I laid her in the dust and took the revolver from her hand. I went over to the Klan member who was dragging Champ toward the crate with the noose around his neck. I put Addie's revolver up to the hood over the Klan man's head and cocked it.

"Turn him loose," I said.

The man turned to look at me through the two holes he'd cut in the hood. When he saw my face, he let go of the rope.

"Hang him. Hang him," Yawley kept yelling.

"Everybody back off," I said. "Drop your guns on the ground or I'll kill this man."

"Don't do it," Yawley said. "Somebody shoot that damn meddling lawyer."

One by one the rifles and shotguns dropped to the ground. The white sheeted members started backing off.

"What the hell are you doing?" Yawley cried out. "He's bluffing. Shoot him. We've got to do what the damn jury ain't got the guts to do. We've got to protect our town. We've got a hanging to take care of."

"It's over Yawley," I said. "Put your shotgun down."

"Damn you, Joel Dean, you ruined everything."

Yawley started bringing the shotgun up to point at me. I swung the revolver around to point right at his heart.

"Don't do it, Yawley. It's over. You're under arrest for killing an officer of the law."

"You ain't running off with my daughter to California. She's all I got left. I'll kill you first."

The click of the hammer on his shotgun was as loud as a church bell. I waited as long as I could. Until I knew I couldn't wait any longer and I pulled the trigger on Addie's revolver.

As Yawley fell over backwards in the dirt, the red spot on his white sheet getting bigger, I heard Estelle screaming as she came running down the street.

"No, no. Daddy. Daddy."

EPILOGUE

LIMB OF THE JUDAS TREE

We buried Addie in a grave beside Ora in the cemetery on the hill overlooking town. The luck of our town went bad after that night under the Judas tree. I had no wish to write this story any longer and I put everything aside.

Now it's 1932 and all of the sadness has softened like a long ago memory. I'm a candidate for the United States Congress this year on the same ballot with Franklin Delano Roosevelt, the man people say will save the country. I would like to help him.

Judge Henry Black eventually declared a mistrial when the jury was hopelessly hung on conviction of Champ. Champ was never tried again for killing Ora.

Not long after the trial when I tried my best to save the life of the one who shot the best man I ever knew, Champ just disappeared along with Nita German. Lonnie came back from a picture show in Jefferson City all excited. He swore he had seen Champ in a one-reel movie playing a singing cowboy. Champ had traded his banjo in for a guitar and had apparently swapped Nita for a palamino that he gave his own name to. I always thought Champ was deserving of his new-found success; he'd already paid for his indescretions up front. He seemed to be trying real hard to be somebody after Addie sacrificed her life for him.

Less than a month after the night Addie was killed, the electrical generating company in St. Louis that had bought out the bankrupt company followed all the original plans for the dam and began a construction project which doomed our town of Linn Creek.

The bullet I fired at Yawley missed his heart, but lodged against his spine and he was paralyzed from the waist down. He spent a long time in the hospital in St. Louis with Estelle by his bedside. It was almost a year before I saw her again. She was pushing Yawley's wheelchair along the porch in front of Yawley's general store and when he saw me, he got very red in the face and began cursing at me. Without a word to me, Estelle pushed him away in a hurry and the last I heard was a stream of condemnation toward me from Yawley. A few days later I received a letter from Estelle. She began it, Dearest Joel Dean and ended it, Love, Estelle. But in between she told me how we could not meet because she had promised to take care of Yawley.

Doyle Savoy became sheriff, albeit a left-handed one. I was appointed by the attorney general to finish Gideon's term as prosecuting attorney for our county, but I did not run for re-election. The attorney general's office appointed a Grand Jury to investigate Addie's killing, but no one was ever indicted. Loyalty to the Klan was a powerful influence in our state and the testimony from me, Doyle and Noah plus a few citizens from our town who had stood by and watched what happened that night fell on deaf ears.

As prosecuting attorney, I got Murdoch and Artis Monger indicted for killing Shorty Mickelson and both served short prison sentences. It seemed Murdoch was at Mamie Crouse's and found out from Champ where they were headed and took that opportunity to cripple Yawley's whiskey delivery and get it blamed on someone else.

And, with great satisfaction, I prosecuted the two city slickers who came to town and bought petition signatures and bribed county officials all over the area. I was an angry prosecutor and I slammed my fist against the table several times in describing the terrible crimes I accused them of. You would have thought I was describing the downfall of the Union. And, I suppose, that was the way I saw it. That was the last case Judge Henry Black presided over before he died quietly in his sleep and was buried in his robe. He gave the men the maximum sentence of five years in prison. I got a measure of satisfaction out of the look of unbelief on the face of the younger of the two. Justice was not complete, however. Within days a higher court freed them.

I represented a lot of people in Linn Creek in condemnation suits against the dam builders. In 1930 people started moving out of town and in some cases, moving their houses with them. Most people went to the new town that the State and the dam people were helping to build. Voters in the county passed the measure to move the county seat to the new town by a five to one majority. Yawley's plan to start another Linn Creek suffered when he couldn't push it. He ended up in bankruptcy with only his house on the hill, above the lake waters, left in his name.

We burned or dynamited all the buildings left in Linn Creek and let me tell you, that was the saddest thing that ever happened to anyone involved. Church after church, store after store turned to rubble and the streets where I played as a boy and the school where I learned a set of principles I have lived by, were now gone forever.

Volly Newell's Shell filling station was the last building in town to be destroyed. When it was evident no more gasoline would be needed by the movers and the bulldozers, and with the lake waters within inches of the station, Volly, Lonnie and I met at the river bank, sat and reminisced for awhile, then got up, set fire to the station and stood down the street and watched without a word. When the gasoline tanks exploded and the still-burning debris landed in the lake waters, that was the end of Linn Creek.

I hear that Yawley is bedridden now and never leaves the house. I have forgiven him for killing Addie, just like I forgave Champ for killing Ora.

I am a patient man. I have waited all these years for Estelle.

It's only a matter of time.

Watch for these thrilling new mystery novels soon to be published by Aux Arcs Novels

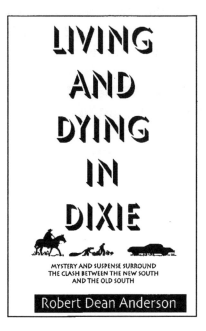

It's been years since Roy Lockhart, a failing California private investigator, has heard from King Fairborne, his roomie and football teammate at Ol' Miss. Now King's son wants Roy to come back to Mississippi and investigate his old roomie's strange death. Roy isn't prepared for the son's bizarre behavior, an encounter with voodoo culture nor the deaths that keep occurring. Just about everybody in town wanted King dead, including his son. Roy concludes from his investigation that he's being used by everyone and no one wants or expects him to solve the murders. This is his last chance to save his marriage, his family and a measure of self-respect. But when it's over, it's not over because Roy knows who the killer is and it is someone that nobody suspected.

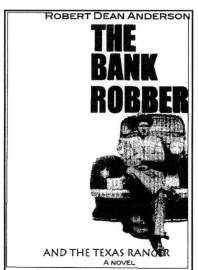

The time is the Thirties, a period of great depression in the nation. Men are desperate for money and some are willing to go to desperate lengths to obtain it. One such man raids the banks in the Texas Panhandle where the riches of a new oil boom are deposited. He leaves money and clues about his next strike for the Texas Ranger who shadows him. A woman, caught in the middle of the cat and mouse game, discovers she has difficult choices to make. A young girl and her entourage of fortune-telling dolls is convinced the Ranger is her father and becomes involved. When the final robbery takes place, the thin line between the guilty and the innocent disappears.

Reserve your copies now and get a $5 coupon—Turn the page for details

Please send me the first five pages of these novels and a $5 coupon to use for ordering one copy of either or both books.

The Bank Robber (A Novel of Suspense in Depression Era Texas)
A bank robber hits Texas Panhandle banks in the 1930's and leaves clues to a Texas Ranger on the location of his next target, but the Ranger knows more than the robber thinks he does.

Living and Dying in Dixie (A Southern Mystery Novel)
A second-rate California private eye is hired to come home to Mississippi where he investigates the strange death of his old college roommate and discovers that the murderer and victim have a lot in common.

Name...

Address..

City..

Tear out page, fold, affix stamp and mail—the address is on the back side.

Aux-Arcs Novels
26183 Indian Creek Lane
Barnett, MO 65011